THE GOOD PRIEST

THOMAS BISHOP

BookLocker

Paperback ISBN: 978-1-64719-042-2
Epub ISBN: 978-1-64719-043-9
Mobi ISBN: 978-1-64719-044-6

Published by BookLocker.com, Inc., St. Petersburg, Florida.

The characters, places, and events in this book are fictitious. Any similarity to real persons, living or dead, or places is coincidental and not intended by the author. Any pronouncements, representations or advice given by any of the characters on any topics should not be relied upon as factual or accurate for any reason other than for an understanding of the perspective of the speaker as the author is not a mental health professional, theologian, canon lawyer, criminologist, or penologist and does not profess, through any of the book's characters, to be offering opinions or advice on any topics.

Library of Congress Cataloging in Publication Data
Bishop, Thomas
THE GOOD PRIEST by Thomas Bishop
Library of Congress Control Number: 2020919281

Printed on acid-free paper.

Booklocker.com, Inc.
2020

For all the children

We never know how high we are

Till we are called to rise;

And then, if we are true to plan,

Our statures touch the skies.

—Emily Dickinson

I

A KILLING

1990 had been a reasonably calm year at the Suffolk State Penitentiary for Father Pat Keefe, now in his eighth year as the prison chaplain. At forty-two, he was physically fit and morally content. His trim frame wasn't showing age except for the occasional white hair intermingled with his generally fair tones and a slight thickening of his midsection. He was comfortable in his ministry. All that was about to change.

He was in his office when the call came. "This is Chaplain Pat Keefe speaking."

"Father Pat, this is attorney Jed Baker. I'm not sure you remember me but we went to the same school in Duncan's Cove before you left for the seminary. I was just a year behind you and friendly with your sister Susan."

"Of course, Jed, I remember you. Don't you come to Mass at Holy Family on Sundays? I think I've seen you there a few times with your family when I'm home visiting. What can I do for you?"

"Well, Father Pat, as you may know I have an office in Duncan's Cove for the general practice of law. Right now, I'm down at the MacDonald Juvenile Detention Center in Westin to see a youngster who's accused of killing a priest. I think I need your help. Could you come?"

"Oh no, that's horrible. Of course, I'll come right away, Jed, but I'm not sure what I can do. I'm a priest, you know, not a lawyer."

"I get it, Padre, but I think this youngster may need more than my kind of help. I know from your sister Susan that a few years after your ordination you returned to school for a master's in social work and now you're the chaplain at Suffolk. Your learning and experience might be very helpful as I try to sort out the best approach for representing him."

After quickly finished his chore, Pat drove to the MacDonald Juvenile Detention Center, about an hour's distance. As he neared, he quickly recalled its fortress-like appearance from his days as a seminarian when he volunteered there as a tutor. The massive stone structure was surrounded by razor wire-topped fencing broken only by a guarded gate. To Pat, the facility was foreboding: anything but welcoming. What a place for parents to come to see their kids, he thought, as he stopped at the closed gate. There, he was met by a guard who checked his identification, then directed him to park in the visitor's area and proceed to the entranceway as the gate swung open.

At the front door, Pat summoned a response by using a buzzer alongside the door. "Who is it?" barked the voice. "Father Pat Keefe, here to meet with attorney Jed Baker, who's representing a youngster just brought here." As the door clicked open, Pat was directed from the unseen speaker to enter the building. Once inside, he was screened by guards before being ushered through another door. There, Jed Baker stood waiting for him: blond, curly hair, short in stature, slight paunch, mid- to late thirties. Just as Pat had recalled.

Face tight, the lawyer silently shook Pat's hand. "This is awful, Father. A kid by the name of Lawrence Jefferson has just been arrested for murdering Father Gregory Mason, a priest in St. Mary's parish in Foxon. He's here now. Thank you for coming."

Pat only loosely recalled Mason, whom he thought he might have met once at a convocation of diocesan priests. Younger, he thought, maybe about five years out of seminary. "Terrible, for sure. God bless this fallen priest and God save this boy" was all Pat could muster as he tried to absorb the enormity of the situation.

"The boy's parents called me for help and I saw him earlier today. He's sullen, minimally communicative, and has an odd calmness about him except when he blurted out that Mason deserved what he got for what he had done to him and he was glad he was dead."

"Would you come in with me to see him? Maybe he'll open up more with you."

"Of course, Jed," Pat sighed, "but I know from what I've studied about sexual abuse of children when I was getting my master's in social work that often they won't open up to someone they've just met. They don't have any trust. And, if he's killed one priest, why do you think he'd talk to another one, and someone he doesn't know?"

"Not sure, Padre, but if you're willing I'd like to give it a try. In this case, the boy has already told his story to the police and his parents and, of course, to a jury in public. So maybe it's different. I know the shooting has something to do with the boy's claim that the victim sexually assaulted him, but right now he doesn't seem interested in talking much. Maybe you can unlock him a little. I think I'll need to really understand this youngster if I'm going to be able to do him any good."

"Okay, Jed. Let's give it a try." Pat smiled warmly.

The two of them were shortly ushered into a room, where the boy sat on a chair by a table, two empty chairs facing him. The lime-green windowless room was otherwise barren of any furniture or adornments. The youngster was hunched over, arms crossed in a protective cocoon; tall for his age, Pat guessed, somewhat overweight, hair disheveled. "I'm Father Keefe, son. I'm not here to judge what you might have done and I want you to know, as well, that I care very much about you. I hate it that some priests abuse kids, and if that happened to you, I hope you will trust me enough to talk with me. I want to help you." That seemed to get the boy's attention as he unfolded his arms and looked up at Pat.

"How do I know you're not just another perv, some other priest who wants to shut me up, keep me from talking about what he did to me? I told all this stuff to the dumb jury and they just fell for what that creep said. I don't want to talk about it anymore. It didn't do any good before."

"That's okay, son, but I want you to know that if you were hurt by another priest, that hurts me as well. Please let me try to help. We know what the jury did but we're new to this. We're here just for you and it would help us if you could talk about it to us."

What followed came out without palpable emotion.

"That bastard tried to grab my dick and then he lied about it, made me look like a liar, and I took care of him for it."

Baker interjected, "Maybe start from the beginning, Lawrence. We're not in any hurry."

"Oh, okay. We go to church at St. Mary's where Mason showed up about a year ago. I was on the parish CYO basketball team and really liked it because I was taller than a lot of the other kids and could get rebounds even though I can't jump very high. After one practice, Mason told me to stay behind to work on my shooting because I was getting fouled a lot in games but not making many foul shots. For about a half an hour, I practiced while Mason got the ball and threw it back to me. Afterwards, I went to the boys' locker room, took my clothes off, and went to the showers, which were big enough for four people. Do I really have to tell this to you? I told it to the jury and what good did that do? I'm tired and just want to be alone now."

Pat interjected, "No, Lawrence, not if you don't want to. Maybe that's enough for today. We can come back."

"Yeah, I want to go to my room now."

Baker and Pat looked at each other in silent recognition that they shouldn't press the boy.

"Okay, Lawrence," Baker said, "I'll be back to see you."

Pat chimed in, "And I'll come too, Lawrence, if you'd like me to."

The boy just stared ahead as the two men left the room.

Outside, Baker suggested they sit together in the room where they first met so he could fill Pat in on the rest of the sad events.

"Here's what the boy told the prosecutor and then the jury. After he had been in the shower for a few moments, Father Mason came in, totally naked, and with an obvious erection. Of course, Lawrence didn't use these words, but this is the gist of it. He approached Lawrence with a bar of soap in his hand and, without comment, started to wash him, first his back and then around to his front, where he put his hand on the boy's penis and began to rub it. Lawrence said he asked the priest to quit but, instead, he continued and then clasped the boy's hand and put it on his penis, directing the boy to stroke him. I guess the boy then got his gumption up and shoved the priest hard while telling him to get away from him. He told the prosecutor that Mason almost fell while backing away. At that point, according to Lawrence, the priest was angry. He threatened the boy that if he told anyone he'd throw him off the team, saying that he caught him trying to steal stuff."

"What happened next, Jed? This is an awful story."

"Well, from what his parents told me, he didn't go back to basketball. When his dad asked him why, he said he didn't like the coach, that he thought he was mean. I guess they just let it go at that. When his mom asked him a couple of times if anything was wrong because his conduct seemed to have changed—staying in his room a lot, not going out with friends, things like that—he just told her he was fine and asked her to leave him alone. She just chalked it up to growing pains."

"Then, how did it finally come out?" Pat asked.

"Well, one time about three months after it happened, he got into a fight with another kid from the team, a boy named Jimmy Koch, and he blurted some things out. I guess the Koch boy was angry with him for quitting the team. He said that because they didn't have any other tall kids, they didn't get far in the tournament at the end of the season. He said it was

11

Lawrence's fault and he called him some unkind names for not sticking with it. Said he was too scared to fight for rebounds, things like that. According to Lawrence, that riled him enough that he just yelled that the boy better watch out for Mason, not to let him near him in the shower because he's a real perv. When Koch asked him what he was talking about, Lawrence just clammed up.

"The Koch boy told his parents what Lawrence had said, and his mom, who also teaches at the school, asked Mr. Evans, Lawrence's homeroom teacher, if he had been acting weird. Mr. Evans reported that Lawrence had skipped school a few days and his grades had taken a nosedive, going from As and Bs to Cs and even a couple of Ds. Evans said he had talked with the boy's parents but no one seemed to know what was going on with him. Then, Koch's mom and Mr. Evans decided to talk to the school social worker and then they called in Mr. and Mrs. Jefferson to discuss the situation. After that meeting, it all seemed to come together for the parents and they sat down with Lawrence. At first he was hesitant to speak with them. Apparently he said he was afraid they'd be angry with him, but, with prodding, he then opened up to them. Next, the police were contacted and a Detective Melissa Barnes from the Foxon Police Department came to speak with Lawrence and his parents. That led ultimately to the arrest of Father Mason."

"That's quite a story, Jed. Was there then a trial, and what happened?"

"Oh yes," Baker replied. "From there it all goes even further downhill, if that's possible.... Father Mason was subsequently charged with attempted sexual assault of a minor and child endangerment. He got a lawyer, Cynthia Towns, who had been retained by the diocese for him, and the case later went to trial, where Mason was acquitted of both charges.

"Some of this I learned from Carl DeMatha, whom I spoke with earlier today. Interestingly, he's the same prosecutor who tried the case against Mason and he's now representing the State in the case against Lawrence. He told me a bit about the trial. Beforehand, he prepared Lawrence. He told him what he was going to ask him and he tried to reassure him about the process. He said he warned him too about the defense attorney, Ms. Towns, by telling Lawrence that she'd be asking him questions too, but he hadn't been prepared for what she unearthed. After some fairly benign questions, she got into Lawrence's school record, and suddenly she started asking him about his suspension from school last year.

"DeMatha admitted to me that he was totally unprepared for this line of questioning. He said he objected but after arguing with the jury out of the room, the judge agreed with the defense lawyer that she could get into the reason the boy was suspended. When it came out that he had cheated on a test, DeMatha said, he could just feel a chill in the courtroom. That fact, combined with Mason's heated denials under oath, likely sealed the outcome. Mason was fairly quickly acquitted of the charges against him."

"I meant to tell you," Baker continued, "that Lawrence did actually talk with me about the trial a little bit when I first met up with him earlier today. He talked about the courtroom itself, how it was, in his words, 'real scary.' He said that when the court person came to get him in the hallway and he had to walk into that courtroom with a lot of people there and the jury sitting by the side, he was shaking afraid. He even described the room itself. Said it was big with high ceilings and a lot of wood, and the judge sat on a bench above everybody else. He remarked to me that everything was so quiet when he walked in and then, when he sat down, there was Mason sitting at a table next to his lawyer and staring right at him. All of that, he said, scared the hell out of him, or words to that effect."

"What was the boy's demeanor in reciting the trial facts to you, Jed?"

"Well, in a way, it was eerie, Father Pat. He spoke in a flat tone, almost at a distance from the content of his account as though he was giving a report about something that had happened to a stranger."

"Did the prosecutor say how the boy did in the trial?" Pat asked.

"Yes," Baker responded. "He said he thought the boy did okay on direct while telling the story of what happened to him but he tensed up once the defense lawyer started asking him questions. Then it all came apart once the jury heard about the cheating incident. He felt very bad about that because he had been unprepared for it. The only other witness he called was the Koch boy, who looked as scared as Lawrence. He recited the facts of his dustup with Lawrence but couldn't add any more. The defense lawyer, Ms. Towns, did what any good defense lawyer would do. She just pointed out through terse questioning that the Koch kid hadn't been in the shower and he only knew what Lawrence had told him. DeMatha said that when she sat down, he could see the slight smirk on her face, which he was sure was for the benefit of the jury."

Baker continued, "Let me tell you more about what the prosecutor said. When I asked whether the priest had testified, he affirmed that he did. He said that he denied the entire incident. He said that Lawrence had been a mediocre ballplayer—so-so, in his words—and that he had benched him because he was lazy and had shown up late for several practices. He said he thought the boy had quit the team probably because he wasn't getting any playing time and that he couldn't handle his coaching style. It all seemed plausible. Certainly, it appears the jury bought it."

"Can you talk about what happened after the trial, Jed, how we got to this point?" Pat asked.

"Yes, I know about that from the boy and from piecing together other information I have received. Oddly, Lawrence was willing to talk with me about this part. Really, he just didn't want to get into the details of the assault itself but he was fairly open about everything else and, strangely, about his own post-trial activity.

"Five days after the trial, Father Mason was found dead in a confessional booth at St. Mary's. He had been shot four times, all in the face. Lawrence seemed proud of this. 'I took care of that dirty bastard,' he said. He went on: 'He did that to me and then he lied about it and nobody believed me. He deserved what he got. It was like he hurt me all over again when he got up there and lied. I don't feel bad about what I did, except I know my parents are real worried and now I'm in all this trouble but I'm okay now.'"

"In recounting this part, did the lad show any remorse?" Pat asked.

"No, unfortunately, he expressed none. I'd say, to the contrary, he seemed satisfied with himself. I actually taped it when I met with the boy earlier. Here's what he said."

Baker then retrieved a tape from his leather tote and placed it on the seat beside them. Without comment, he started it.

"I was really kinda relieved. A week after the trial, I got a gun from the drawer of the table next to where my parents sleep where one time I saw my dad put it. I grabbed it when I knew they had gone to the movies. I took that gun to church on that Saturday afternoon 'cause I know that's when they usually hear confessions and, pretending that's why I was there, I went into the confessional and knelt down and I asked if the priest on the other side of the screen was Mason. Once he said yes and started to ask why I wanted to know, I pointed the gun right at his face and yelled at him that he lied in court and made me look like the bad one. I blasted him a bunch of times, then dropped the pistol right there in the confessional and ran from the church.

"A little while later, a cop car came along and asked where I was going. I guess I mumbled something to the cop like 'he had it coming to him' because the cop got out of his car and had me stand up against it while he felt me all over and then he put handcuffs on me. As soon as I got in the car, I said I wasn't surprised that it didn't take them very long to find me and I asked if the prick was dead. I told the cop that Mason deserved to die as he had hurt me and then lied about it in court and made the jury believe him."

Baker then stopped the tape.

"At that point," Baker said, "I ended the interview. I assured him that I was going to try to help him but that it might take a while. In the meanwhile, I cautioned, please don't talk any more about this as that could only make matters worse."

"As you might gather, Father Pat, Lawrence's identification as the shooter is not a question; he's admitted it to several people and his handprints are all over the Glock semiautomatic he used. A pretty vicious weapon, by the way.

"His legal culpability and appropriate punishment are still up in the air, however. Normally, a fourteen-year-old kid charged with a nonviolent crime would be sent to juvenile court where the proceedings are not open to the public and the punishment cannot extend beyond the person's eighteenth birthday. But in the case of a serious violent crime, the prosecutor has the option to ask the court to transfer the case to adult court where a person, once convicted, can be sentenced just like an adult. In this case, that could mean years of confinement. Sorry for the lecture but I'm just trying to say that keeping the case in the juvenile court would be much better for Lawrence, and Padre, that's where I'm hoping you can help—on the mitigation side of things."

Pat nodded. "Hard to be sure, but Lawrence certainly fits the profile of a kid who's been abused. From what I know so far, I haven't heard any other reason for his sudden change in behavior after he left that team. Of course, you know you'll have to do some more work on that score, but I'm very interested in helping, Jed. Lawrence seemed oddly calm when we met with him as though, in his mind, a terrible wrong had been redressed. He did not seem overwhelmed with guilt for having killed Father Mason. Rather, he appeared to be flat, almost uninterested in what might happen to him. He certainly didn't show any kind of remorse or any introspection about the enormity of what he did. I think you might want to consider getting a psychiatrist to see Lawrence in order to give you an assessment of the boy's mental state."

"Yes, I've thought of that, and I've already reached out to someone for that purpose—a psychiatrist I know. Someone I've worked with before. She's very good."

While the two men were speaking, Mollie and Tim Jefferson arrived in the anteroom where Baker introduced them to Pat as a priest and an old friend from Duncan's Cove. He quickly added that Pat had an advanced degree in counseling and was now a chaplain at the men's prison in Suffolk. The Jeffersons, both in their early forties, were blond, trim, even athletic looking, and smartly clothed—she in blouse and skirt and he in an open-collared shirt, blazer, and slacks. They just nodded in tacit acceptance of Pat's presence. When Baker asked them if they'd like to sit down and talk after their visit with their son, they seemed eager.

After less than a half hour, while Jed Baker and Father Pat waited, the parents returned to the anteroom. Mrs. Jefferson was in tears, trembling; Mr. Jefferson was quieter, stiff-lipped, but to Pat's practiced eye, shaken as well, struggling to hold it in.

"He seems so quiet, maybe sullen. I'm afraid he's not feeling at all sorry for what he did. What do you think will happen to him?" Mr. Jefferson asked.

Calmly, Pat responded, "I'm only a priest, Mr. and Mrs. Jefferson. I think Attorney Baker would be the better person to answer you, but in my view, there's room for mercy in the justice system. Lawrence is just a youngster. Even though he's charged with a terrible crime, his age and the circumstances could be factors in what happens next."

Mrs. Jefferson told Pat that they were good Catholics and thought they had raised their son right and just couldn't understand what could make him do such a horrible thing. Here, Pat thought he could be more helpful. "Mr. and Mrs.

Jefferson, let me ask you about Lawrence as a youngster growing up. Did you ever have issues with him being truthful?"

"Absolutely not," Mrs. Jefferson said, with her husband in nodding agreement. "He was no angel but our issues with him were his attention to his schoolwork, and we often had to prod him to make his bed and do his share of household chores, but his faults were more things he didn't do. We didn't think he had a mean bone in his body. Yes, he did cheat that one time last year and we had a long talk with him about it. Not to make any excuses, but he had a test right after he had been sick. Anyway, that incident was an anomaly. Lawrence was never like that."

"What about basketball?" Father Pat asked. "Did he seem to like it, and what did he tell you about quitting? "

Mr. Jefferson answered. "Lawrence has not ever been what you'd call real athletic, but we have a basketball hoop over our garage door and once in a while we'd play HORSE together or just mess around for fun and I thought he had some talent, particularly because, at five-feet-ten, he's tall for his age. So I encouraged him to go out for the basketball team. I thought it would be good exercise for him and maybe, if he had any success at it, give him a bit more oomph. We were really surprised when he came home and told us he had quit and, boy, we now wish we had pressed him to tell us why instead of just letting him be, thinking it was a teenage thing that he had to work out on his own."

"When did you find out about the incident with Father Mason?" Pat asked. He wasn't surprised when they said it wasn't until they had gotten a call from the school counselor.

"Then," Mr. Jefferson said, "he told us the whole story. He was really angry at Father Mason and so were we. We were pretty hot, thinking this guy, a priest after all, had assaulted our Lawrence. Actually we were mad as hell, Father. And, you know, I can't get it out of my mind that it was my gun he used. I just bought it a few months ago because there have been some robberies in our neighborhood. We live in a very nice area and I guess some people think we're ripe for the picking, so I got this gun. We have some pretty good stuff in the house but I never thought..." His voice trailed off as his head sunk to his chest.

Baker responded, "Mr. Jefferson, I can imagine how you may feel about the gun, but you owned it legally. You have a right to protect yourselves. I know that can be a hard spot for you but please don't go there. Now, the focus has to be completely on Lawrence."

Jefferson just nodded. They talked about the trial for a few more minutes and then Mrs. Jefferson asked, "Father, if he did this thing, and I guess he did, what about his soul? We're good Catholics and we're really afraid he's damned himself by killing Father Mason."

Pat thought for a minute and then said, "Mr. and Mrs. Jefferson, God is merciful and forgives those who have done even terrible things so long as they repent and truly feel sorry for what they have done. I will come see Lawrence again and I will pray with him and, in time, I hope he will come to understand that what he did was very wrong, something he probably knows deep down from his upbringing, though now he seems to be in a kind of spiritual shock. When he's ready I will hear his confession, through which I believe he will receive God's forgiveness.

"He will have to be punished for this, however, and you need to steel yourselves for that reality. When we get to that point, I can talk with you about our penal system for juveniles and what happens there because I have worked both in this place and in the adult prison as a chaplain. Of course being locked up, kept from home and community for some period of time, is no fun for anyone, but let's hope he can be in a place where he can continue his high school studies. We can talk some more when you'd like."

With that, Pat gave Lawrence's parents his card, identifying him as the chaplain of the Suffolk prison and providing his work telephone number. They embraced as they parted.

Pat left these searing meetings concerned for Lawrence's well-being, not only in terms of his likely punishment, but also for his spiritual welfare.

Within a week, the psychiatrist, Dr. Meagan O'Toole, came to visit Lawrence in the company of Jed Baker. As they entered the room where Lawrence had been brought, he just looked up at them, his eyes expressionless. "Lawrence, this is Dr. O'Toole. I have asked her to meet with you as she is going to work with us to help you. I'll be right outside, but I think it's best if you and the doctor speak alone." And with that, Baker left the room.

O'Toole was prim, mid-forties, with her hair tightly pulled back in a bun, but once she spoke, warmth radiated from her. She took a seat across the table from Lawrence, smiled at him, and then asked, "Lawrence, it's nice to meet you. Can you tell me why you think you are here?"

"Yeah, 'cause I killed that shit priest," he quickly answered without looking directly at her.

"Gosh, Lawrence, that must have felt weird, doing that," she suggested.

"Not really. He had it coming for what he did."

"I'm wondering, Lawrence, how does that make you feel now?"

"What do you mean? I'm happy he's dead if that's what you mean. Otherwise, I'm okay—a little sad because I miss my parents and don't like it here. They keep me pretty much to myself," he answered flatly.

"Do you want to talk about your parents, Lawrence? It sounds like you might be close to them." She tried another tack. But to no avail.

"What for? They had nothing to do with this. I don't feel like talking about them," he sullenly answered.

And so the conversation continued. Dr. O'Toole probed to unearth Lawrence's feelings but, to her, he seemed castled off, a moat around his emotions. After about forty-five minutes, O'Toole told Lawrence that she was pleased she got to meet him and said she'd return in not too many days.

Outside, she sat down with Jed Baker. "Well, Jed, these are only first impressions, of course, and I don't really know the boy, but he seems walled off. There's no sense that any coping mechanisms have kicked in, probably not just from the killing of the priest but from the trauma of being assaulted, as you explained. My hunch is that after the assault, Lawrence probably just didn't have the resources to get back into emotional balance. He got knocked off his pins and still hasn't recovered.

"Killing this priest may have been seen by him as the only way out. I think you might want to get a psychologist to give him some tests, as they might give you some useful information in defending this kid. Of course, I'd be very willing to work with him. He is going to need a lot of therapy to regain his balance, and, based on my experience with other abused kids, if he can't get his equilibrium back fairly soon, his life's path from here on could be very rocky."

After about a month, Baker called Pat at the prison. "Hi, Padre. I just wanted to bring you up to date on Lawrence Jefferson's case. A psychologist administered several tests, which basically confirmed Doctor O'Toole's initial assessment. While Lawrence's fund of knowledge, his basic I.Q., is intact, he's at sea emotionally, just floundering without a beacon. Dr. O'Toole has seen him again a few times. Her initial impression is the same. She thinks that he never recovered from the assault and then, metaphorically, felt assaulted again at the trial by the defense lawyer's questioning his honesty and Mason's fabrication, and that the combination of those factors likely overwhelmed his coping ability."

Pat replied, "Well, that's what you and I sensed; it's useful to have it confirmed by the pros. Where do you go from here?"

"Well, my next step," replied Baker, "is to meet with the prosecutor. I've asked Dr. O'Toole to write up her impressions.

That, and the testing results should help in my discussions about what might happen to Lawrence in court."

Pat next heard from Baker ten days later. He said that he had met with the prosecutor, who was willing to talk about trying to work out a plea agreement. "I think I told you when we first met at the Center that the prosecutor, Carl DeMatha, is the same one who had represented the State in the trial against Mason for assaulting Lawrence. When I spoke with DeMatha, he said his boss believed he should now handle the charges against Lawrence because he already knew so much about the underlying facts. I was really happy to hear DeMatha say he had believed Lawrence, that he had in fact been assaulted by Mason in the way he claimed, but that the trial just didn't go his way. He explained it's often tough to convince a jury beyond a reasonable doubt when it's just a one-on-one crime with no witnesses and, maybe, the fact that Lawrence had that cheating incident on his record really hurt him with the jury."

"Well, that's something," replied Pat. "Actually maybe a very good omen for the youngster."

Baker said that he was buoyed by the prosecutor's apparent sympathy for Lawrence and that he had scheduled another meeting with the prosecutor.

"Would you be willing to come, Padre?" he asked.

"Of course, Jed, but to what end? I'm no lawyer and can't really talk about the legal punishment."

"I know," said Baker. "I would like you to explain, on the basis of your education and experience, what happens to these kids who are assaulted, as that may help the prosecutor and me come up with a reasonable plan for Lawrence in terms of his sentence. Your physical presence, combined with the reports from the mental health folks, could go a long way in achieving a reasonable outcome for this kid."

"Sounds good to me, Jed. Just let me know."

A week later, Baker and Pat visited Carl DeMatha's office, which was located in a ten-story, early twentieth century stone building adjacent to the Foxon courthouse. On the second floor, the elevator opened into a small waiting room where a gray-haired woman sat guard at an oversized oak desk bearing a computer and a telephone next to a pile of small sheets of paper that looked like phone messages. When Baker identified himself, she smiled and pointed for them to continue into the inner part of the office, where they found the prosecutor seated at a large metal desk strewn with manila folders—each one, Pat later learned, representing a criminal case pending in court. The look of a busy man, Pat quickly decided, and maybe not a very organized one. DeMatha's physical appearance matched his desk—unkempt, uncombed hair flopping over his ears, haphazardly dressed in a tie that clashed with his shirt with a wrinkled jacket draped over his chair. With a quick glance around the room, Pat saw more files on an adjacent table and books in shelves piled every which way.

As they entered, DeMatha stood to extend his hand to Baker in a warm greeting, revealing pants that looked like they had never met an iron. "Good to see you, my friend, and, Father, I'm Carl DeMatha. Please, let's sit so we can talk."

"You know, don't you, Jed, this kid is going to have to serve some time. We can't just put him on probation after killing someone no matter how bad a guy Mason was."

Baker was prepared. "I don't disagree with you, Carl. I'd like to talk with you about where Lawrence will have to serve his sentence and, of course, how long it must be."

"What do you have in mind, Jed?" And so the plea bargaining began.

"Well, he's just fourteen now, Carl. Maybe a sentence of four years to be served here at the juvenile detention facility to be followed by a period of probation."

"Oh, I don't know," replied the prosecutor. "Four years for a murder seems way too short even if he is a kid."

At that point, Baker asked if Pat could talk about what happens, generally, to kids who have been abused.

"I think I told you, Carl, that Father Pat has a master's degree in social work and works full time as the chaplain at Suffolk."

"Yes, of course, Jed," the prosecutor responded.

Pat started slowly, wary of appearing to be a know-it-all and not wanting to patronize.

"Well, Mr. DeMatha, in my master's program, I studied about child abuse with particular attention to its long-term effects on the victims. Unfortunately, there is an increasing body of literature on this subject. I'm certainly no expert but what I've learned is that these kids' lives often spiral into dysfunction. Lots of reasons for that but one constant appears to be the lack of early intervention. That's not surprising because so many victims bear their burdens in secret. Here, you have the chance to fashion a disposition for Lawrence that could actually help guide him back so that whenever he's released from custody, he has a chance of a reasonable life. Living with the knowledge that he took a life, of course, will be a heavy burden for him. But if he doesn't get intense counseling now, I fear that his life will just descend into a miasma of despair and then who knows in terms of his social conduct."

As though on cue, Baker added, "And, Carl, you know that the men's prison would provide none of that. Perhaps the juvenile facility might work so long as the boy can get the counseling he needs, and, of course, sending him there for a reasonable period, I hope, could satisfy the State's need that he be punished, confined for a while."

After more good-natured and earnest back and forth, including a discussion of the reports from the mental health experts, the lawyers agreed that the case would be transferred to the adult court, where DeMatha would recommend that the youngster plead guilty to manslaughter, a lesser charge than murder, and that he would be sentenced to a period of twelve years, suspended after serving four years, to be followed by eight years of probation to include continuing counseling as recommended by the probation department. While Baker said he thought the top end of the sentence, twelve years, seemed a bit high as any violation of probation, even for a minor violation, could expose Lawrence to eight more years of incarceration, he didn't push his view because he was relieved that all of the boy's incarceration would be served at the juvenile center, where education and counseling would be available to him.

Later, Baker told Pat about his subsequent meeting with Lawrence, when he told him what was likely to happen. Baker reported, "The boy seemed unmoved, almost uninterested in his fate. It was an unnerving kind of interview, Padre, one I'm not used to with my adult clients."

Once hearing this, Pat wondered to himself whether Lawrence's outcome had already been determined in that shower room at his school. He knew the boy had broken one of God's sternest prohibitions, but he could not reconcile the damnation of the boy's soul with the goodness of a forgiving God. He resolved to periodically visit the youngster and, over time, try to gentle him back to spiritual equilibrium. He sensed, as well, that he had been emotionally dislodged by the horrific tale of an abusive priest and his violent slaying by a boy whose innocence had been stolen from him. What was the value of his role in this nightmarish tale, he wondered, and could this youngster ever recover? Only time would yield the answers.

II

LOST AT SEA

A few days after seeing Lawrence Jefferson, Pat returned home to Duncan's Cove for a long weekend with his younger brother Sean, sister-in-law Maggie, and their teenage son Chris. Although Sean was five years younger than Pat and seemed cut from a different bolt, the two brothers shared a kinship bond of mutual affection. Unlike Pat, Sean had been boisterous as a youngster, a great high school athlete, full of energy, a magnet for friends. He had carried his energy and bravado into adulthood, outfitting his lobster boat, *Keefe's Folly*, with an oversized engine so he could participate in lobster boat races on weekends. He savored competition and his occasional victories with a gusto often beyond Pat's understanding.

He and Maggie had been high school sweethearts and had married young, anxious to begin their life together. In time, they had settled into a comfortable family life raising Chris, who seemed to carry both of his parents' traits—full of energy, respectful of his parents, and bursting with the promise of life. Weather permitting, Sean lobstered throughout the year while Maggie had worked her way up the employment ladder at the fisherman's cooperative to become its much respected manager. For Pat, the occasional weekends at home with them were always a welcomed respite and often full of fun devised by Sean for their amusement.

After the weekend, Pat returned to his prison duties, wearied by his experience with the young priest killer, Lawrence Jefferson, but buoyed by the liveliness of Maggie and Sean's home. Though he had become somewhat inured by his growing comfort in working with felony inmates, nothing in his formation or earlier assignments had prepared him to deal with such a tragically wounded youngster as Lawrence Jefferson. He had needed this break.

He had little time to dwell on these recent events, however, because shortly after he returned from Duncan's Cove, he received an urgent call from Maggie that Sean had not returned from fishing in the afternoon as normal, and he had not been seen the rest of that day or night. Pat was overcome. He immediately rushed home and quickly joined in the search on a friend's lobster boat. By this time, the Coast Guard was also conducting a search operation. Pat learned from Maggie that Sean had left earlier in the morning than normal because he had a double workload. He was helping an older friend, Mark Philips, who was ailing and not able to fish. Sean would tend Mark's traps as well as his own and, in return, he'd be paid a percentage of Mark's share in the cooperative's profits with Mark sharing the cost for fuel and bait. In this way, Mark's traps could still be active and both he and Sean could reap some benefit from the continued work while Mark was too sick to go out.

On this particular day, Sean had set out amid dark clouds and a worsening marine forecast. He left in spite of Maggie's urging that he remain in port, arguing that both he and Mark needed the income and the traps could not be left unattended lest the lobsters caught in them become too weak for market. As Maggie reported, the day had darkened and the wind quickened, likely making Sean's boat an unstable platform, a dangerous workplace in a changing sea.

She and their fishing friends all feared the worse. And, sadly, their fears were realized. After three days of searching, Mark's boat was found ashore in a place called Seal Cove, a vacation, home-lined retreat for seasonal residents about fifteen miles south of Duncan's Cove. The boat was wedged between the rocks close to shore, her hull partially holed and taking on water. On later inspection, it was determined that the boat had run out of fuel. There was no sign of Sean. Two days later, Sean's body washed up ashore several miles away, hardly recognizable except for the clothes still clinging to his distorted and bloated body.

At Maggie's request, Pat conducted the funeral Mass. Holy Family Church was packed with family and nearly all of the fishing community. Pat's mom and dad, now looking elderly, had flown up from Florida, where they were living in retirement. Pat's homily dwelt on fishing. He decided that since many of Christ's disciples were fishermen and several parables found their metaphorical roots in fishing, his focus on Christ as a fisher could be comforting, maybe even reassuring to his family and friends. The notion of putting out nets to gather in the faithful and also to gather substance to reap God's bounty resonated with this grieving assembly as they celebrated Sean's life while mourning his death. Pat spoke too of the honesty, the earnestness of fishing as a way of work. His words rang true as most knew his upbringing, his credentials as a part of this close-knit community.

When he voiced his awareness that danger is always a part of being at sea, as the community had once again experienced through Sean's death, they knew he spoke from the heart. Pat talked about Sean in a personal way as well, his exuberance, his love for Maggie and Chris, and how even he, as a priest, felt great grief and confusion that Sean had perished too young. He offered a prayer that he and the entire congregation could be reconciled in the faith that God's plan is not always seen.

After church, the community gathered at St. Elmo's hall next to the fisherman's coop where families shared homemade stews, casseroles, breads, and desserts, and all had a chance to visit and reminisce. This experience saddened and warmed Pat. He felt at home in this setting, sorrowed by the loss of his brother but embraced by the community of his youth.

After a week or so trying to help Maggie and Chris regain their footings and a few dinners with his sisters Susan and

Ruth, Pat returned to his prison ministry, sad to leave his hometown but comfortable once again to be with his prison congregation. He was not prepared for what happened next.

III

TREACHERY

Pat resumed his prison work, attempting to immerse himself in the needs of the inmates even though his concerns for the fate of Lawrence Jefferson and the loss of his brother were never far from his mind. *Is it odd?* he wondered to himself, *that I'm more concerned about what happens to this kid than the fact that he took another person's life, a priest at that.* Food for contemplation and prayer, Pat concluded.

He was surprised one afternoon when his old seminary mentor, Father Stanley Mathews, called on behalf of the diocese with a request. Father Stan said that the diocese had decided to sponsor a weekend retreat at the chancellery for priests of the diocese. He asked Pat if he would be willing to share insights gained from ministering in a prison setting. Pat initially was skeptical. "What can I tell these priests that would be relevant to their parish work?"

"Don't take such a narrow view of your ministry," responded Stan. "The people our priests serve—whether in parishes, hospitals, or prisons—are all part of Christ's flock. I'm sure you know that. I think you'll have a lot to say that's meaningful. You might even inspire a few."

Pat's loyalty to Father Stan overrode his reticence. At the welcoming gathering in the chancellery's paneled meeting hall, there were priests and seminarians roaming under the crystal chandeliers, enjoying the hors d'oeuvres and libations, amicably mixing with old and new friends while awaiting the first session of the retreat. Pat saw some of his classmates, including his old roommate, Luke Reardon, whom he hadn't talked with since ordination in spite of their mutual promises to stay in touch. "Luke, so good to see you. Where are you assigned? Do you enjoy your parish work?" The usual chatter between old friends now grown apart.

To his surprise, Pat thought his talk went well. He had even been inspired while preparing for it. Perhaps, he now remembers thinking, there's some benefit, once in a while, to gathering myself, taking stock, the quiet reflection required in advance of a speech. Based on the reactions of the retreat attendees, Pat felt glad he had accepted this invitation, although he thought he likely benefited most from the experience.

To Pat's surprise, Luke approached him after his presentation. He looked about the same as he did in seminary except for a few pounds added to his mid-sized frame, his sandy hair now cut short, his eyes a paler blue. Pat thought their initial chat had been vapid, a meaningless gloss on a past friendship. This time Luke's demeanor was different, quiet. Without any preliminaries, he asked Pat if he would hear his confession at some point during the weekend. "Why would you want me to do that, Luke? I'm sure the retreat organizers have planned for that possibility. Certainly there are priests at the meeting who have been designated to hear confessions during the weekend. They'll probably be some announcement about that later today or tomorrow." But Luke was insistent. "No, Pat, I was inspired by your talk and I trust you. Please do this for me."

And so, on Sunday afternoon, once the formal retreat had concluded, Luke and Pat met by pre-arrangement in the private chapel at the chancellery, the bishop's special place for prayer and meditation. Unlike the garish meeting hall, the chapel was quiet in muted colors, adorned only with two stained glass windows and fronted with a plain wooden altar. Sitting side by side on a pew toward the front, they were alone with most of the retreat participants in process of leaving. Luke asked Pat if he could talk for a while about his own priesthood before getting into the specific reason he wanted to make an act of contrition, but he emphasized that everything he said from that point needed to be considered as part of his confession. Pat agreed, curious about Luke's obvious preoccupation with secrecy.

"At least outwardly," Luke started, "my priesthood has followed a traditional arc. After ordination I was assigned to St. Mary's Church in Hopstown, where I assumed the routine duties of a parish priest—saying Mass, hearing confessions, performing baptisms, weddings, and funerals. I also volunteered to coach adolescent youngsters in the parish-sponsored Catholic Youth Organization, where I could share my basketball skills. That was fun for me. I got along well with the kids under my tutelage. The rector, Monsignor Cummings, thought I was particularly suited by age and personality to work with the youngsters of the parish. And the kids, in turn, appeared to take to me."

Pat was curious as to where the narration was heading, but he remained silent as Luke spoke. What Pat next heard was deeply shattering.

"I became attracted to one of the kids on the basketball team. I don't want to say his name, but we became friends. I liked to give him treats, candy bars, that sort of thing. One time I even invited him into the rectory for ice cream when I knew the others were out." At this point in Luke's narration, Pat was stunned, but he remained quiet, dreading what he feared might be coming. "After a while, I decided to invite him to my coach's office, where I put my arms around the boy and kissed him. When I started moving my arms and hands around him, he pushed me away, yelled something unkind to me, and ran from the office. I think he was crying."

At this point, Pat couldn't resist asking, "What did you feel then, Luke, about the boy and yourself?"

Luke's response was telling. "I didn't know what to do. I was scared that something might happen to me. I guess he must have told his parents because just a week later I was transferred to St. Anselm's in Johnstown. No one ever told me why. The monsignor just came to me one day and said he had received a message from the chancellery that I was immediately to go to this new parish, and so I did. Once I got there, it was just like nothing had ever happened. I guess because I was the youngest priest, I was again assigned to work with kids, this time the parish Boy Scout troop. And it happened all over again. I became fond of another lad, paid particular attention to him, complimenting him on his achievements, giving him special help in his work toward merit badges. One weekend I took the troop on a campout, where I arranged for this boy to have a tent to himself. After bedtime I went to this boy in his tent, bringing him a special candy bar I knew he liked. We talked for a while and then I just lied down next to the boy, caressing him. I asked him to touch my penis and rub it while I did the same to him. Once, the boy said he thought what we were doing was wrong, but I just told him it was just about becoming a man, and that it was okay because I'm a priest."

Pat was repulsed not only by the contents of what Luke said but by his calm demeanor, as though he was giving a book report, talking about some benign subject. Luke continued, "I guess this kid must have told somebody because this time I was called to meet with Monsignor O'Brien at the chancellery. He really ripped into me, told me that he wouldn't tolerate any more misbehavior by me, to get myself under control. He then dismissed me, saying I had just one more chance before something might happen to me. Next thing I knew, I was sent to St. Charles Parish in Medford where the rector welcomed me with open arms, said he was happy to have a younger man to help with the youth activities. I guess nobody told him about my troubles."

Luke's recitation continued, now with disheartening familiarity, as he retraced his steps from parish to parish to his present assignment. He said that he had tried to control his urges in his later assignments, with some success, as he was afraid of getting into more serious trouble. So far, he said, he had not heard further from the chancellery. Pat surmised from this sordid account that Luke's abuse of children continued through multiple assignments, unabated and unseen, except by his victims; Monsignor Vincent O'Brien, who was the bishop's right-hand man; and maybe the bishop himself. Also aware of Luke's destructive behavior, as it related to their own sons, were probably the families who were too daunted by the authority of the Church to make waves beyond their own parishes and far too hesitant to make pubic their children's experiences. Pat surmised that the parish rectors who had reported Luke's behaviors to the chancellery ellnnwere likely cowed by fear, misplaced loyalty to the Church, or personal ambition to report Luke's misdeeds beyond the confines of the Church.

After confessing his predatory behavior without expressing emotion, Luke asked Pat for absolution. He admitted to Pat that at times he felt besieged by sexual urges toward young boys that, sometimes, he felt were beyond his control. Luke vowed to try to quell his urges as he continued in his priesthood.

Pat's first response was to question Luke. "Why now, Luke? Why seek absolution after all that? What has brought you to this point?" Luke's response was disarming. "I'm not sure, Pat. I know what I've done is wrong and I'm sorry for it. I just have these urges that sometimes engulf me, but I want to be better. I'm hoping for a fresh start."

Pat asked, "Luke, have you ever seen a mental health counselor for this, thought about taking a break to try to heal?" Luke shook his head. "Oh, no, Pat. I think I can be right now. I know I want to try."

The dilemma of knowing these horrible secrets while being ruled by silence unsettled Pat's moorings. Steeped in the Catholic tradition and Church law regarding the sacrament of penance, Pat knew that in hearing Luke's confession he was acting only as God's agent and that whatever Luke confessed to him could not be revealed. Nevertheless, Pat was deeply troubled not only by the realization that Luke had committed such shocking acts, but by Luke's failure to demonstrate any genuine remorse for his victims. Pat worried that Luke's misconduct could be out of control. Moreover, he grieved for Luke's many victims, whose lives no doubt had been immeasurably affected by Luke's depravity.

In his prison ministry, Pat had counseled inmates who were adult victims of sexual abuse, often by male relatives in positions of power to them—fathers, stepfathers, mothers' boyfriends. Common among all these inmates were feelings of despair, unworthiness, and anger—and in some, thoughts of suicide. Hearing these stories, Pat had learned how the damage of abuse had affected and tormented the lives of these men. In the prison setting, Pat could offer solace and reassurance that those men as children had been victims, even if later in life they had victimized others in the same or other ways. His recent unhappy experience with the youngster who had killed his abuser gave him yet another perspective on the devastation wrecked by the adult abuse of children.

Pat had learned in seminary that not all sinners were entitled to absolution, the cleansing of their souls of their sins. For absolution, he knew, a sinner must not only confess his sins but must be contrite with a firm resolve not to sin again. To him, it appeared Luke only wanted to unburden himself of his sinfulness, clean the slate, assuming that absolution would then be automatic. But Pat reasoned differently. He told Luke, "As God's representative, I will grant you absolution only if you agree to take a personal leave from your responsibilities and to seek mental health counseling from a qualified therapist, returning to ministry only with the concurrence of that counselor." Luke readily mouthed his agreement with Pat's conditions and then abruptly left the chapel, leaving Pat filled with concern for Luke's victims and dread that Luke's appetite might be insatiable.

Pat was in a quandary. If he kept silence, could he somehow be morally implicated in Luke's evil acts? But if he reported Luke's confession, he'd be guilty of breaking the holy seal of confession and subject himself to the harsh penalty of excommunication from the Church he so loved. Caught in the apparently insolvable conflict between his fidelity to his priestly vows and his moral sense of outrage and foreboding, Pat was immobilized. On one hand, he had, for the years of his priesthood, embraced the seal of confession, but, he was burdened with the fear that Luke's preying on youngsters could be continuing, and that thought tormented him.

In his education as a social worker and counselor, Pat had learned the value of consultation. But that resource did not seem available to him without violating his priestly vow.

Unable to report Luke's misdeeds to any third party, Pat resolved to speak directly with Luke, to learn if he had at least started counseling and whether he had sought a leave from his parish assignment. A week after the retreat, Pat drove to Luke's parish in Gainsburg and met privately with him.

"Luke, I've come to see you to follow up on our meeting last week. Please tell me what steps you've taken as we've discussed and as you agreed."

Luke's response was cold, hostile. "When we spoke, Father Keefe, it was in confession and what was said there stays there. I'm not interested in any further discussion with you about that. If you have no other reason for being here, then your trip has been wasted, and so has my time. I think you should go." Pat reeled as though he had been struck in the face.

"Luke, you promised to get counseling, to seek a leave of absence in order to receive absolution for your sins. Have you lost interest in the holy sacrament of penance?" He knew his response was harsh but he was trying to stir Luke from his impassiveness.

Not the penitent he projected to be in the chancellery chapel, Luke responded: "Remember the sanctity of the confessional, Father, and that you're bound to silence no matter how uncomfortable you might be with my secrets. I think we're done here. Please go." Luke opened the door to his room, leaving Pat standing, agape.

On his return to the prison, Pat considered his unhappy meeting with Luke. He knew that Luke relied with cunning on Pat's faithfulness, his commitment to the tenets of their shared faith. He concluded that Luke probably felt confident that he wouldn't report his confession to anyone lest he compromise his own priesthood. The more he considered Luke's demeanor and words, he felt that Luke had been surprised that Pat had not simply given him absolution without penitential requirements. The conditions he had imposed on Luke, he now realized, were more than Luke was willing to abide, a troubling omen for Pat.

Luke's arrogant resistance to Pat's entreaties was dizzying. What else could he do? After considerable puzzling over the issue, he decided that he could perhaps speak with his mentor, Father Stanley Mathews, talking only in hypotheticals without revealing Luke's identity or the specific acts of his violence. Pat chose Father Stan because he knew that in addition to his grasp of philosophy and scriptures, he was a canon lawyer, trained in the law of the Church. He also deeply trusted Father Stan because he had served as his confessor from time to time while he was a seminarian. He knew from this personal experience that Father Stan would be a wise and reflective listener. Two days later, Pat drove to the seminary and went to Father Stan's rooms, where he was warmly greeted.

The older and balding, but still trim, professor was seated comfortably in his reclining chair, books and journals strewn about in literary disarray. Immediately he put aside what he was reading and warmly greeted Pat. "Have a seat, Pat, you look terrible. I think you might have more white hairs than just a while ago when I saw you at the retreat, and you're blanched. Are you ill? What's wrong?" These were Father Stan's first words as he looked quizzically at Pat.

"Thank you for seeing me on short notice, Father Stan. I'm deeply troubled, Father, because I feel morally vexed and, yes, I think it might be affecting me physically, too, but I'm not worried about that. Can I give you a hypothetical situation and then talk with you about what's eating at me?"

"Of course, Pat. Fire away."

"Recently, Father Stan, I heard the confession of a priest—no names as I don't intend to violate the seal of confession. But this man told me in confession that he has sexually abused several youngsters in his charge. Although he promised that he'd take a leave of absence and get therapy, I'm afraid he won't do either. I'm so worried this man may still be abusing children, and yet I'm silenced by my vows. I'm even thinking of leaving the priesthood, if that's what it takes, so that I can report this man if that would save even one child. And, yet, Father, I love my vocation. What can you say to me?"

Father Stan was quiet for a few moments and then he sighed. "Well, of course, Pat, you cannot break the seal of confession unless this man has told you he actually intends to continue his harmful ways. That's the only exception to the seal, Pat. A confessor who states an intention to commit a future crime or sin is not protected, but, in this case, your worries, valid as they may be, are not the same as a statement from this man of his future intent. And, please, God, don't think about leaving the priesthood over this. You are too good a priest for the Church to lose, and I don't want you to lose yourself either."

Father Stan continued, "You know, Pat, there's a difference between breaking a rule of the Church and violating one of God's truths. Let me give you an example. Priestly celibacy is a rule of the Church organization but it's only a temporal law subject to change. We know from our study of Church history that there were married clergy for the first several hundred years of its existence and the rule came about only as a result of the deliberations of a church council. Indeed, the history of the Church reveals that even some popes had illegitimate children. But the sexual abuse of children is an outrage, so much worse than merely violating a rule created by the leaders of the Church.

"This man violated God's eternal law. Remember what you learned from the psalms, Pat, that children are a heritage from the Lord. In many places in scripture we see that the abuse of children is viewed as an abomination. In short, Pat, this man is not merely violating a vow, a rule of the Church; his conduct violates a tenet of God. An abomination, indeed. Nevertheless, no matter how vile the act, once revealed to you in confession, your lips are sealed."

In saying this, Father Stan made reference to the section of canon law on the subject that holds, he reported while reading from a text, that the sacramental seal is inviolable and that it is unpardonable for a confessor to betray a penitent, for any reason whatsoever, whether by word or in any other fashion. "Remember, Pat", Father Stan pointed out, "the notion of confession is that the confessor is God's representative on earth and that by confessing his or her sins, the penitent is seeking God's grace, a reunion into God's house, which can only happen through confession and absolution. So, there's a good reason that the seal must be sacrosanct. If it weren't, many people, we fear, would not seek absolution and communion with the Church. So, you're stuck, Pat, because this man did not say he intends to keep molesting; you must keep silence about what he confessed even though you withheld absolution, as I certainly would have under the circumstances."

"I understand that, Father, but this man's confession, which I now doubt was sincere, probably does little for his soul, and my silence only makes me an abettor in his evildoing."

"No, Pat. Do not be so harsh on yourself, and give God His due. This man will have his comeuppance, now or much later, and your silence does not fuel his wickedness."

"Well, maybe so, Father, but my concern for this man's victims is what has me thinking the impossible."

"No, Pat, please put that out of your mind. The punishment for violating the seal is excommunication and losing your priesthood. This man you're speaking of is not worth the loss of your soul. Trust in God, Pat, that he will be punished."

"Not much solace, Father, for his victims, but I understand and respect your counsel. That's why I came. I need to pray and think more on it. Thank you for seeing me. You are wise, as always. I guess I was just hoping for some magic." They embraced as Pat left, still disconsolate.

In the end, Pat concluded that Father Stan had been receptive but had provided him no vision for solving his dilemma. Indeed, his advice only confirmed in stark terms Pat's awareness that the seal of confession was sacrosanct. He hadn't been sure, however, that the rule of silence trumps even the civil law that requires certain caregivers to report abuse to children. Father Stan had explained that the overarching purpose of canon law is to set the contours of the Church organization in order to protect regularity in the Church, and, in that manner, to help preserve and protect the majesty of the Church, a value greater, doctrine holds, than the mandates of civil law. Confused and conflicted, Pat drove back to work uneasy with the sense of conflict between the constraints of his priestly obligation and his concern for Luke's unknown victims.

Battered by Luke's admissions, Pat resolved to seek a leave of absence in order to create space from his daily obligations and to make time for quiet contemplation. He thought that perhaps a period of prayer and meditation might light the way ahead. He knew that he could not continue until he regained his own equilibrium. He needed to come to some resolution of this intractable dilemma between his faithfulness to Church dogma and his more temporal concern for Luke's unknown victims. How could he hear anybody's confession, counsel any inmate or student, when he felt personally so unsteady in his vocation? Until he could regain his spiritual footing, he did not feel suited to the duties of his calling.

Pat decided to seek a meeting at the chancellery of his home diocese in order to gain permission to take a leave of absence. He knew that even though he was working in an adjacent diocese he was still under the thumb of the bishop, to whom he had taken a vow of obedience. And, he correctly assumed the bishop had delegated to his vicar the authority to grant or deny Pat's request. He was hoping that since he was not actually serving in the diocese, the bishop would not have any work-related objections to his absence. And, he was correct. When he arrived at the chancellery, he was escorted into Monsignor O'Brien's office, an ornate room filled with religious-themed oil paintings on the walls and even a small statuette of the Virgin Mary atop a table by a window. The white-haired, burly monsignor remained seated at his oversized desk as he summoned Pat to have a seat. The meeting was brief. Pat told the vicar only that he was facing a personal and spiritual unease that required him to step back and embark on a period of prayer and contemplation. The taciturn vicar listened without comment or question. Once Pat had finished speaking, the monsignor simply nodded his assent. That simply, Pat's request was granted. After informing Warden Tucker at Suffolk, Pat returned home to live with his sister-in-law Maggie and her son Chris.

When Pat first phoned Maggie to ask her about staying with her, she was understandably concerned.

"Why are you leaving your priesthood, Pat? What terrible thing has happened to make you quit doing what you so much love?"

Pat replied, "First, thank you, Maggie for your caring. To be clear, I am not leaving the priesthood, at least not now. I am just taking a respite, a leave from my work, for some quiet time. If you'll allow it, I could just stay in your basement apartment and mostly keep to myself as I need a lot of time to think and pray."

"Well, if you're not quitting, Pat, are you sick? Something serious must be going on for you to be leaving even if just for a while. What about all those inmates who depend on you?"

"Well, Maggie, right now I don't think I'd be useful at the prison. The warden told me he could get a minister to come in, a retired friend of his, who could be there at least part-time while I'm gone."

"But then, Pat, what has you so upset that you feel you have to be away from what you love so much? Of course, you're welcome in our home. Chris will be thrilled to have you around. He so misses Sean. So, if you come, you can have your quiet space in the basement but you can't isolate yourself all the time. You will come as part of the family, even if a quieter presence than we'd like."

"Thank you, Maggie. Here's what I can tell you. I learned from someone that he's done evil and I can't repeat it because it was in confession, and I'm deeply bothered by it. I need to think and pray my way out of this dilemma." "Wow, what this person said to you in confession must be horrible. Surely you hear lots of sordid tales at Suffolk."

"That's true, Maggie, but for sheer evil, this one is the worst. I can't talk about it because it arose in confession where my lips are sealed. So, that's my problem. Please don't ask me any more about it. I need you to trust me on this, Maggie."

"Oh, Pat, trusting you is easy. Just come and be at home with us. We look forward to seeing you. I'm a good ear if you want to talk about any of this, but I think I know how to yield space too, when that's desired." Pat thanked Maggie and let her know when he'd be arriving, and they talked about his basement quarters.

Maggie's mid-century two-story home was on Back Cove Street, a tucked-away dead end with many similar houses nestled close together, a fishermen's enclave not yet discovered by the big money-from-away folks. From this home, it was only a short walk to the harbor. The home had a finished basement, which Pat now occupied. It was fine for him: a bedroom, a bath, and a small reading room with a television and a separate entrance, making it easy to come and go without affecting the family routine.

On the main floor, in addition to the bedrooms, there was a small combination dining and living room with a television and radio of uncertain age and a wood stove, now only a resting place for magazines, car keys, and the like. Chris' room was decorated with posters of hockey players, and a large Boston Bruins banner nearly covering one wall. Now thirteen, already five-foot-nine and broad-shouldered with his mother's curly blond hair, Chris showed competitive verve playing defense on the town's rec league hockey squad.

Maggie and Sean had bought this home in the early years of their marriage with financial help from Maggie's parents, Tom and Gail Calhoun, who had owned the Toyota dealership in town. Pat was comfortable in this home, which he had visited during his vacations over his student years and during his priesthood. None of his assignments to date had been too far for a family visit. He appreciated Maggie's hospitality to him during his leave. She was a good soul and Chris was lively and engaging, a family comforting for Pat in this most troublesome time in his life.

At Maggie's, in addition to taking daily walks, Pat prayed and read. He mixed in somewhat in Maggie and Chris' lives, and he occasionally got out into the community, but his inner turmoil was a constant block to any real sociability. Although he was close to his sisters Susan and Ruth, the fact that he could not tell them what was nagging at him only increased his sense of isolation.

From time to time he'd walk to the library to read magazines or journals dealing with social policy and current issues. One day he came upon a text about community organization, the notion that policy changes can be initiated in a community from the bottom up and not merely imposed from those in power, a different view of society's organization. While that subject had no direct relevance to his dilemma, the idea of rousing a community to action, of power from below and instead of from on top, gave him an inspiration. If he could not motivate Luke to step aside, and if he could not report Luke's abuse to any authority, perhaps he could find some way to make the community inhospitable to Luke's malevolence.

He came upon the idea of soliciting a public statement from the priests of the diocese in support of victims of sexual abuse by the clergy and affirming their commitment to protecting God's children, whom they were ordained to serve. His idea was that if he could obtain such a statement from a substantial number of priests, the publication of the statement in parish bulletins would energize the lay community to be more protective of their children's activities and watchful of wayward priests. He hoped that perhaps that change in the temper of the Catholic laity would embolden victims to speak out—and maybe, even, awaken the Church hierarchy to their ministerial duties.

Without making any reference to Luke's confession, Pat decided to speak with his old parish priest, Father Mike O'Donnell, about the increased reporting of clerical sexual abuse across the nation and the doubt now being cast on the good works of priests who were true to their vocations. Father Mike received him warmly. "Come in, my friend. I heard you were home on some sort of a leave of absence. Can I do anything for you?"

"Oh no, Father, but thank you. I just want to ask you about an idea I have."

"Fire away, Pat," The kindly priest responded.

After Pat described his notion of getting priests to join in a statement to be placed in parish bulletins, Father Mike showed concern. "Be careful, Pat. Tread lightly, as the good bishop might not take too kindly to a public discussion of this problem. As you can imagine, the increased attention to priest child sex abuse is a sore spot for Church leadership, and if you're seen as antagonistic to the Church, your standing could be jeopardized. I'd be wary of stirring the pot." Pat thanked his old mentor but decided that the risk was worth taking.

In his basement quarters, he prepared a statement with the intent that if he could obtain the support of enough priests, the statement would be published in the weekly parish bulletins of all the churches of the diocese. The statement read: "As priests in the Fishburg Diocese, we affirm our support for all victims of sexual abuse and our belief that the molestation of children is an abomination. We support victims of clerical abuse and we urge any victims to report such instances to their parish rectors and to civil authorities. We affirm our love for all of God's children in this public manner so you may bear witness to our shared commitment to all the faithful of the diocese to chaste lives in service to God and to all his people."

Pat first showed the draft to Maggie. Her reaction was spontaneous. "I don't know what's troubling you, Pat, but what's in this statement needs to be read. We're beginning to hear more about this problem and the Church has been silent about it. Good for you. I hope you can do this."

When Pat showed this draft to Father Mike, he was not surprised that the reaction was more muted. "This is very bold," said Father Mike, "and risks creating havoc with the diocese. If many victims are to be emboldened by this statement to come forth, you will not be popular at the chancellery. But nobody will be able to accuse you of veering from a Christlike path."

Pat took this as tacit approval but with a warning. He didn't care. His quandary had morphed into anger. He was caught in a conflict between canon law and civil law where he thought the latter had the moral upper hand, but he was limited so long as he continued in the priesthood he cherished. His plan, he thought, offered the possibility of frightening Luke into counseling and abstinence from his base misconduct while also offering abuse victims some hope of support from their church. "Thank you, Father Mike," Pat replied to him. "I know it's a bold step but I think this problem requires it. I'll take my chances with the good bishop."

"Godspeed" was all Father Mike said as they made their goodbyes.

Satisfied with the draft statement, Pat's next challenge was to find a way to embolden parish priests to publicly embrace it, a necessary prelude to presenting it to the Diocesan leadership for publication. He feared that some to whom he might send it could actually be abusers, while others might feel a loyalty to the Church hierarchy greater than their concern about the subject of clerical child abuse. He pondered how to make the first step.

Pat came upon the idea of sharing it with one of his seminary friends, Father Steven Walker, a priest he remembered from seminary as very devout and whom Pat had been in touch with from time to time, more for comradery than consultation but, nevertheless, someone with whom Pat thought he could share the draft and discuss possible steps forward. He remembered a particularly enjoyable conversation with Father Steven at the retreat when Steven was telling him of some interesting initiatives he had undertaken in his present assignment. And he thought this man would give Pat an objective yet caring critique of his proposed announcement.

Pat miscalculated. Not long after sending the draft to Father Walker, he received a summons to the chancellery office from Monsignor O'Brien. When Pat arrived, the burly O'Brien was seated at his desk, bare except for a telephone, a large blotter fronted by a pen and pencil set, and an inbox with neatly stacked papers. The scene immediately reminded Pat of the first time he had been in the room seeking his leave. Without any salutation, the scowling vicar shuffled the papers on the blotter before him and then held one up to Pat. "Is this your handiwork, Father Keefe? I thought you were on a leave of absence. What's this all about?" he asked.

"Yes, it's a draft I prepared. Don't you think, Monsignor, that we need to do something about the growing problem of sexual abuse in the Church?"

Obrien harshly replied, "No, I don't think WE should be doing anything about this problem. I'm sure you have your hands full at the prison, from what I read in the papers about that place. And now you're dealing with some sort of a personal problem that requires you to take leave from your responsibilities. I suggest you leave leadership to your leaders, Father, and we'll all be better off that way."

The monsignor then launched into an oration while seated with Pat standing, uninvited to take the chair immediately across from the monsignor's desk. "Your duty is one of loyalty to Church and to the bishop. That's what you should be concerned about. That's certainly not what this so-called bulletin item suggests."

What alarmed Pat was that at no time did the monsignor touch on the harm to victims of clerical abuse. His sole purpose with Pat seemed to be to put him in his place. And, when Pat attempted to broaden the discussion to get into the substance of the issue of priest child sex abuse, the monsignor was dismissive. "We know what's best for the Church, Father Keefe. Just do your job." Pat did not go quiet. "I think I understand my vows, Monsignor, and I hope I have been serving God's church in my prison ministry, but shouldn't we all be concerned when evil is being done in the name of the Church?" he asked.

"Let me repeat this to you, Father Keefe, slowly and clearly, so you'll have no misperception. You do your job and, in this building, we will guide you in your ministry. Your task is to obey. We will provide God's leadership to you. We are your shepherds and, in turn, you administer to your flock—in your case, a building full of felons and other miscreants."

Without directly threatening Pat, the monsignor suggested that further circulation of the draft by Pat to other priests could put at risk his prison work and could even subject him to an order of silence from the bishop. It was a difficult, dispiriting meeting. Once the monsignor's lecture was completed, he unceremoniously tore up Pat's proposed bulletin entry and dismissed Pat, who left disheartened and angry. If this was to be the reaction of Church officialdom, the laity deserved to know that their parish priests, the men who had constant interaction with their children, were, in the main, people of holiness and generosity who would bring no harm to their children. If such a message would not come from the top, then it must be generated from below. But, for now, he knew that avenue had been closed.

This tension was causing Pat great anxiety. In his lifetime, he had never experienced the discomfort of being at odds with his church, and the notion that diocesan leadership was on the wrong side of a moral dilemma was disorienting for him.

At home, Pat found some comfort and balance from his family interactions. On earlier weekends back in Duncan's Cove, he had watched Chris grow into adolescence, and now he had the opportunity to know him better. He enjoyed helping him with homework assignments and attending his school-related events. With his growing athletic talent, Chris was a star on the rec league hockey squad. His team played their home matches at the Duncan's Corner ice rink, and they traveled to other towns, an adventure for Chris and his mates. Pat enjoyed going to Chris' practices and talking with him about sports. He also met with the coach, James German, and tried to sort out whether he was a good influence for the kids. It was hard to know, but from what Pat could see, German acted respectfully and amiably. He seemed totally appropriate.

How little we know, mused Pat to himself. On the outside someone can seem normal while still leading a secret life of wickedness. Pat resolved to keep an eye on Chris for any signs of disturbance. Happily, none appeared throughout the season. Although Pat had only been minimally involved in sports as a student, he had enjoyed watching sports on television, sometimes at the penitentiary with the inmates or on

Sunday afternoons at the rectory with the other priests. This shared interest with Chris enhanced a growing bond between them. Chris, in turn, seemed to relish having an adult male in the household, a dad figure, Pat supposed. It was an unfamiliar role for him but he embraced it as well as he could.

In the evenings, at times, having coffee in the living room, Pat and Maggie would talk about Sean and the loss to Chris. Maggie commented that having Pat around was an unforeseen godsend for him. In time, it appeared to Maggie, Chris had begun to look up to Pat in this way. From Pat's perspective, he enjoyed these family interactions. He had not been in such close contact with a youngster since his early home life. And Maggie, whom Pat had known since she and Sean were dating, was easy company. Bright and pert, trim with curly, straw-colored hair, Maggie had not lost any of her teenage allure. Such a young widow, Pat thought, a full life ahead of her, but now without her beloved Sean.

During the day she worked as the manager of the lobster coop as the store's retail manager, a job she returned to after a brief period of mourning. She was full of ideas about how to modernize the lobster coop operation and to make it more attractive to tourists as a way to increase its earnings, which were shared with the fishermen who belonged to the coop. They talked too about literature—prose and poetry—as Pat discovered that Maggie was an avid reader whose learning belied her limited formal education. He discovered that they shared a love for Dickinson and Frost for their connection to nature, another common interest. This new awareness of their mutual enjoyment made life with Maggie amiable.

And as Pat eased into the relaxed relationship of a close family, so too Chris grew in his attachment to him and willingness to talk with him about himself and his life as he approached his teenage years. Pat liked the feeling of being a dad figure to this engaging youngster.

IV

INTROSPECTION

During his leave of absence, Father Pat often hiked up Fish Trap Hill to sit on Sean's bench. In early May, weather permitting, he'd come to this perch overlooking his hometown harbor to ponder, and to fret. Soon after his brother Sean's death at sea, the fishing community of Duncan's Cove had commissioned Art McDonough, a local furniture maker, to craft the bench. He had skillfully built it in the traditional way, fitted together only by wood dowels, made to last. With the town's blessing, this commemorative bench had been placed in a conspicuous spot, easy to view and to remind, and it afforded a panorama of the harbor.

On calm mornings, after the lobster fleet had gone, the remaining boats alternately tugged and eased at their moorings, swayed by the breeze and current. The water lapped the harbor's shore, its many private docks, and the Duncan's Cove lobster coop, a commercial operation now managed by Maggie. Fuel, bait, and ice were sold there, and lobsters were stored in pens tied alongside the dock, pending sale.

Often, Pat was able to view the swooping of terns and osprey divebombing from high aloft. On the water, cormorants dunked and resurfaced as they hunted. Of course, the gulls, gray and white-backed, were ever-present. When Pat came in mid-morning, the fishing fleet would be gone, just pleasure craft and a few idle lobster boats still in harbor. In the afternoon, he could watch the boats return, gulls in pursuit, and line up to discharge their catch at the lobster coop and replenish their bait supply for the next day, a familiar rhythm of activity soothing to Pat.

He recognized the routine that unfolded before him from his high school days, when he helped at the pier after school and on weekends—a happy and innocent memory. On clear days, the bench offered a near view of the mooring field as well as the harbor's distant outlet to the sea. But on others, when the harbor was befogged or misted by light rain, only shapes were visible, less settled and more like Pat's frame of mind. Since taking a leave of absence and coming home to stay with Maggie and Chris, it had become Pat's habit to go to this place, where he would sit, sometimes in prayer or meditation, never free of the angst that vexed him, as he pondered his uncertain way forward.

Never did he imagine in his formation and early priesthood that he would find himself at this crossroad in his priesthood, conflicted between duty and the right, between obedience and conscience. In this early spring, he needed to get out at least once a day to breathe the salt air and smell the promise of summer in the greening of lawns and the flowers now beginning to bud. Seeing the white and yellow daffodils, and the narcissus and the rhododendron buds swelling red and white along his way, prompted him to recall his mother's love for nature's beauty and her enjoyment in tending her small flowerbed in their postage stamp front yard.

These reminders of his childhood place helped to gentle Pat as he ambled along familiar walkways. He liked to think about his upbringing in this town of happy memories, his family and friends, of his calling and formation as a priest, and his ministry at the state penitentiary, from which he was now on indefinite leave. For Pat, retracing his life's path helped center him as he strove to make sense of his dilemma and to try to visualize his way forward.

Sometimes Pat let his mind wander to his upbringing in Duncan's Cove. Born in 1948 to Angela and Joseph Keefe, he had mixed memories of his early years as the oldest of four in a close-knit family. They lived in a home less than a mile from Maggie's in a small grouping of similar homes on a back street, not unlike Maggie's. Neither Angie, as she was known, nor Joe had much formal education beyond high school. Having met in nearby Millard Junior College, they completed two years and then decided to get jobs so they could afford to be married. With a little pull from his well-situated family, Joe was hired by the post office and stayed on for a full career before retiring. Angie worked first as a bookkeeper at the lobster coop but then stayed home while rearing the four children while they were young, returning to the coop once the last had fledged. Now living in central Florida, Pat's parents had moved south after Joe had taken an early disability retirement caused by an accident at the loading dock at the post office. They hardly traveled now, last seen by the family at Sean's funeral, a sad homecoming for them.

Joe and Angie's New England cape-styled house had been just adequate to accommodate the family. Pat the oldest and Sean the youngest, less than six years apart, shared a bedroom as did their sisters, Susan and Ruth, little more than a year apart. In the mornings before school, adequate time in the home's one bathroom was often a challenge to harmony but, overall, by the grace of God, their close living added strength to the family bond. Although quiet in manner, Pat sometimes played the role of peacemaker, particularly when all four kids were competing for bathroom time in the morning rush for school, urging his siblings to be patient and considerate and to keep any uproars down lest their father overreact with his occasional sternness.

While Pat generally had fond memories of his upbringing, he remembered his dad most for his controlling ways. He ruled the roost, to be sure, but he was never abusive, at least in a physical way. Thinking back on his elementary school days, Pat now realized how strict his father had been. In the household, his word was always final. His parents seemed, at least to a kid, to have a loving relationship. Often, pleased that he so capably fulfilled his role as the oldest, they both marveled that their quiet son had such people skills. "That boy's got strength in him," Pat once heard his dad say. And his mother: "Perhaps a bit of goodness as well for his gentleness. He surely will make us proud one day."

He liked it that they thought of him in that way, although he was uncertain until he was a teenager what his parents had in mind for him. While breakfast was often on the run, the family traditionally ate dinner together, always protein, veggies, and carbs, followed by dessert as their mom delighted in baking. The children took turns leading grace before dinner and, by seniority, did kitchen cleanup afterwards.

Family entertainment at home was simple. There was a radio and a phonograph player in the living room, no television until the mid-'50s, and a small backyard with a patio and a grill and a net for badminton. Along the white picket fence girding the back area, Pat's mom had planted rose bushes, which she lovingly tended each growing season. From his early days, Pat enjoyed listening to music on the phonograph or the radio while indoors and playing pickup games in the milder months of the year. At physical play, Sean and Susan always dominated Pat and Ruth, the usual pairing for badminton. Those two were more or less the aggressors while Pat and Ruth typically were more passive, less compulsive about coming out on top.

More than sports, Pat enjoyed music. His taste as a kid and now was eclectic. Growing up, he liked to listen to whatever was available on a clear FM station; anything— classical, jazz, soul, or folk. As he matured, he turned more to folk and now, sometimes when he took his walks, he'd take his Walkman and earphones so he could listen to his favorites— Joan Baez, Bob Dylan, Arlo Guthrie, Mahalia Jackson, and Odetta—as they sang songs of America, of struggle and of unity, music he'd heard on his wondrous and meaningful trip to Washington, D.C., back in 1963.

To the close-living fishing community, the Keefes were a family to admire. All students of Holy Family Grammar School, the children were closely tutored in the Catholic religion of their parents' upbringing and attended the rituals of the Church throughout the year. On Sundays they would together attend the 9 a.m. Mass, following their father to the front, close to the altar and in full view of their Catholic neighbors. Pat, and later Sean, served as altar boys at Mass, funerals, and the rituals of Holy Week, endearing the family to the parish priests. While they didn't look at all alike, Pat, thin and small, and Sean, robust, their bond was unusually strong for boys with such an age gap between them.

Susan and Ruth were as different in looks as they were in personality. Susan was the family's only redhead, but not the first in the extended Irish family. She was often raucous, full of fun and sometimes a bit of a devil, as, from time to time, she'd get into one kind of mischief or another. Never malicious, always good-natured, Susan was nevertheless a handful for her parents and a constant source of excitement in the family household. Ruth, on the other hand, was as easy as her name. She was quiet, short on words, but sharp-witted. She was black-haired and diminutive, a kin in appearance to her maternal grandmother, Nonna Rosa.

Once a month, on Sunday, the family would drive to the nearby town of Darwin in the family's white Ford sedan to visit with Angela's mother and father, Rocco and Rosa Deluca. They lived in an art-filled home overlooking the ocean with a statue of St. Francis by the front entranceway and a large marmalade cat usually nestled on a living room chair. It was a tradition that, after a brief, late morning visit to the home for coffee or juice and, most times, delicious gooey cinnamon rolls, they would all then drive to Rocco and Rosa's restaurant, Deluca's. There, they always occupied the circular table in the rear, where the wait staff treated them as royalty. Deluca's, once a small neighborhood diner, had grown in size and popularity over the years so that it had become a favorite gathering place, particularly for the locals who knew that Rosa made the best marinara sauce on this side of the ocean. Pat remembered as well the cheese-topped garlic bread and tiramisu, both of which added to the allure of this warm and friendly place. Those Sunday dinners with Nonno Rocco and Nonna Rosa grounded Pat in the special value of family. The memory of those many Sundays was now a comfort to him.

Pat remembered that it was around seventh grade when his parents started talking to him about the priesthood. "You're such a good boy," his mother said more than once. "Maybe you should consider becoming a priest. How wonderful that would be for your dad and me." The idea was not totally alien to him. He enjoyed the rituals of the Church, and he liked putting on a black cassock and white surplus, the uniform of an altar boy, as it made him feel a little holier than when he just attended church in his regular clothes. Often, he was in awe of the aura of the Church when he served as an acolyte during Mass and especially during Holy Week, and he kept at it long after his classmates had stopped, as they yielded instead to sports and social life and particularly to the increasing allure of girls. *Maybe Mom and Dad are right,* he remembers thinking. Maybe that's my destiny.

He remembered now that even as he went through puberty, his sexual awakening seemed less urgent than his peers. He was friendly with a few girls, mostly pals of his sisters, and found some of them attractive, but the idea of intimate physical contact with them did not impel him as it did most of his similar-aged pals. At first, he kept these feelings to himself but, in time, he confided in his mother that maybe he might want to become a priest. She, in turn, suggested he speak with Father Mike, short for Father Michael O'Donnell, the youngest and most accessible of the three priests assigned to the parish. "Go see Father Mike," she said. "He'll give you a good listen and he'll point the way for you."

The bespectacled O'Donnell had grown up in Mackerel Cove, a coastal inlet two towns away, and had come from a family not unlike the Keefes—large, oriented to the sea, and deeply fervent in their Catholicism. Tall and gangly, his face still marked with vestiges of the acne that pocked him as a youngster, Father Mike's physical appearance was uninspiring but his warm smile radiated an affectionate manner. As he had once explained it to Pat, it had been a natural for him to enter the priesthood as it was a tradition in families like his to give at least one child to the Church. Once ordained and immediately assigned to Holy Family, he thought he'd be a good fit for his home parish, where he knew everybody and felt accepted like a brother or son. "Something like that could be in store for you, Pat," he remembered Father Mike responded when he asked the priest about a vocation. "Pray on it." He encouraged Pat. "I'll be available whenever you want to talk with me about this or anything."

Over time, and with his dad's encouragement and Father Mike's coaxing, Pat inched toward a sense that he had been called to the priesthood. He remembered that as he grew into his teenage years, his parents seemed avid for the idea of his becoming a priest. Thinking back now, Pat surmised that in addition to the honor of having a priest son, having one mouth fewer to feed and one fewer body competing for place in their crowded home had not been an unwelcome prospect for his folks.

After graduating from Holy Family, Pat started at St. Mary's Prep, the same all-boys Catholic high school his dad had attended. He stayed there for two years, achieving success in his classroom work and mixing sociably with his fellow students, even dating once in a while.

Pat remembered one particular time when he was about fifteen, after he had gone to the movies with Janet Frazier, a friend of his sister Susan. She had invited him to her home, suggesting they could be alone there because her parents were away for the weekend. Pat knew from Susan that Janet was very social, always talking about boys and who among her friends was involved with what boy, and he did think she was cute. She looked older than fourteen, well filled out and with a pretty face. Not sure how to respond to Janet's invitation, but mildly curious about what might happen, Pat went along with the idea and, before he had much chance to think about it, found himself on the living room couch with Janet, who was aggressively kissing him.

Then without notice, she had reached for his pants, opened the zipper, and was stroking his penis all while moving his hands under her blouse to her breasts. Pat was enthralled, feeling her soft fleshiness and the hardness of her nipples while she quickened the pace of stroking him until he suddenly ejaculated, his first time. Janet laughed as she pushed away, straightening herself and standing. "That was great," she panted. "I really liked doing that. You're not such a stick in the mud as Susan claimed when I told her I wanted to go out with you. I think you're fun and cute! Let's get together again, real soon."

Pat was speechless. While he liked the exuberance of the sexual release, he felt guilty for his sin, torn between excitement and dread and he was embarrassed by his wetness. What would his parents and Father Mike think of him now? Quickly, he arranged his pants, said good night to Janet, and went home. Doing that with Janet was so thrilling, her breast so soft, and his release so complete, an experience he now recalled that he fantasized about again and again, reliving its pleasures. He remembered too his apprehension after this episode. He was rethinking becoming a priest. If he chose not to enter the seminary, surely his parents would have been disappointed. As Pat now looked back on those days, he remembered his consternation, his conflict between what he thought he was supposed to do and his more immediate urges. As he reviewed those days in his mind, he concluded that his greatest impulse had been to please his parents. Their desires for him to be a priest had become the driver of his choices.

Pat recalled that as a teenager he didn't pay much attention to national news, as he, like most kids his age, was more interested in community, school, and family activities. But one August Sunday in 1963, the summer after his sophomore year, Father Mike stopped Pat after Mass and asked him if he'd come to the back of the church for a brief chat. There, Father Mike told him that there was a march on Washington for civil rights coming up that he was planning to attend. He asked Pat if he'd like to come along. Pat was puzzled as there hadn't been much talk about civil rights in Duncan's Cove and it wasn't something his parents discussed, even though they had seen reports on television of growing racial unrest in the South.

"What do you know about slavery?" Father Mike had asked him. When Pat started to say that it was something that had happened in the South, Father Mike interrupted him: "True enough, Pat, but did you know we had slaves in New England right up until the middle of the nineteenth century, and, at any rate, even if the conflict we read about and see on television is taking place in the South, where there are a lot more black people than around here, I think the problems of equality—in education, in employment, in housing, and in voting—are not regional. They're a national issue, and a moral one for all of us. I know as a priest that treating someone differently just because of what he looks like or where he comes from is un-Christian. So, I'm going to the march be part of it, to bear witness as well."

Pat remembered being taken aback, a bit overwhelmed, but he was curious and excited about the prospect of seeing Washington, D.C. Father Mike had further explained that, although he was from New England, he had a particular interest in race relations as he had been appalled, as a student of sociology in college, to learn about the country's historic mistreatment of people of color and the evidence that it was still continuing in many areas of the country. Father Mike continued with an energy that he didn't often display in his normal parish ministry and, particularly, in his homilies, "I believe that how we, as a country, respond to the growing voices for equal treatment, for equality across the board, will reflect what strength of character we have as a nation. This could be a wonderful opportunity for you to see, up front, an important event in this struggle for civil rights, if the predictions for a large gathering are correct." To Pat, Father Mike's enthusiasm had been inspiring.

Pat remembered asking his parents about it. Their initial reactions, particularly his father's, had been skeptical. "Why should you get involved in something like that?" asked his dad. "We have no problems here in Duncan's Cove. Why don't we just let other people take care of their problems?"

But Pat's mother thought differently and with surprising verve responded: "If Father Mike thinks it's important for you to see this, that it's something significant for your learning, then I'll put my trust in him." And, so, early in the morning of August 27th, Pat and Father Mike set out by car for a long day's trek to Washington, D.C., stopping at St. Ann's church in Greenbelt, Maryland, not far from Washington, to stay the night as guests of an old college friend of Father Mike's, Father Timothy Cohan, and the next day the three of them took the crowded train the rest of the way.

Pat's recollection of the day in Washington was a kaleidoscope of images and sounds. He remembered seeing thousands of people, mostly but not only African Americans, marching toward the Lincoln Monument, some with their arms locked together, others holding up placards with demands for equal pay or for voting rights, and many that just had the word "Equality." Some of the people were in groups and they sang, as they marched, "We Shall Overcome," a song he later learned had become the anthem of the civil rights movement. Others were singing hymns he didn't recognize but which Father Mike later told him were Negro spirituals.

He remembered being in an ocean of people, crowded on either side of a large pool, which was framed at one end by the

Lincoln Memorial. He had never seen so many people in one place-black or white. Because of the distance, he could only see images on the steps of the Memorial, but there was a speaker system set up so he could hear the goings on. He was moved by the power of Mahalia Jackson and the urgency of Joan Baez, songsters he had heard about but never seen or heard in person. And he heard Martin Luther King's now famous "I have a dream" speech, which seemed to bring so many people, arms raised, to cheers and clapping, and chanting "Amens" as the cadence of King's voice quickened, arousing the fervor of the throng. It was mesmerizing.

A day to remember, he now reckoned. He was always grateful to Father Mike for lifting his eyes to the world beyond Duncan's Cove. He was uncertain, however, that he had been adequately prepared for the challenges now vexing him.

V

FISHING

Aware of Pat's continuing angst but not its cause, and fearing that he was becoming increasingly despondent, Maggie came up with the idea that it might be useful for Pat to have an activity to divert his attention away from his dilemma. Whatever it was, it was clear to Maggie that it was eating at Pat's spirit. On a late May day, she told Pat about an old family friend, Timothy Chandler, now in his mid-seventies, who was still lobstering but now going out alone because he had lost his crewman, a situation she thought was perilous. Maggie was very sensitive to the dangers of fishing as the sea had so recently taken her husband. It never left her mind that Sean had been fishing alone when, one early morning, he left port and never returned. The supposition in the fishing community was that Sean had somehow fallen overboard after the wind had come up and caused the seas to build, making the boat an unsteady platform. To herself, she hoped that was all there was to it. "Chandler is now fishing just part-time and alone because he can't afford to pay the extra cost of a mate. Maybe you could offer to help him."

"What a good idea." Pat seemed instantly cheered. He had fond memories of going to sea as a teenager to help pull lobster traps, and he thought the physical activity would be good for him. He knew this would be hard and hearty work. Pat called Tim Candler and asked if he could talk with him.

"Of course," responded Chandler. "Always time for an old friend, and a priest at that. I'd say that's a bonus."

Tim greeted him at the door. Medium height and wiry, he had the look of a man who lived by the sea. His tanned face was cracked; his bushy eyebrows accented his gray-blue eyes and his fulsome beard and every-which-way tufts of white hair radiated warmth and wisdom. While sharing a cup of tea, they agreed that Pat would go out with Tim three days a week through the lobstering season until the cold set in. They met at dawn at the coop dock where Tim kept his dinghy, the last wooden skiff in the harbor, hanging an outboard motor of uncertain vintage. Each trip started with a ride to Tim's mooring, where the *Roberta Ann*, named for Tim's late wife, was tethered to her mooring. It was a thirty-two-foot lobster hull, white with a green cabin, bright in the style of the fleet..

Their harbor departing routine was pleasant in calm days. While Tim guided the *Roberta Ann* to sea, Pat sat aft, able to take in the natural beauty of their surroundings.

In their first few days, Pat noticed that Tim drove out to sea before reaching his string of buoys.

"Why so far?" Pat asked on their first trip. "I remember as a teenager the boats lobstered much closer to shore, easy to get to and get back to port. Doesn't going further out just cost you a lot more in fuel and time?"

Tim responded, shouting over the engine, "That's for sure, but with the water warming, most of the lobsters have migrated into deeper and colder waters. So, we go where they go . All the guys now fish off shore, most further out than me. I set my traps about ten miles from the harbor's entrance, further than I like, yet closer in than many of the others with their more powerful engines, which move them along pretty fast. I found a good spot, though, not too deep but in colder water a little nearer to shore. So far it's been good to me. You'll see. When it's foggy," Tim explained, "I can still find my string of buoys with the radar as each buoy, green and red striped over white base, is topped by a radar reflector."

Once the *Roberta Ann* got to their fishing area, Tim lined the boat up to come alongside the buoys, and here Pat had to go to work attaching each buoy to a drum and then hauling up the pots connected by line to the buoy, one at a time. As a trap came to surface, Pat had to quickly retrieve the lobsters and then rebait the trap before muscling it back overboard. He had to repeat this task many times over as Tim maneuvered the boat from buoy to buoy, string to string until each of his traps had been inspected, emptied, and refilled.

For Pat, who had thought he was still in reasonable shape, hauling lobsters was backbreaking, but the environment helped him regain his moral anchor. The work was straightforward and unswervingly true. It was a balm to his soul.

One time, while returning to the harbor, he asked Tim why he still fished. "That's a funny question, Pat. I do it because it's what I do. What else can I say?" Pat listened quietly. "Nothing, I guess, Tim. In a way I envy you. You know why you're doing what you do. Sometimes I wonder. Life ashore can be more complicated, I think; too many cross currents."

Often, while steaming back to port, Pat sat in quiet reverie. He had learned over the years to practice meditation. When he could, he'd try to put himself into neutral gear, thinking of nothing, just sensing his place. In these moments, he felt a closeness to God that no church afforded him. Reflecting on those moments, he often felt Maggie's idea for him to go fishing might have come from divine inspiration. Nowhere else, not even perched on Sean's bench, did he feel more centered, more at peace than when at sea aboard the *Roberta Ann*, fishing the waters for their bounty.

On the few days Pat and Tim were out in weather, Pat's mind was constantly on Sean. But in the good days, in calm seas and sunlit sky, Pat sometimes wondered to himself what life could be like, living in his hometown, close to Maggie and Chris, maybe even opening a therapy office while fishing from time to time in his own version of the *Roberta Ann*. What a life that could be, he mused, until some motion out of rhythm with the gentle sea startled him back to his realization of place and time.

Toward late fall, Tim indicated that he was done for the season. "Time to put the *Roberta Ann* to bed," he said. "This seventy-five-year-old body doesn't like the cold so much anymore and my legs aren't as steady in the seas that usually come up this time of the year."

"Thanks for the ride, Tim, and the conversation. You can't know how much it helped me."

Tim looked at Pat quizzically. "No, Pat, I'm thanking you for your good work. Couldn't have kept going without you. If you ever decide to quit ministering, you got a job with me." He grinned broadly. Pat just smiled back, nodding. He thought to himself, however, that his taste for the sea, dormant since he had left Duncan's Cove, had been awakened by this brief experience. He resolved that, if possible, he would try to get on the water once in a while no matter what path his vocation took, just for the clarity and purity of the challenge in the embrace of the sea he loved.

When he returned from fishing, although somewhat refreshed, he was not yet ready to resume his ministry. Instead, he reverted to his interactions with Maggie and Chris and his daily musings at his favorite spot overlooking the harbor, ever searching for inspiration.

VI

A FAMILY SECRET

One morning when Pat was home alone, he was upstairs in the living room rummaging for a pencil as he wished to make sideline corrections to an essay Chris had asked him to review. When Pat opened a side table drawer his eyes were drawn to a folded leaflet with the heading "AL-ANON." Curious, he began to read and then sat down as the implication of the booklet struck him.

Pat had heard of Al-Anon during his master's program but had never given it much thought. He knew it concerned groups of people who periodically come together to provide mutual support around the issue of alcohol abuse by family members. *What is this about?* wondered Pat. Does Chris have an issue with alcohol? If so, thought Pat, he was not as close to the boy as he had thought.

He resolved to ask Maggie about it when she came home. Her answer shocked and saddened him. Pat had replaced the booklet in the table drawer and returned downstairs to await Maggie and consider his approach to what he knew would be a very sensitive subject. He decided frank honesty would be best. A little while after he heard Maggie upstairs, he called for her to join him on the rear patio where, he said, he'd like to discuss something with her. In that way, he thought, they could have privacy even if Chris came home from hockey practice early.

"What's up, Pat? It's not like you to summon me in such a way. This must be serious."

"Oh, I'm sorry, Maggie. I didn't mean to convey that. I guess I'm more transparent than I realize. Anyway, I think this could be a serious conversation and I want to apologize ahead of it for seeming intrusive. Earlier, I went upstairs looking for a pencil as I couldn't find any down here and when I opened a drawer next to the sofa, I found an AL-Anon leaflet and my wheels started churning. If there's an issue with Chris, I'd really like to help if that's possible. I think he and I are developing a great relationship."

At first Maggie just stared at Pat, perhaps thinking about what to say and then she just started weeping. "No Pat, it's not about Chris. It was Sean. Oh, poor Sean! He had a terrible drinking problem but he tried to hide it and so, unfortunately, I did too. Sean would come home from fishing and just as soon as he changed his clothes he'd be into the vodka and he wouldn't stop until he went to bed. Oh, I'm so worried it played a role in his death. I was praying that no one would find any bottles on the boat. I guess they didn't because I think I would have heard.

"Anyway, at some point about six months before the accident, when I thought I couldn't take it anymore, I confided in Father Mike—you know him, from the parish. He's older now but still full of wisdom. He told me about Al-Anon and that's when I started to go. I still go to meetings even though Sean's gone because friends there are such a great source of support. I was so embarrassed when I first decided to go that I found a group about twenty miles from here in Beaverton where I thought I'd be more comfortable. I'd go right from work, telling Sean one excuse or another about being late. He really didn't question me. Probably the vodka."

Pat was dumbfounded. "But, Maggie, I never knew. When did this start?"

"Sean was always a drinker, Pat. After he had a few, he'd start in on your father, how you were the golden boy and how he could never measure up or please him in any way. He thought your dad never forgave him for marrying early and not going on to college. Poor Sean was never happy with himself but he was too proud to seek help. So he drank, always alone and never around Chris. At least that part is good. I'm so sorry."

"Maggie, my heart goes out to you. How hard for you to have endured this in solitude. I'm so glad for you that you found Al-Anon, and I hope it's been a good find for you. I know the ability to share can be more than just soothing but healing as well. Your secret is, of course, yours to keep. Just know I'm here if you ever want again to talk about it or if you have questions about whether to bring Chris into your confidence. No doubt that's a hard area for you."

"At least not yet, Pat. Chris seems well adjusted and happy with himself. I don't see any reason to burden him with this as I'm afraid how it might affect his memory of Sean. But I'll keep an eye out."

They then both stood and embraced as Maggie thanked Pat for being a good listener. He just nodded as she returned upstairs.

VII

A DEATH TOO EARLY

One late afternoon while he was quietly listening to music, Maggie called from upstairs. "Pat, there's a call for you. It's Jed Baker. You can pick it up on the extension down there." Pat was curious since he had not seen the lawyer for a while. "Hello, Jed, what can I do for you?" he cheerily began.

Baker's voice was somber. "Father, I am so sorry to tell you this but Lawrence Jefferson took his own life two nights ago at the juvenile detention center. He was found hanging in his room during evening bed check rounds. They could not revive him."

"Oh, pray God, Jed" was all Pat could say as he bent over his desk, his breath constrained.

The lawyer continued, "As you know, Pat, the boys at MacDonald are kept in rooms that are open during the day, allowing them access to common spaces and programming, but at nighttime they are locked down. Apparently, sometime during the early evening, the boy took a bed sheet that he fastened into a noose and found a way to take his own life. So terribly sad, Padre."

Pat was still. His mind raced to his last visit with Lawrence, about a month ago, when the boy had seemed no different from the first days of his detention. Quiet, sullen, expressionless. Afterward, Pat called the psychiatrist, Meagan O'Toole, who said she shared his concern that the boy seemed emotionally stagnant. "It's still early, Father. Only more time and continuing counseling will bring this boy back. I've alerted the detention center to my continuing concerns and that told me they are keeping a watch on him." Pat knew from his intern days that the center was a reasonably well-run facility, but no place, he surmised, could be totally safe.

"Have you spoken with the boy's parents, Jed? This is unbearable."

"Yes, Padre, a few times. They're in shock but I think they are strong. I came to admire them in our dealings about the disposition of the charges against Lawrence. As you might expect, their anger at the Church is unabated, but I think they have their legs under them. Tim called me a few moments ago and wanted to make sure you know. His view of you is not at all tainted by his antipathy toward the Church. In fact, he asked me to see if you'd be willing to lead a memorial service for Lawrence. It won't be in Church because they've stopped going; rather, it will be a hall someplace in town."

Pat instinctively agreed to the Jeffersons' request. "Of course, Jed. Just let me know when and where and what they would like me to do."

"Oh, I know a little about that, Pat," Jed responded. "They don't want a regular funeral Mass and yet they haven't given up on Lawrence's soul. They're so hoping you agree that his final act of self-murder should not serve to condemn him."

"No, Jeb. The Church's attitude about suicide has changed as we've learned more about its causes. Now the Church recognizes that some suicides are not genuinely intentional but rather acts of psychological impairment. That's certainly my view here, Jed, from what I've learned about this boy and what happened to him. It appears this poor youngster had no real chance of recovery. I will talk directly with the Jeffersons when it's appropriate."

Once he and Baker said their goodbyes, Pat went upstairs, where he told Maggie, "Something terrible has happened, Maggie. A youngster I had worked with, a boy who had killed a priest after he had been abused by him, has now taken his own life. This is dreadful. I will be going to a funeral service for him in a couple of days. For now, I think I just need to get some air."

"Oh, my dear," Maggie reacted while reaching for Pat, giving him an embrace. I am so very sorry, Pat. You already have so much on your platter, whatever it is, and now this. Bless the poor boy's soul. Anything you need, you know Chris and I are here for you."

Pat left the house and strode to the calm of Sean's bench, where he sat in silence for nearly an hour, barely noticing the harbor below. Nevertheless, the air, the feeling of salt-borne wind in his face, helped to steady him.

Two days later the service of remembrance took place at the Foxon Community Hall with a sparse crowd of family and friends, each holding a candle while forming a circle around the urn containing Lawrence's ashes.

In the center, Pat led the rite, which was poignant and brief. When he spoke, he was gentle. "I will not try to console you with meaningless clichés taken from a standard funeral rite. The Psalms of the Bible say much about untimely death, and a quiet review of them may bring solace to some of you. Today, I'd rather speak from my heart of the grief we all share for Lawrence's untimely departure from us.

"Surely in our mourning for the loss of this young soul, we can be assured that God has welcomed him into His arms. The assault on Lawrence was more than anyone should have to bear. For that burden, we all must all take some responsibility as there is no place in our society for the abuse that was visited upon him or an environment that permits that to happen. My teaching leads me to believe he is at peace with the Lord. Now is the time for us to affirm our mutual love for one another and our shared support for making our communities places of love where we can nurture and be nurtured."

With that, Pat sprinkled holy water on the urn and then to the congregation as he intoned: "Let us each pray in our own way for the soul of this lad and let us take hands in solemn commitment that we will seek the good in his memory." As Pat extended his arms to the gathering, he concluded with a blessing: "God's peace to you all and may God gentle Lawrence's soul unto His bosom."

After a few private minutes with Tim and Mollie Jefferson, Pat left the hall, holding in his emotions until he reached the safety of his car, where his tears flowed freely. Once composed, he drove directly to Duncan's Cove.

VIII

PREDATION

One late afternoon, only a few weeks after the memorial service, Pat was reading in his room when Chris came in and asked if he could talk about something bothering him. "Of course," welcomed Pat.

"I have this close friend from school, Robbie, Uncle Pat. He tried to help me a lot after Dad died. He's really my best friend. Sometimes we shoot hoops at his house down by the fire station. He's about the same age as me. One day, for some reason, he was ranting about priests, how you can't trust them. When I asked him why, he first said he didn't want to talk about it so I just dropped it. But, then a couple of days later, he said something else about priests, how you can't trust them, so I sort of went right back at him and told him about you.

"I said you're really great and I can trust you with anything so don't say those things as though you know about all priests. Then he just started stammering about something really bad that happened to him. He said that one time, he and a bunch of Boy Scouts had been on a campout with Father Malley— Father David, they call them. He was their scout leader and a priest at St. Anthony's in Trenton. I guess he's not there anymore. Robbie told me there aren't enough boys for each parish to have its own troop so the kids in Duncan's Cove and Trenton are in the same troop. I'm not really into that so I don't know much about it.

"Robbie told me that he and Father David had become buds, and that after scout meetings, he sometimes stayed behind to help clean up and Father David would give him little things, mostly candy bars, stuff like that. Then he told me that on one campout weekend, they had a campfire where they toasted s'mores and Father David told ghost stories, which were cool and weird. A few hours later, Robbie told me, when he was asleep in his single-person tent, Father David came inside, lighting the tent with his flashlight, and the next thing he knew Father David was on the ground next to him, his breath reeking of something, and he began to cuddle with him, eventually putting his hands down the front of his pajama bottoms and rubbing his thing.

"Robbie said that Father David then took out his own thing and told him to rub it until some white stuff spurted from it. Then he just got up, Robbie said, but before he left the tent, Father David told him that what they did was a natural part of becoming a man and that they needed to keep it a special secret just between them. Uncle Pat, he was real nervous once he started telling me all this. I've never heard him lie to anyone before. Do you think this could be true, a priest doing that?"

Pat felt like he had just been hit over the head by a two-by-four. His mind raced back to Lawrence Mason. He took a moment to get his balance. "Chris, that's really a horrible story. What a terrible thing for your friend to have experienced. And yes, I'm afraid so, Chris, we priests are supposed to be people you can look up to, trust, but sometimes it doesn't work that way. I'm so sorry. Can you tell me what happened next with Robbie? How did it end with him?"

"Yeah, Uncle Pat, after Robbie said he didn't tell anyone else about this because he felt real dirty, I didn't know what to say. When I asked him about his parents, he said he was afraid to talk with them because he felt he had done something wrong. He didn't think they'd believe him and he'd just get into a lot of trouble for saying a priest did that. He said he only told me after that priest, Father Malley, was gone from the parish and it just sort of came out. He said he guessed he just needed to tell someone because he couldn't get rid of the bad feelings he had from doing this with Father David."

"Well, Chris, what a good friend you are to Robbie, and you're so right to come to me. Let's see if I can help somehow. It took a lot of trust for Robbie to tell you about this. Do you think he might be willing to talk with me? Maybe I could help him figure out what to do. It sounds like he might be calling out for help without knowing that's what he's doing."

"I don't know if he'll talk with you, Uncle Pat, but I'll sure ask him and I'll tell him how easy you are to talk to, just like you and I do sometimes."

"Okay, Chris. What a great friend you are," Pat repeated. "Please let me know what he says when you ask him about seeing me."

How horrible and sad, thought Pat, but perhaps in all his turmoil an opportunity was coming to him to personally help a victim. Even if counseling Robbie wouldn't allay his concern for Luke's unknown victims, providing comfort to this boy could at least give him some sense of renewed purpose.

A few days later, Chris caught up to Robbie walking home from school and told him how he had always been able to talk with his uncle, Father Pat, about things and that his uncle had never gotten mad at him for anything. He told Robbie that Pat always seemed to understand and to give him good advice. He suggested that maybe Robbie could talk with his Uncle Pat, that maybe he could help him to feel better about things. Robbie said he'd think about it and maybe he would go see Father Pat, but he wasn't sure. He asked Chris not to tell anyone else.

About a month later, Robbie did call. "Father Keefe, my name is Robbie. I'm a friend of Chris who's told me about you. Can I come see you?" The phone then went silent except for the sound of Robbie breathing.

"Of course, Robbie, I'd be happy to meet with you. And you know, I'm a priest so if there's something you want to talk with me about that's private, that will be just between us. When do you think you'd like to come over?"

"Right away," Robbie rushed to answer. "When can I come?"

"Well, how about tomorrow right after school? I live in the basement of Chris' house, but there's a back door just for me. You can come there and we'll be by ourselves so you can talk just to me—that is, if you want to be alone. Or, Chris can be there if you want."

"No," said Robbie. "Just us please, Father."

The next day Robbie appeared. "Hi, Robbie," Pat greeted him at the door. "Do you want to sit out here on the patio? Don't worry about anyone hearing us. You can call me Father Pat, if you'd like."

To Pat, this small, freckled, red-haired boy seemed so young, so vulnerable. Robbie was anxious in his manner and halting in speech as he blurted out that Chris said he'd be a good person to talk to about something that was bothering him. Pat tried immediately to put Robbie at ease. "Sit wherever you like, Robbie. It's not fancy around here but it's comfortable. Would you like a soda or something like that? I have a small refrigerator here."

"Oh, no thank you, Father. I'll just sit here on this folding chair." Once they were seated facing each other, Pat asked Robbie about his family and learned that he lived with his mom and dad, older brother Mark, and younger sister Roseann in a house on Main Street, not far from the fire department where his father worked. Pat also tried to ease Robbie into safe areas for him in a way to begin to build trust. He asked what he liked in school, and they talked for a while about sports. But Robbie was clearly distracted. To Pat, it was clear that Robbie had come with a purpose.

"I love my mom and dad but can't tell them about what I told Chris because they'll get mad at me. They probably won't believe me anyway because they go to church all the time and think the priests are so holy. I'd never tell my brother or sister either because they'd probably just tell my parents even if they promised not to."

Pat listened quietly and then said, "Robbie, I know from Chris that something terrible happened to you and if you want to talk about it, I'm here to listen and to answer any questions you might have. I promise you I won't get angry at you no matter what you tell me. And, Robbie, whatever we talk about here will be confidential, sort of like confession, and I won't repeat it to anyone else unless you decide you want me to. It's okay too if you just want to think about it and come back another time. I don't want you to feel any pressure from me." This seemed to calm Robbie.

"Thank you, Father, but I'm here. That was the hard part and I think I really need to talk about this. I feel like I'm getting crazy."

Pat suggested to Robbie that he could start at whatever place he wanted. As Robbie began to tell his story, his speaking pace quickened, words came faster and faster as though he needed to purge himself of the horrible event. He told Pat that all the kids had liked Father David because he was fun to be around and always had good stories to tell. He said that in the Boy Scouts, Father David seemed to know a lot about the outdoors and at meetings he talked about how much fun it would be to go on hikes and to camp in tents, and so when he suggested the Boy Scout troop go on an overnight in the state forest, he was excited about it. "My dad even went to the outdoor store with me where we got a sleeping bag, new boots, a pup tent, an outdoor eating kit, and a canteen. I was real excited about going on my first campout with friends. The first day was great. We hiked through some woods, even stopped to swim at a lake before we got to the campsite."

Pat listened quietly as Robbie talked all around the event most troubling him, letting him tell his story in the way most comfortable to him. "We had a campfire after we all found enough kindling and stuff, then, ah, cooked burgers and dogs over the fire. It was real fun. After it got dark, we had s'mores and Father David told some scary stories before we all went to our tents. I had a single one, by myself. I was kind of scared, being alone, but I felt real brave too."

Pat then interrupted. "Take your time, Robbie, you're doing fine."

"Well, a while later, I guess an hour or so, Father David came into my tent. I sat right up because I didn't know why he was there. I was real surprised and thought maybe something bad had happened." Pat noticed Robbie had grown more fidgety, plainly uncomfortable now. "It's okay, Robbie. I know this must be hard for you but I think it would be good for you to get it all out. You know, I'm not going to get upset at anything you say."

Robbie nodded and continued. He then told Pat the details of what Father Malley did just as Chris had reported to him, halting at times, almost stammering. At one point, he was shaking as Father Pat told him just to take a breath. "You're being so brave, Robbie. This was such a terrible thing to happen to you. Do you want to tell me what happened after Father David left?"

"Well, nothing really. I just lied down, kind of shaking, not knowing what had happened. I know I felt sort of dizzy, like I didn't know where I was. Then I guess I just fell asleep. The next morning, when I woke up and went outside from my tent, I saw Father David with the other kids and he just acted like nothing had happened. That was so weird."

"What about when you got home, Robbie? What did you say to your parents?"

"Nothing much," Robbie said. "I just said "hi" and went up to my bedroom. Later, at supper, when someone asked me about the campout, I just said it was okay, not great, because by then I had decided to quit the Boy Scouts. I never wanted to see that Father Malley again. When my parents asked me why I wasn't going on any more campouts because they knew, from reading in the parish bulletin, that some were planned, I just said I didn't want to do it anymore, that it wasn't much fun and I really didn't care about trying to get any more merit badges anyway. I was afraid that maybe my dad was mad at me because they spent so much on camping stuff and that just made me even more afraid to tell anyone what had happened. And, I thought maybe nobody would believe me because Father David was so popular with everybody." Now sobbing, he blurted out, "I think maybe I'm just no good; I did something really dirty. I don't know, I'm all mixed up. I even took a scissors to my leg a couple of times and made myself bleed. I feel really bad, Father."

Pat's heart was breaking for this youngster as he listened. Robbie continued, "Ever since, I've been real mean to my little sister a couple of times because I'm always mad. I never used to be like that. I can't even think about liking a girl as this whole thing has really messed me up. There's no one I can talk to, at least up to when I told Chris about it, and now you."

Pat saw that Robbie was now shaking, his eyes awash in tears freely riveting his face. He tried to gentle Robbie but there was little he could do to help or say other than to smile warmly and tell him he was going to be okay.

"I'm so sorry this happened to you, Robbie, but I think it's really good you came to see me. Let's see how I can help you. But first, please let me say to you that you're very brave to be here. I know it took a lot of guts for you to see me when you don't even know me. And me being a priest too."

"Well, Father, I knew from Chris that you are now living with him and his mother, and Chris says he really likes you. I guess that was enough to get me here, him telling me about you. I really feel like I have to tell somebody. I don't know what to do."

In listening to Robbie's story, it seemed clear to Pat that because Robbie's parents hadn't closely questioned him about his newly acquired dislike for the Scout troop, he was left on an island of confusion, fear, and guilt, and he had become more isolated before he just blurted it out to Chris. Thank goodness, thought Pat, for the human spirit, for our instincts for self-preservation as shown in Robbie's spontaneous outpouring to Chris. And what a shame, he thought, that the Jefferson boy didn't have a friend like Chris.

In hearing Robbie's story, Pat's initial reaction, in addition to sorrow for Robbie, was revulsion that another priest had sexually abused a child, this one so obviously a vulnerable prey. The memories of poor Lawrence Jefferson came flooding back, which stoked his anger that this child had been wounded. From his schooling in social work and his learned instincts, Pat had no doubt believing Robbie's account. His social worker training kicked in as he reassured Robbie that he had done nothing wrong and that he was, instead, a victim of abuse, which was particularly harmful as this Father Malley had been an authority figure for him, someone he looked up to. This reaction seemed to quiet the boy and encourage him to further engage with Pat.

"How could a priest do something so bad, Father? I just don't understand. Now I'm afraid of the other priests in the parish, particularly the new one, Father Foley, who showed up after Father Malley went away. Father Foley now runs all the youth activities in the parish but I don't want to go to anything now because I didn't know anything about him. What if he's just like Father Malley? Now, I spend most of my time in my room, sometimes shooting hoops in the driveway, but I don't leave the house much except when I have to."

Gently, Pat tried to move the conversation forward. He gently probed with Robbie the idea of telling his parents and trusting that they would understand that he had done nothing wrong in the incident with Father Malley.

"You know, Robbie, from what you've told me about your family, they sound wonderful. I bet they wouldn't want you to be suffering so much alone. I think you can trust them not to be angry, at least not at you. Maybe you should decide if it's safe to tell them. And, if you want to come see me again, now you know where I live. Just call to make sure I'm here and I'd be happy to see you anytime. Of course, everything you and I talk about alone is just between us. But, if you tell your parents, and I really hope you will, I'd be happy to meet with them too, as they'll probably have lots of questions."

This first meeting with Father Pat somewhat settled Robbie and, sure enough, just a few days later, he called Pat and asked if he could meet with him again and, this time, if he could bring his parents. When Pat asked Robbie if he had told his parents, he said no, but he did want them to know, and he was hoping Pat could do that for him when they met together. He said he'd just tell his parents he'd like them to meet Chris' uncle whom he thought they would really like.

They agreed to meet at Pat's apartment at two o'clock on the next Saturday which gave Pat time to scrounge a few more chairs from upstairs, telling Maggie only that he was having a family meeting with a youngster Chris had asked him to see. Pat told Maggie that it was a confidential matter but that Chris had been a really good friend to a school chum who needed help and that's what the meeting was about.

At exactly 2 p.m., Robbie appeared at Pat's door with his parents, who introduced themselves as John and Mary Fallon, late thirties, both trim, the look of physical activity in them. They were clearly curious about why they were there, but they were friendly as well. John Fallon said, shortly after they were seated, "I was a good friend of your brother Sean from the Lions Club, Father. None of us could believe what happened to him because he was such a great guy, strong too, and he knew his fishing. But we know there are safer jobs to have."

Mary added: "John and I went to the funeral mass and heard your homily, Father, which I still remember for tying the parables about Jesus to life in a fishing community. How true and comforting for us all. My dad and his before all fished. There's a draw to it, a lure that some can't resist. I'm happy John didn't go in that direction. It feels safer even though I know what he does has its dangers too."

After the initial chitchat, the Fallons asked, almost in unison, why they were there. "All we know," they said, "is that

Robbie told us he had talked with you and he asked if we'd come here to meet you. But there's got to be more to it than that." Pat smiled and assured them it was not because Robbie had done anything wrong. Very much the opposite, he told them. "Robbie had something terribly wrong done to him that he has been afraid to tell you and he wants me to talk with you about it with us all together."

Pat turned to Robbie and asked if he wanted him to proceed. "Yes, please, Father. I think you can tell it better than I can." With that, Pat outlined the story as Robbie had related it to him.

The Fallons were initially incredulous.

"This can't be true. There's something wrong with this story," Mr. Fallon blurted out. "No priest would ever do such a thing. Robbie, maybe you just dreamed this or maybe you just misunderstood what happened that night during the campout."

But Mrs. Fallon just looked at Robbie, who was now sobbing. Their eyes met. "Mom, I would never make up a story like this. I'm so sorry, but it really happened. He did what Father Pat just said, all of it."

"Mr. and Mrs. Fallon, I'm so sorry to have to say this, but not every priest lives up to his calling. This has happened before with other children and other priests. It's so very sad. I studied some about child abuse when I was in graduate school. What Robbie told me about how he feels, the changes you must surely have noticed these past months, they're all consistent with abuse. And, sad to say, how Robbie told me about it, it all rings true."

Pat noticed that Mrs. Fallon had a look of terror on her face. He risked a question to both parents: "In the past, have you had any difficulties with Robbie telling you the truth?"

"Never," quickly responded both parents in unison. Mrs. Fallon added: "Robbie's always been such a wonderful boy, never any problems with his behavior. He would never make up such a story." And then they caught each other as the implication of that statement hit them. Mrs. Fallon spoke as her husband sat, shaking his head in obvious disbelief. As she spoke, Mrs. Fallon looked directly at Robbie, whose face was puffed and red. She got up and embraced him, followed quickly by her husband. As Pat quietly sat, the three Fallons clasped in a family hug as though trying to hold on to each other against a stiffening breeze.

Once they sat again, Pat continued. "I think it would really be good for Robbie to be able to talk with a counselor about this. I have some education in social work but I think someone who specializes in seeing children would be best. Perhaps Robbie's pediatrician could recommend someone for you." They seemed receptive to this idea, yet fixated on this startling news.

"And what about this Father Malley? Shouldn't something be done about him, to punish him for what he did to Robbie and to keep him from doing anything like this again? Do you think we should go talk with someone at the bishop's office? Where should we go?" Mr. Fallon asked with machine gun vehemence.

"I've been thinking about that question," responded Pat, "and, yes, I think you should report this. In fact, I think you should go to the police. What Father Malley did to Robbie is a crime, and he should have to face up to that." Pat's response startled the Fallons.

"Get a priest arrested?" Mr. Fallon asked in unfeigned shock. "Can a priest actually be arrested for this?"

The quickness of Pat's response surprised even him. "Yes, we priests are not above the law. We have no more right to abuse people, to rob from them, to violate them, to hurt them any more than any other person does. There's nothing about being a priest that insulates us from the criminal law. If you go to the police, feel free to tell them that you have talked with me and that I urged you to report this incident to them."

"But what about the diocese. Shouldn't we also tell the bishop about this?" continued Mr. Fallon.

"You can do that, Mr. and Mrs. Fallon, and maybe you should, but if you want something done about this, I think the most important places for you to go are to a counselor and to the police." As upset as Pat was with the seeming indifference of the diocese to the bourgeoning issue of clergy sexual abuse of children, he was not yet prepared to openly speak his darkest thoughts about the Church of his calling. And never far from his mind was the tragic death of Lawrence Jefferson, a victim of a priest defended by the Church.

In addition to urging the Fallons to report to the police, Pat suggested they meet with an attorney to talk about what other recourse could be available to them and Robbie for what Father Malley had done to him. While Pat had no legal training, he had read other stories from places where suits were now being filed against the Church for clergy abuse. While he wasn't sure how he felt about this, he saw no harm in steering the Fallons in the direction of a civil lawyer who could advise them as to their rights. When he suggested they also see a lawyer, Mr. Fallon was quick to respond. "Absolutely, we'll do that. But we don't really know any lawyers. Do you?"

Pat gave them Jed Baker's name. "I've known him since we were kids and I know that he now attends Holy Family here in Duncan's Cove and has a small practice here. He's a very good person, Mr. and Mrs. Fallon, and I know he has some experience in dealing with kids who have been abused. I think you'll find he's a skillful and ethical lawyer. A nice person too."

"Oh, I think I know who he is," said Mrs. Fallon. "His wife Betty and I work together in the PTA's annual book sale, where we raise money for the kids' extra activities. She's very nice and I'm pretty sure her husband's a lawyer."

"Good," replied Pat. "Having that connection may make it an easier meeting with Attorney Baker. I think you'll find him a good and wise ear."

After their meeting with Pat, Robbie's parents did, in fact, consult with Jed Baker, who in turn called Sergeant Alice Fay, a detective in the Trenton police department. She called the

Fallons and asked them to come to the station and speak with her. At that meeting, Sergeant Fay was solicitous of the Fallons, and particularly of Robbie. She told him she had spoken with Attorney Baker and she asked Robbie if he'd retell the events of the campout to her.

By this time, having told the story to Father Pat alone and then with his parents and to Attorney Baker, retelling it was not as difficult, though nor was it easy. At first, Detective Fay asked Robbie to talk about himself, questions intended to put him at ease, and then she asked him just to narrate the story in his own words. Afterwards, she went back over his account, to give her more details so she could obtain the complete picture. Throughout the meeting, Robbie's parents sat respectfully quiet, letting the detective do her work as she was obviously very competent as well as visibly compassionate. Afterwards, they answered her questions about Robbie as a boy growing up, his behaviors around the home, and how well he did as a student.

Within a month, Father Malley was arrested and charged with having sexually assaulted Robbie as well as a more general charge of child endangerment. This news brought mixed reactions to Pat: sadness that another fellow priest had fallen so low that he now faced imprisonment and banishment from the Church, but relief as well that at least one child molester was no longer free to prey.

Once Father Malley had been arrested, Attorney Baker informed the diocese of his intention to bring a lawsuit against the diocese for its failure to properly supervise the conduct of Father Malley. In Attorney Baker's subsequent lawsuit, Robbie's parents sought a large financial judgment against the diocese.

In spite of these developments, Pat did not feel complete relief from his angst. He was concerned that there could be many more victims who were suffering in silence while offending priests continued their marauding, preying on more innocents. He pondered how he could help other as yet unidentified victims.

He was driven, as well, by his need, somehow, to right the wrong that had taken young Lawrence Jefferson's life. Pat knew from reading the papers and from television that the scourge of priests sexually assaulting children was becoming more wildly known as each new case was headlined in the popular media. He wondered, with dread, about the Church's possible role in keeping this stain under wraps. Those thoughts angered and energized him.

Without asking Robbie for any names, Pat told him that he'd be happy to meet with anyone else Robbie thought had been abused by any adult. He gave Robbie his phone number with the suggestion he share it with anyone he thought might want to talk with him. Pat said the same to his nephew Chris.

Not long afterward, Pat received a call from someone obviously young who identified himself as Mickey Davidson. He asked Pat if he could come to talk with him. "I know Robbie" was all he had to say to alert Pat to the nature of his quest. Pat arranged to meet the boy at Sean's bench where, he thought, the youngster might feel less intimated. They set a meeting for 3 p.m. the next day. Pat got there early to watch some of the boats returning from fishing, always a centering site, as he thought about the youngster coming to see him. Within minutes, a lanky, dark-haired boy in high-top sneakers, jeans, and a T-shirt with an indistinct imprint approached somewhat out of breath. He stopped at the bench and asked Pat if he was Chris' uncle. Introductions over, the boy took a seat on the ground next to the bench.

"Tell me, Mickey, how I can help you," Pat opened.

"I know Robbie's older brother, Mark. We met one time at a swim meet with a bunch of YMCAs and now we see each a lot and we talk about stuff sometimes. We both swim freestyle and sometimes race against each other even though he's a little older than me. It's real cool. I think he's better than me but sometimes I win. We were at a meet a few weeks ago when I heard him telling another kid that his little brother went to the police, saying that a priest had done something bad to him. I tried to talk to Mark after the meet when I was waiting for my mom to pick me up but all he said was I should talk with Robbie if I want to know more. We live in Harrowston and go to St. Michael's, not too far from here. I can usually get a bus to Duncan's Cove. That's how I got here today."

The youngster continued in his somewhat disjointed way.

"So I called Robbie and he didn't want to talk with me either but he gave me your name and your phone number and that's how come I'm here. But I don't really know what I'm doing here. I'm all mixed up."

Pat tried not to flinch.

"Why don't you take a breath, Mickey. We have lots of time to talk and I want to help if I can with whatever is on your mind." Pat's calm demeanor seemed to slow down Mickey's pace. He then appeared to brace himself.

"Well, Father, I guess I'm here because something like what happened to Robbie happened to me but I'm afraid to talk about it. Do you know Father Reagan? He was at St. Michael's where I go until he left a while ago. Up till I told Mark, I didn't tell anyone. I'm scared and feel dirty and just didn't want to talk with anyone until I heard about you, Father. I think I just need to tell someone other than another kid like Mark 'cause it's making me crazy."

In order to give Mickey time to get his bearings, Pat asked him to talk about his family. "You know, Mickey, I'm not planning on going away or anything. If it's too hard to talk about today, you can come back tomorrow or whenever you want. I'll be here. Sounds like it's important for you to be able to talk with somebody, but you should do it only when you're ready."

"Okay," the boy responded. He got up and started to walk away. "Can I call you tomorrow? I think I just want to go home and ride my bike around for a while now."

"Of course, Mickey. We can have our talk whenever you want."

And with that, the boy left. Pat wondered if he'd see him again but he didn't have long to wait. Two days later he boy called back.

"Father, can I come see you this afternoon? I really want to talk about this."

"Sure, Mickey, I'll be at that bench around two in the afternoon. Does that work for you?"

"See you then, Father. Thanks."

And the next day along came the boy. He was no sooner seated on the grass before he started in:

"Well, I live alone with my mom in Harrowston. It's just the two of us. I didn't talk with her about this because she's busy all the time. After my dad left, my mom had to work two jobs. I haven't seen him since he left but my mom's always griping that he doesn't ever help her with anything so he must be around someplace."

"Where does your mom work, Mickey? It sounds like you don't have it too easy."

"She works two jobs, one at the fish processing plant in Duncan's Cove and a part-time one in the supermarket on weekends. She's hardly ever home. And when she's around, I don't want to bother her. I know she loves me and all that, but we don't talk much about stuff."

Pat's immediate reaction to this recitation was that, in some ways, Mickey seemed mature beyond his years, which he estimated to be around twelve or thirteen, and that life was not easy in his home. Trying to move the conversation into the reason for their meeting while still giving the boy space, Pat asked where he went to school.

"I go to Mayflower Middle School but go to Catechism classes at St. Mike's on Wednesday afternoons taught by Father Reagan. I can take the bus there. He wants us to call him Father Ralph. I guess he's only been at St. Mike's for about a year but he's kinda young and the kids all liked him because he shoots hoops after religion classes, stuff like that. When he asked me to help him in the church, straightening up the sacristy, I felt real honored. A couple of times, he even took me out to McDonald's for a hamburger and fries after all the other kids left and then gave me a ride home. He said he knew that my mother was divorced and wasn't around much because of the jobs she had. I thought he was real nice, kind of like the father I wished I had. I really liked being around him, particularly going to get meals after school and getting a ride home so I didn't have to take the bus."

Now Pat sat quietly, not interrupting, letting the story come out in Mickey's way. Less confidently, Mickey continued: "Then one time, when we had gone to McDonald's, Father Reagan drove back to the rectory where he said he wanted to show me something, but when we got to his room, he got all creepy. That's when he said he loved me and he tried to kiss me and he pulled me to him. And then he started pawing me all over, reaching down my front, and he pulled me into his bed. I couldn't believe this was happening right where Father Reagan lived, but he was so strong. He pulled my pants and underwear off and suddenly he had his mouth down there, you know, which made me feel weird."

The boy then turned to Pat with a different look in his eyes.

"Do I have to tell the rest? It makes me feel icky even thinking about it. Oh, well. I guess I might as well just say it. My thing got hard and then some white stuff came out of it, going all over the place. After that, Reagan just got up and said I should leave and that if I told anybody about this, he'd say he kicked me out of religion class because I wasn't paying any attention to my work and I was acting up. He said he didn't think my mother would want to hear that. So I ran out of there with my pants half off. I was really scared and just ran all the way to the bus stop. After that I quit Catechism but I didn't tell my mom. I don't think she could handle knowing what had happened and she'd probably never know I wasn't going anymore anyway."

Pat sat motionless. Finally, he said, "Mickey, I'm so sorry this happened to you. It's a terrible thing Father Reagan did to you. I'm glad you have come to talk with me about it. I'd like to help you."

To Pat, Mickey's story was depressingly similar to Robbie's in the way that the offending priests had groomed the boys and then, in a flash, had attacked them, turning their worlds upside down. Mickey continued, "I'm worried, Father, that I'm going to hell because I did that with a priest right in the rectory and because I'm not going to religion class anymore. I feel real sad about what happened and even thought a few times maybe I should just kill myself. I know my mom keeps some rat poison in the garage and think sometimes maybe I'll just eat some of it or maybe I'll just drown myself even though I know that would be a sin. But I really love my mom and don't want to hurt her. She has so much to deal with anyway."

Once Mickey was spent, Pat gently assured him he had done nothing wrong and that he was completely a victim. Although Pat didn't know Mickey's mother, he suggested she was probably stronger than Mickey thought, and he offered, if Mickey wanted, that he'd be happy to meet with her any time she was free. He urged Mickey to trust that his mother would want to know about what had happened to him.

And Pat was correct. The next day, Jennifer Davidson called. She identified herself as Mickey's mother and said that he had said some things about Father Reagan only in vague terms, but enough for her to know that something bad had happened. She said she was anxious to speak with him. The following day, they met in Pat's quarters. She was a tall, lean woman, mid-thirties, Pat thought, with a look of wariness about her. She appeared fraught, harried. After greeting her, Pat asked. "Where's Mickey? Is he coming along?"

"No, Father. Mickey knows I'm here. He asked me if he had to go and I said he didn't. Should he be with us?"

Pat was curious about Mickey's absence but he just smiled and invited her to have a seat.

"He just doesn't want to talk whatever is bothering him anymore, I guess." She said she had assented to Mickey's wish but with misgivings as she really didn't know what was going on. Gently, Pat took her through Mickey's story, pausing from time to time. When he was done, he sat quietly waiting for her reaction. Like Robbie's parents, Mrs. Davidson appeared dazed, confused, and uncertain of her bearings.

"This is so terrible, Father. It's hard for Mickey not having his dad; the son of a bitch does nothing for us. Oh, sorry, Father, I got lost for a moment. I thought this Reagan was a godsend, Father, I mean literally, and then I find out that he did this to my Mickey. I'm so mad I could spit." Her red face and clenched hands matched her voice.

"I know Mickey told you I'm a single parent. Having this happen to him just makes me feel inadequate all over again, just the way I felt when Josh, that's my ex, walked out of our lives. But it's worse now. I thought we were doing okay. Mickey's such a great boy. It's not fair what happened to him."

Pat responded. "I've only met Mickey twice, Mrs. Davidson, but I was so impressed with how much he cares about you. He seems like a really good boy. Of course I'm upset that this happened to him, but I'm glad he came to see me. I want to help if I can."

As he did with Robbie's family, Pat suggested that Mickey could benefit from counseling from a person specially trained to deal with adolescents, and he steered Mickey's' mother to Jed Baker as well. "I think you should talk with the police too, Mrs. Davidson. What happened to Mickey is a crime." He gave her the name of Detective Fay, at the Duncan's Cove police department.

While aware that the allegations against Father Reagan concerned criminal conduct in Harrowston, where St. Michael's Church was located, he assumed that detectives from the departments talked with each other. And sure enough, once

Mickey and his mother met with Sergeant Fay, she called her colleague, Detective Julia Fortney of the Harrowston Police Department, who, in turn, contacted Jennifer Davidson and asked if she and her son would meet with her at the police station.

Detective Fortney also called Pat, confirming that Mickey and his mother had visited with her and that Mickey had revealed to her the misconduct of Father Reagan. When asked for his impression of Mickey, Father Pat thoughtfully responded that Mickey's tale sadly rang true. He spoke of Mickey's demeanor, his obvious concern for his mother as likely being a strong factor in Mickey's delayed reporting, and the details of his story being unlikely for any normally healthy child of Mickey's age to contrive. Pat agreed, as well, to support Mickey at trial should that occur.

Once Mickey and his mother met with Detective Fortney, she prepared a warrant for the priest's arrest, which shortly later was signed by Judge Damon Rucker and served upon Father Reagan at the rectory the same day. He was charged with sexual assault of a minor and child endangerment, like the charges against Father Malley, felonies carrying prison terms upon conviction.

A few weeks later, Pat received a surprising phone call.

"Father Keefe, this is Joe Sorella from the *Daily Gazette* where your sister works. She gave me your phone number where I guess you're now staying."

"What can I do for you, Mr. Sorella?"

"Well, Father, I've been following the arrests of those two priests for sexually abusing kids, and when I spoke with the mother of one of them, she couldn't stop talking about you, how wonderful you've been. I was hoping you'd make some comment about these cases. You know, being a priest and all, that's kind of unusual."

Pat was weary. "Mr. Sorella, I'm not going to comment on those cases or any role I may have played in bringing them to light. I just don't think it's my place to do that."

"But, Father, you're already in these cases. I spoke with the prosecutor, who confirmed that you will be helping the State in the prosecution."

Oh boy, thought Pat. "Well, Mr. Sorella, I can't help what others say, but I think my role here is more private. I really prefer that my involvement, whatever it may be, not become a matter of public comment."

"Too late for that, Father. But I understand if you don't want to talk about it. I don't blame you."

And with that, the conversation ended. Pat wondered to himself how long it would be before the chancellery sought him out.

In a world where the unexpected seemed to be happening more frequently to Pat, the next call should not have been a surprise. Maggie called downstairs to say the phone was for him.

"Hello, Pat, this is Jim Peterson from St. Ann's in Maynardsville. You probably don't remember me because I was a couple of years behind you at Trinity, but seeing your name in the paper a few days ago made me want to reach out to you."

"How did you find me?" was Pat's first response.

"It wasn't too hard. I called the warden at Suffolk who told me you were on a leave of absence, and once he knew I was a fellow priest he told me how to find you. And here I am."

"Well, then, Jim Peterson, what can I do for you?"

Paterson then explained that he had been sent to St. nconcoAnn's in Maynardsville a few months ago, without any advance notice, and that he had been told that he was replacing George McNamara, who had been transferred elsewhere.

"I think his leaving happened suddenly as well. There were rumors around here about McNamara, that he had gotten into some sort of trouble with the bishop, but I didn't know anything about it until a parishioner came to see me. His name is David Colsen and we're old Navy buddies. I'm sure you have no idea, but I went to the Naval Academy before I decided to become a priest. Long story for another time, but Colsen and I got pretty close when we were shipmates."

Paterson further explained that Colsen's wife had reached out to the Navy to get him compassionate leave from his ship as she said there was a family emergency.

Peterson continued: "Poor guy—had no idea until he got home. He said his wife was a mess. Apparently their son, Carl, had just told her that this fellow McNamara, my predecessor, had molested him and she believed him. I guess she had gone right to the chancellery when she found out but the monsignor there just blew her off, suggesting it was probably all in Carl's imagination. He even said that she should discipline him. That put her over the edge and made her reach out to the Navy to get David home.

"Now the whole family's in a stew. They believe their son. David says he's a good kid who just doesn't lie. Now they have no idea what to do, where to turn, and so here I am, Pat, looking for help. I heard you went on to get a master's in social work after seminary and I was just hoping you might have some insights for me. I really want to help this family."

Pat thought to himself, *Oh, boy, here we go again. Yet another priest. When will this end, or are we just at the beginning? What's happening to Mother Church?* His response to his colleague was warm.

"I tell you what, Jim, if you would like me to meet with the family, I'd be happy to take a ride over to Maynardsville. As you've learned, I'm on a leave of absence, so I have lots of time. Do you think the family would be willing to meet with me?"

"Oh, that would be great, Pat. And, yes, I know they would. I already told David Colsen of my intent to reach out to you. They just want to get to the bottom of it. They're pretty upset as you can imagine. I guess their son has some learning disabilities, which makes this even harder for them, if that's possible."

Three days later, Pat took the two-hour trip to Maynardsville, an inland town he didn't know. When he got to the rectory, he was met by a tall, sandy-haired man who introduced himself as Jim Peterson.

"Thanks so much for coming, Pat. I hope the drive wasn't too bad. The family is in here."

Immediately, he ushered Pat into a large sitting room where a man and woman and young boy were already seated. "These are the Colsens, Father Keefe—Jim and Rita and their son Carl."

Pat shook hands with all, having to look up to meet eyes with the erect and fit looking Navy man standing next to his obviously distraught and quite thin wife. To Pat, Carl seemed a fragile-appearing youngster, tall and thin for twelve, his age according to Jim Peterson. Pat found it a little awkward to be meeting the entire family at once, as he suspected this youngster might not be comfortable talking with a stranger, but he didn't want to ask Carl to leave. Instead, he suggested that perhaps the parents and Father Peterson could go to another room for a while so that he and Carl could chat. He turned to Carl and asked if that would be okay with him. "Do I have to?" the boy seemed to stammer.

"No, not at all," Pat quickly answered. "If you want your parents to be here with us, Carl, that's just fine. We'll do it that way." Father Peterson got the cue as he quietly left the room.

With the whole family present, Pat decided to try to talk directly to the boy. "Carl, I'm glad you came. Could you tell me a little about yourself? I'd like to get to know you if I can."

"Well, all right. I'm in the seventh grade here at St. Ann's. I like it okay but it's kind of hard. I have a tutor sometimes. She's real nice. I guess I do all right but I don't have a lot of friends. Some kids say I'm weird but I have a couple of friends anyway. At least up to when this happened. Now I just stay in my room. I like to listen to music, but most of the time I just sit around feeling sad, sometimes really scared that it might happen again. I dunno."

When Pat asked Carl if he wanted to talk about it, the words began to tumble out. "When Father McNamara came to the parish and took over the CYO basketball team, he seemed really nice. He acted just like one of us kids, you know, always fooling around, giving us hugs, sometimes pats on the butt when we did something good or sometimes for nothing at all—like he was kidding around. He was real friendly. He'd ask me about his family, about my dad's work in the Navy and how I was doing in school, and he even offered to help me a few times with my homework. I thought that was neat since my dad is away a lot and my mom works all the time."

Pat asked him about his daily routine, what his life at home was like.

"Well, you know. I'm the only kid so I'm alone most of the time. After school I'm home by myself. I used to feel lonely sometimes but now I kinda like it that way."

When Pat tried gently to nudge Carl into talking about what had happened to him, he began to sob. "Do I have to tell it? I told my mom and dad—why can't they?" Pat thought for a moment and then looked at the boy's parents. They both nodded. "Okay, Carl" Pat said. "Would you feel okay about going outside to shoot some hoops? I saw an outdoor court when we came in. I bet Father Peterson could find a ball for you."

"Yeah, sure," Carl quickly responded. "That's our play yard. We go out there for recess. I don't mind being by myself there. Can I go?" When both parents nodded, Pat got up and went looking for Father Peterson, who was close by in another room, reading. "Hey, Jim, do you think you could find a basketball and show Carl how to get outside to the play area? He'd rather not be with us right now. I think he'd prefer to be by himself out there, but maybe you could keep an eye on him."

"Sure thing, Pat."

Pat returned to the room to fetch Carl. "Father Peterson will show you the way outside, son. And he'll get you a ball.

You can just hang there for a while if that's what you want to do."

"Yes, please, Father. I want to do that."

After Carl had left with Father Peterson, Pat turned to the Colsens and asked if either of them could talk about what had happened to Carl. Mrs. Colsen said she'd do it.

"Well, one day after I came home from work, I called upstairs to say hi to Carl but I didn't hear anything back so I went upstairs and knocked on his bedroom door. Still, he didn't say anything. So, I opened the door and there was Carl curled up on his bed and sobbing into his pillow as though trying to keep it quiet. Immediately I went to his side and just rubbed his back a little until he seemed to get control. When he sat up, I could see that his face was all puffy. After a while, he just started telling me this horrid story.

"He said that one time when the team had an away night game at Chamberlain, Father McNamara invited him to drive with him while the assistant coach, Mr. Levine, took the other kids in the church van. At one point during the ride home, they stopped at a drive-thru for burgers and fries and a malt, which Father McNamara paid for. After they got their food, Father McNamara drove for a while but then pulled onto a road in the back of a big parking lot that seemed empty. Carl said he thought maybe the stores had closed. Father McNamara said they were stopping there so they could eat as it wasn't safe to eat and drive. And this is the really hard part." Pat could see her tense and, gently, he nodded for her to continue.

"Once they were done with their food, Carl said this man, this creep, just leaned over and began kissing him. He undid his belt and reached under there to put his hand on Carl's penis, and he kept saying that he loved him. Carl said at that point that he was real scared and didn't know what to do. So he just pushed the priest hard away from him and then jumped out of the car on his side and just stood there with the door open. I guess he was panting. When McNamara told him to get back in, he did because he really didn't know where he was.

"He said then that the priest started all over again. This time, he said McNamara unzipped his own pants, and pushed my son, my dear son's face, down to into his lap, and told him to put his mouth around his penis. Of course that's not the word he used, but it's obvious what he meant. When that happened, Carl said he pushed back real hard against the man and said he wouldn't do that because it's dirty and I guess he asked him why he was acting like that. Carl said that Father McNamara then seemed to suddenly change. He got real angry. He started the car up and yelled that Carl was ungrateful for everything he had done for him. Then he said that if Carl told anyone about it, he'd just say he was making it up because he's lonely and, he said, he'd throw him off the team, telling anyone who asked that he was lazy and not good enough to be on the team. The nerve of that so-called priest.

"Carl said then they just drove back to St. Ann's, neither of them talking, but when they got to the church Carl said he just jumped out of the car and ran all the way home. He told me that's why he quit the team and he said he was sorry for first lying to me about that. Dumb me, I didn't ask him anything about it even though I thought it was kind of odd. He had seemed to like it so well. The other thing is that when Carl sat up I saw the scissors in the bed, and then I saw the cut marks on his legs. That was absolutely terrifying. Right after that, I reached out to the Navy to get David home."

At that point in her recitation, Rita Colsen was trembling, her voice trailing to a whisper. Her husband quickly went to her side and held her hand.

"I know that was very difficult for you, Mrs. Colsen." Pat remarked. "It must have been really hard for Carl too, to tell you all this."

"Oh, yes." Mrs. Colsen smiled through her tears. "I gave you the sanitized version. Poor Carl was stammering, starting and stopping, and sometimes just sobbing as the terrible ordeal came flooding out of him. We were both exhausted when he was finished and we just sat there embracing each other for a good long while. He's such a dear boy. He struggles, you may not know, but he has lots of get-up-and-go. How dare that priest do this to him?!"

David Colsen then spoke up. "Father, do you think there's any possibility Carl just made this up?" His wife just silently shook her head.

Pat responded: "Let me ask you this. Before this incident, would you have described Carl as being hysterical, the sort of child who would make up stories just to get attention, anything like that sort of behavior?"

"Never," both responded. David Colsen added: "Carl's always been a straight arrow. I know I'm not around much, but he's never been any kind of a behavior problem—isn't that right, dear?"

Rita replied without hesitation. "Carl struggles as a student. He has some learning disabilities that we're trying to help him with, but I don't think he's ever lied to us about anything. That's just not him. And, he's always been a mostly content boy, at least he was before this happened, but now he's in a nosedive. We've never had any issues with him. He's about as perfect a son as any parent could have. Why did this have to happen to him?" What's wrong with this priest?"

Pat spoke carefully. "I understand that one of you went to the chancellery. Can you tell me what happened?"

"That was me," Rita said. "And what an eye-opener that was. I was ushered in to meet this Monsignor O'Brien, I guess the bishop's right-hand man, and he just patronized me. It was galling. He suggested that Carl might be making it up because David's away so much and I work, and he said we should have a stern talk with him. Maybe, he suggested it's part of his learning disability that, somehow, he must have found out about. That was really offensive. When I told this man that I thought Carl was telling the truth, he acted as though I had just committed blasphemy. He suggested I leave and pray for forgiveness for making such an accusation. And that was that. Except that in a week's time, that priest, McNamara, was sent someplace else. I guess maybe that monsignor thought that might be the end of it. But not for us it isn't."

Pat's voice reflected his sorrow. "I can't justify what happened to you at the chancellery, Mrs. Colsen, and I won't even try to because that would be an act of hypocrisy on my part."

"Well, what do you suggest we do now, Father?" David interjected.

Pat responded that he thought it was very important to continue to reassure Carl that he had done nothing wrong, and he said he thought it would be important for Carl to meet with a counselor to help him deal with the aftershock of this incident. He also urged the Colsens to talk with someone at the Maynardsville Police Department because what Father McNamara had done was a crime.

When Rita Colsen asked about trying to meet with the bishop personally, Pat's response was bracing, even to him. "You can talk with the bishop, Mrs. Colsen, but I don't have any confidence your reception will be any different than it was with his aide. I do think it's very important you report this to the police as that may be the only way Father McNamara is going to be brought to justice. I'm sorry to say this, deeply sorry, but I wouldn't rely on the diocese as it appears Father McNamara is gone and the circle has closed around him. Anyway, what Father McNamara did to Carl is a serious crime. Going to the police will be the best way to make him accountable and to stop him from harming anybody else."

"But what about Carl?" Mr. Colsen asked. "Who's going to pay for what happened to him? So the priest gets arrested— that doesn't help Carl very much."

At that point, Pat gave the Colsens Attorney Baker's contact information and told them that Baker would be able to answer their questions about any other claims they could make. Pat was curious about Father McNamara's sudden exit from St. Ann's and he made a mental note to tell Attorney Baker about it, as it seemed a noteworthy repetition of what had happened to the priests who had molested Robbie and Mickey. To Pat, it appeared to be a trend in how the diocese dealt with the accusations related to all three boys.

Soon thereafter, the Colsens followed Pat's advice. They met with Detective James Cooney of the Maynardsville Police Department, and just as in the case of the other two priests, Father McNamara was ultimately arrested for child endangerment and sexual assault. In a sense, Pat thought once when thinking about all three boys, he had become a way station in the recovery of these youngsters, and a conduit to the help they needed and deserved, a role he sadly welcomed.

And then one day Pat received a summons from the chancellery, this time to meet directly with the bishop. Pat knew he had a problem as he feared the bishop might have sensed that he was operating a kind of underground railroad for victims of priest abuse and the bishop might order him to stop. He knew, as well, that he had taken a vow of obedience when he was ordained and yet, in spite of what he had learned about the bad actions of other priests, or perhaps because of it, he was steadfast in his commitment to these children. He felt strongly that he walked in Christ's path and that if anyone had lost direction, it was the diocesan leadership. This sense was very disquieting for him. Before now, he had never questioned the authority or majesty of the Church, the holder of eternal truths. Who was he, one priest, to question the holiness of the organization that had carried the faith through the centuries?

What to do? He discussed his dilemma with Maggie, who showed her usual practical wisdom. "Before meeting with the bishop, go see Attorney Baker, Pat. He's a wise man who might have some ideas about how to deal with the bishop without jeopardizing your priesthood." And she was right. Although it felt odd, even disorienting, for Pat to be consulting with a lawyer about his dealings with the Church hierarchy, a new undertaking for him, Baker was thoughtful and insightful.

Baker's office was located in a midcentury house converted into an office on a tree-lined street mixed with homes and other lawyers' offices, all within walking distance of the courthouse. Once inside the front door, he found himself in a waiting room attended by a young woman who looked up and smiled at him. "Father Keefe, is it?" she queried.

"How did you know?" Pat smiled ".And what is your name?

"I'm Melissa, Father, and, oh, we don't get too many priests in here so I just made a good guess. I'll let Mr. Baker know you're here. Please have a seat."

Shortly, Jed Baker appeared and guided Pat to his small office. "I'm no canon lawyer, Father Pat" was his first reaction once Pat outlined his concerns. "I bet you studied something about canon law in the seminary. If so, you may know that's a very specific body of law, created by the Church for its organization and governance. There are people who study it, become specialized."

"Yes, I know, Jed," Pat replied. "I don't think my problem relates to church law. The bishop's got all the cards there. I think I'd just like to talk this out with you because, well, I trust your judgment and I appreciate your taking on these cases. My sense is that you might have some insights just based on the way you think about problems generally."

"Well, maybe, Father Pat. Let's just brainstorm together for a few moments."

They talked then about the bishop, what his concerns might be about the reputation of the Church and also its finances. After some back and forth, Baker reasoned that the bishop might be in an awkward situation with Father Pat.

"If he orders you to stop seeing victims of priest child abuse," Baker suggested, "that step could be viewed as evidence of culpability in the lawsuits I've brought against the diocese on behalf of the boys. No jury would want to hear that the diocese, a defendant in a civil lawsuit, had attempted to silence the person who, in effect, brought this misconduct to light. Maybe in your conversation with the bishop, Father Pat, you could sort of wonder out loud about that. If you can pull that off, you might be able to sow seeds of doubt with the bishop about trying to block you from helping the kids and threatening retaliation against you."

What an awkward feeling that gave Pat to be in an adversary position with the Church, which had sheltered and nourished him in the years of his priesthood. And yet, for Pat, the moral imperative was clear. He was confident his concern for the victims was borne of a Christ-like care for the oppressed. It tormented Pat that his faith in God and the institution of the Church might be at odds, but his conscience was clear as was the path he felt he needed to take.

"Thanks, Jed," Pat expressed as they shook hands goodbye. "In an odd way, maybe this is what tough love looks like. Only this time it's not a lover, or a child; it's Mother Church. Maybe a heavy dose of medicine today will be a cure for a long time to come."

"We'll see," said Baker with skepticism in his voice.

On the appointed day, Pat set off for the chancellery to meet with the bishop. He had been there before but this time he took more note of his passage. To get to the building itself, he had to turn off Sacred Heart Way, which divided the cathedral from the chancellery. There he entered a long driveway bracketed by two stone pillars, stationed as guards to salvation, Pat was amused to think. One pillar displayed a bronze plaque lettered in ornate typeface: "Chancellery of Fishburg Diocese." The matching pillar had a bronze Irish cross affixed to it with letters "ihs" in the center of the cross. A humble entranceway, Pat chuckled nervously to himself. The driveway then made an arching turn until it opened onto an expansive lawn fronting a gothic three-story building complete with gargoyles, little monsters perched by the eaves. What a grandiose structure, thought Pat, as he remembered the building and grounds had been donated to the diocese early in the century by an industrial baron whose name he didn't remember. How utterly out of sync, thought Pat, with Christ's message of humility.

When he was ushered into the bishop's office, he faced, for the first time alone, the short, rotund, and red-faced prelate, Bishop Edward Ryan, decked out in a floor-length cassock with purple buttons and a color-matched sash girding his considerable midsection. A quick glance of his spacious office revealed oil paintings of familiar religious figures on the walls in gilded ornate frames speaking of an earlier time. This is a room of splendor, Pat surmised, a statement of grandeur and place in history. Behind the bishop's oversized, rich mahogany desk, Pat noted a picture of the bishop with the pope, and another with the current governor—a curious juxtaposition, Pat mused to himself.

As Pat entered the room and approached the desk, the bishop was standing next to his chair, erect for a rotund man, presenting a picture of sternness. While Pat didn't know what to expect, he was not prepared for such an inhospitable and frosty greeting. Without inviting Pat to have a seat or greeting him, the bishop said in an accusing manner, "Father Keefe, I hear you've been making trouble for the diocese and the Church by getting some of our priests in trouble without coming to me first."

Pat was prepared. "I'm sorry you believe that, Your Excellency, as I think my recent activities have been in the long-term interest of the Church, even if it may not seem that way."

The bishop was not moved to ask Pat to explain. Rather, in a huffy manner, he told Pat that he had strayed from his calling and that he was in danger of being silenced by the diocese for his conduct. "You must stop seeing these youngsters," the bishop proclaimed, "and having any dealings with the police or the courts. When you're ready to end this leave of absence of yours, and get back to your duties, I'll find a suitable parish for your next assignment."

To Pat this was a double-barreled assault. Not only was the bishop threatening to silence him, he was also telegraphing his intent to remove him from his prison ministry. This both frightened and emboldened him. Remembering what Attorney Baker had told him, Pat spoke. "Your Excellency, I am grieved that you are displeased with my pastoral work with these young boys, and, of course, I bow to your superior authority. I wonder though, how silencing me could be understood by others. Perhaps that could put the diocese in a bad light."

If the bishop could have reddened any more, he did by Pat's seeming impertinence.

"Young man, do you know who you're speaking to? Don't you dare threaten me."

"Oh, Excellency, that is not my intent. I am only thinking of what might be the unintended consequences of what some might view as retaliation for my work in assisting these children."

At this the bishop plopped down in his chair, without inviting Pat to sit as well.

"What are you implying, Father Keefe?"

"Well, Bishop, I think my role by now is well known and I will be expected to provide assistance in the coming legal actions, as I have served as a priest to these young boys and they told me about the abuse by priests in their parishes. I just don't know, respectfully, Your Excellency, that you'd want to be seen as interfering with the judicial process as that might not be good for you or the diocese. I am sorry to speak so directly, Excellency, but I just want to be sure you have an appreciation for the scope of what's happening in court. And, of course, if it became known in the coming civil lawsuits against the diocese that I have been silenced, maybe sent away, that information might just inflame a jury, the people who have to decide the families' claims for monetary compensation."

The bishop was unprepared for such an insolent reply. No priest had stood up to him in this way. After all, he was omnipotent to these priests. They owed a vow of obedience to him. The diocese was no democracy. He was not elected to his position by priests, but rather chosen by the pope. His position was derived from divinity. Total obedience to church hierarchy was an enduring precept of the Church. What did this upstart think he was doing by talking back to him in this way?

And yet, what Father Pat said to him made him fearful. Had Father Pat obtained legal advice? Was he correct that by taking punitive action against this priest, he could personally be in trouble and he could be further jeopardizing the position of the diocese in the civil litigation sure to come, increasing the risk of a substantial financial judgment against him? And if that happened, what would be the position of his own superiors in Rome? This dilemma perplexed the bishop. While it did not cool his ire, in fact it likely stoked it, the bishop decided he might have to be more careful with this Father Keefe. Time for him later, thought the bishop.

Emboldened by the bishop's pause in his rant when Pat suggested the harm that might befall the diocese if the bishop were to punish him for his aid to victims of priest abuse, Pat decided to turn the tables.

"I have been told, Bishop, that priests who have abused children and whose misconduct has been reported to you have been transferred and sent to distant parishes with no warning to the receiving rectories. That can't possibly be true, can it?"

The bishop was apoplectic. While he huffed at the cheekiness of this challenge, he decided it was a moment to teach this naïve lowly priest.

"Let me tell you, Father Keefe, the Church was founded by Christ and has continued for more than two millennia to bring Christ to millions of souls all over the world. In all that time, there have been priests who have sinned, indeed popes, but none of that has brought demise to the Church. We continue in our holy mission unabated by the misconduct of a few. Our overarching charge is to preserve the continuity of the Church so God's gospel may be heard. And your task as a priest is to be God's disciple in this holy mission. That's your job. It's not to go on some unholy crusade on behalf of these so-called victims. You don't even know if they're telling the truth."

Pat was offended. How dare the bishop question these youngsters?! "Bishop, in God's plan, what do you think should be the proper role of a priest who learns that his fellow clerics have gone astray and harmed others in the process if it is not to console and bring aid to those victims?"

The bishop glowered at him. "We are done here, Father Keefe. You had better watch yourself. I have no patience for impudence from priests in my diocese."

And so, just as tersely as the bishop greeting him, Pat was dismissed. As he left, he passed Monsignor O'Brien, who was on was way into the bishop's office. They nodded to each other, two ships passing, although perhaps now from different navies.

No sooner had Pat left the building the bishop turned to Monsignor O'Brien. "Why that little pipsqueak. What gall he has, questioning my authority. Make a note, O'Brien, that we need to take care of this fellow once all this abuse business is over. We'll put him in his place."

As Pat drove away from the chancellery, he thought to himself, *Well, that went really well, I wonder how far he can send me!*

After more conversation later in the day, the bishop and his aide decided they needed to speak with John Hill, the attorney who was representing the diocese in the pending litigation. "Sorry to say, Father Keefe is correct," Attorney Hill advised the bishop. "Exercising your power over him to silence him could easily be seen as a hostile response to the plight of the victims, only aggravating a jury even more than the facts of each case. And, if you are hoping to settle these claims without the publicity of a trial, disciplining this man, the one priest whom they probably think is a saint, will only embolden the victims. My suggestion, respectfully, Bishop, is that your tread lightly, at least while this litigation is pending."

And so, the bishop and Father Pat were at an impasse. Even though the bishop had complete authority over Pat, he could not exercise it lest it cost the diocese in court and maybe him personally.

Pat didn't know about the bishop's meeting with his lawyer and that the decision had been made to leave him alone for the moment. He felt at sea, uncertain of his duties. All of his adult life had been in service to the institution of the Church, which to him was his medium for service to God. And yet, now, he and his church seemed to be not just at legal odds but out of spiritual sync.

In the days after his meeting with the bishop, Pat searched his conscience to try to detect any manner in which he might have allowed his ego to overwhelm his duty of fidelity, but he kept coming back to his sense that his conduct was Christlike. Even Christ, in his times, Pat mused, was not always in tune with the authorities of his day. Pat took solace thinking of the life of Jesus, and while he did not consider himself as a Christ figure, it gentled his soul to believe his course had been true to the teachings of Christ, notwithstanding the unfortunate stance of the diocese. In Pat's mind, while he had no doubt the bishop thought he was protecting the Church, Pat believed that, to the contrary, the bishop's impulses of self-preservation were, in the long run, likely to cause the Church to suffer.

It was time, he thought, to go see Father Stan again. Perhaps Father Stan could help him think through the consequences of testifying on behalf of the children, and in particular how to harmonize the diocese's threats with his own feeling of support for the kids who had been abused.

The meeting with Father Stan was sobering. He discussed with Pat the parameters and limitations of his vow of obedience to the bishop. "What if, for example, the bishop ordered you to commit a crime?" Father Stan proposed. "We know that you would not be obligated to follow such a clearly wrong-minded order. The question for you, therefore, is one of conscience. Do you have a moral obligation to these victims that outweighs your duty of obedience to the bishop? Or by testifying against the diocese, would you simply be acting on your own preferences without any moral mandate that trumps your vow of obedience?"

In formulating the question in this manner, Father Stan was bringing home Catholic teaching that, while a vow of obedience to one's bishop is an integral part of one's priesthood, the obligation could not extend to the commission of any act that violated one's informed conscience. Pat knew this principal to be true from his studies at seminary; but for him, debating the notion in class was far different from a firsthand confrontation with the dilemma of choosing obedience or conscience.

"Do you remember that we talked about Dietrich Bonhoeffer in one of our classes in which we talked about activism?"

"Yes, I think so," responded Pat, "but wasn't he a Protestant? What does his life have to do with my problem with the bishop?"

"Well, yes, he was a Lutheran, but in his life he was very much engaged with Rome. Here's how he's relevant. Bonhoeffer was a cleric and a theologian during the Second World War in Germany. He was vehemently opposed to Nazism and frequently spoke out against its antisemitism from the pulpit, even in the face of opposition from his own church, which was undoubtedly afraid of Hitler's power. Ultimately, Bonhoeffer left his church and started another. Of course, that's not what I'm suggesting, Pat, but Bonhoeffer is a great example of courage, of following one's conscience in the face of opposition. In his case, he was executed by Hitler shortly before the end of the war. In my book, Pat, he is a saint for following his conscience without regard to the consequences. That's why I bring him to mind to you today."

Back in the seminary, Pat remembered having wondered why Father Stan had talked about this non-Catholic cleric who had defied his own church, started a new one, and ultimately died at the hands of the Nazis. In time and with later experiences, he learned of Father Stan's wisdom and gained an appreciation of his message of action when driven by personal conscience and conviction. While the opposition he now faced with the bishop was not life-threatening, coming to terms with what road he might take did require him to think deeply of his moral imperative. No matter the pushback he had received from the bishop in his quest to help children who had suffered from clerical abuse, Pat still felt a deep commitment to his Catholicism—but the bishop was now testing it.

Buoyed by Father Stan's wise and affectionate counsel, Pat knew he needed to think about what Father Stan had said, particularly the part about informed conscience, to ensure himself that his own ego was in check. That if he decided to assist the State in its prosecution of the priests and Baker in his civil claims, he'd be acting out of conviction and not merely the will to see the perpetrators and the diocese punished. He wanted to be certain that his action, whatever he decided to do, would be based on a moral decision and not on his own ego needs. A few days after seeing Father Stan, he returned to Sean's bench, where he prayed while absorbing the purity of the beauty before him. In those moments, he resolved to assist the children and to bear the consequences no matter what might come.

IX

FORMATION

In Pat's quandary, he had the recurring thought that his seminary studies had ill-prepared him for the challenge he now faced. He tried to retrace the steps of his early formation for cues to any insights he may have gleaned from his formal education. He was doubtful.

At the end of the summer of Martin Luther King's now famous speech, Pat had left St. Mary's to attend St. Thomas Academy in Stapleton, a minor seminary for boys on track for eventual priesthood. His first two years were akin to being a junior and senior at St. Mary's. There, he completed his high school and then two additional years before moving on to the major seminary.

Pat remembered doing well at St. Thomas. At the suggestion of his social science teacher, Father Richard Finneran, Pat volunteered once a weekday afternoon in his last high school year at the MacDonald Juvenile Detention Center in Easton, only a bus ride away.

For Pat, unwise to the habits of juvenile detention, the incarceration of kids close to his age had been bracing and eye-opening. How early in life for these kids to be derailed, he remembered thinking. His experiences at MacDonald provoked in him a yearning to learn more about teenage crime and its consequences. Perhaps, he now thought, the experience at MacDonald had planted the seed to his later studies in social work.

At the Center, his main task had been to tutor the students in high school courses. He was surprised at how relatively illiterate and far behind grade level many were, particularly in reading comprehension and mathematics. Without knowing more, it was apparent to Pat that many of these kids had received horribly inadequate educations in their early years for reasons he couldn't fathom. But he enjoyed tutoring and was cautiously accepted by the teen inmates once they realized he was only trying to help them. He felt over his head, though, because he did not understand the routes these boys had taken that had careened them into the justice system.

He had good moments, though. Looking back, he remembered that he particularly enjoyed one kid, Hector Mayo, with whom he sometimes got into conversations about sports when they were supposed to be working on math. A brown-skinned teenager, Mayo already had tattoos on both muscular arms, one signifying membership in a Latin gang. Short, at about five-five, his swagger made up for his size. Mayo's favorite star had been Jim Brown, the running back from the Cleveland Browns who tore up the field. When asked why, Mayo explained, "My gran had been from Cleveland and everybody in my family still roots for them." Mayo even had a Cleveland Browns cap he wore with evident pride. "A couple of kids here tried to grab it off my head once but I made them pay for it. I guess they didn't like it because it's not from around here but I showed them."

When Pat had asked what happened to him after that dustup, Mayo just shrugged: "I got put by myself for a few days but it weren't no big deal. It was worth it. You should have seen them kids when I jumped them. They didn't know what hit 'em." To Pat, trying to understand Mayo's nonchalance about fighting was part of a steep learning curve. "This place is run by gangs," Mayo had told him, "and if you're not in one or, worse, in the wrong one, it's a bad place. Now, I just try to mind my stuff, and wish the time to go faster." On the surface, Pat remembered thinking the Center didn't look like a dangerous place but, he concluded, little did he know.

In tutoring Mayo, they often talked also about nothing. Hector wanted to know about his life. "Why do you want to be a priest, Pat?" he remembered Mayo once asking him, and he found it difficult to give a simple answer.

"Well, Hector, because I love God and I want to serve Him through working with people, like you." That response seemed a little thin to him and it didn't work for Mayo. "That's crazy, man. You can do that without giving up being a man, not having a woman, being by yourself. I know the church my mom goes to has a pastor with a wife and kids. Why can't you?"

"Good question," Pat remembered responding. "It's the tradition of my church that priests shouldn't marry so all their attention, their whole lives, can be dedicated to God without the distraction and responsibility of a wife and family."

"That's bullshit," Mayo shot back. "It just sounds like you don't want to live in the world like the rest of us. I guess I just don't understand. My mom really likes our pastor and told me he's helped her deal with all the stuff I've caused her."

"That's great," Pat had responded. "We just come from different places on that one, Hector, but I think we wind up together. Sounds like your pastor cares just like I do. We have different religions with different rules, but we're really a lot alike when you get to the really important stuff, like looking out for each other, showing respect."

Pat remembered that particular conversation. It came bubbling back as he pondered his strife with the chancellery, causing him to question the need to cabin himself into celibacy in order to do Christian work when so many other good people of kindred faiths did not share the impediment of abstinence. Maybe that kid, Mayo, had something—something Pat more than once considered but just as often had put aside.

Pat remembered that two weekends a month he took the bus home to be with his family and to see some of his former school pals. In his fourth year, he particularly enjoyed going to the matches where Susan, just a sophomore, was already a standout soccer player at the Sacred Heart Academy, which she and Ruth attended. He also remembered with fondness going to concerts in which Ruth, a budding violinist, now played as a youth member in the Chamberlain County community orchestra. In season, when Sean was on the football field playing in a community league for kids up to age fourteen, Pat cheered from the sidelines as his younger brother romped up and down, showing talents beyond his years. He remembered one time when he and Susan were at a game; Janet Frazier sauntered by arm-in-arm with a boy Pat didn't recognize. She gave him a flirtatious wink and then a broad smile as they ambled along. Seeing Janet had provoked his memory of their earlier encounter, which he now remembered had so excited him.

To Pat's mentors, he was the ideal candidate for the major seminary. And surely enough, after this period of preparation, Pat was admitted to the Trinity Seminary in Johnston, about twenty-five miles from his home, a place of study and formation that drew students from several dioceses in the Northeast. At Trinity, Pat's studies focused first on philosophy and then theology. His life and learning became more rigorous, his environment nearly cloistered.

Pat was assigned to live in a double room with Luke Reardon, who had come directly from high school in St. Johns, a distant town in Pat's geographically spread-out diocese. How ironic, Pat now thought, that this perpetrator had been his seminary roommate. Even the thought of it chafed him. At the time, Pat had seen Luke as garrulous, playful, and seemingly immature—traits that Pat found difficult to harmonize with the life of study and prayer he embraced. Luke was different too. Unlike the other seminarians Pat befriended, Luke talked little about his family, just that he had moved around and that his dad was not in the picture.

For a person so talkative, Luke seemed oddly quiet about his family, but it wasn't Pat's manner to pry. He wondered now if Luke's home life contributed to his wayward conduct. Luke also played the guitar and seemingly had memorized nearly all the popular folk songs of the day, an attractive aspect of him that Pat enjoyed as they shared similar musical tastes. This ability sometimes made their room a magnet for other students.

In one of these sessions, he met Jerome Robinson, then two years ahead of him, a black man, only one of five in the seminary. At six-feet-two and pushing 250 pounds, robust and energetic, Jerome was a presence in any gathering. He was a delightfully new experience for Pat, who never before had had a close relationship with an African American. In time, Pat and Jerome became good friends as they talked about themselves and their families. But mostly, they shared a love for music. Jerome had a phonograph in his room and a decent collection of folk and Negro spirituals that they often listened to together.

Other than what he had heard at the March on Washington from the marchers when they strode together and then from Odetta on the distant stage, Negro folk music was unfamiliar to Pat. He remembered thinking when he first heard one of Jerome's albums how the music synced the body and soul, the whole person, not just the brain. He thought now how eye-opening Jerome's descriptions had been of life as a young African American in the largely white community of his upbringing, of the snubs he and his family endured as part of daily life. Pat was particularly moved by Jerome's description of the warnings his father had given to him early in his adolescence. "When you're outdoors, Jerome, even just walking around, don't stare directly at white people. Be extra courteous so no one has any mind to stop you, ask you what you're doing." Jerome remembered his father's voice being strict and sad all at once, something he didn't then understand. His father had also told him, "When you get old enough to drive, Jerome, you will become a target."

"What do you mean?" Jerome remembered asking.

"I mean white cops will be thinking you're up to something, even if you're just driving from one place to another. So, always be courteous—don't give anybody any reason to mind you." Pat was shaken by Jerome's account of his father's advice as it was alien to him, having come from a town with no significant black population, and he was sad for Jerome's father to have to give that sort of advice. In all, Pat was grateful to Jerome for unwrapping a life so different from his own.

Pat now remembered one particular afternoon in the dorm. He had been headed to his room but was distracted by the music coming from Jerome's room. When he knocked and Jerome invited him in, he found him sitting on the edge of his bed, his upper body swaying in sync to the easy tempo. He nodded to Pat and gestured for him to have a seat next to him where, together, they listened to Aretha Franklin intone the lyrics to "Amazing Grace." Suddenly, as Pat now recalled, Jerome reached over, put his arms around him, and kissed him squarely on the mouth while pushing him down on the bed. Pat remembered jumping up, breathless and shocked. He pushed hard at Jerome, scowling in surprise.

"What are you doing, Jerome? Where did that come from?" he gasped.

"Oh, so sorry, man", Jerome said, his eyes pleading. "I just really like you and thought you might feel the same."

"Jerome, you're my friend and I do like you, but not in that way. That's just not me."

"My mistake, Pat", Jerome said. "I guess I got it wrong. I thought you might have the same feelings for me that I do for you and guessed you'd probably like to take it physical. Please don't hold it against me."

"Well, I'm not gay, Jerome. I just like being your friend, you know, listening to music, talking, that kind of stuff, but not this." Pat's voice was stern, unyielding.

"You know, Pat, I'm not the only one around here with these kinds of feelings; I've seen other guys who I know are gay. It's not like I'm the only one," Jerome said defensively.

"Not my issue," replied Pat. "I don't hold it against you for being gay or anybody else. It's your life and not mine and I'm not interested in going there. But I'm not trying to judge you either. Others can do that. I know the Church has issues about homosexuality but I'm not really concerned about other people's personal lives or preferences so long as they don't bother me or keep me from being the priest I hope to be."

"That works for me, Pat. And, thanks," Jerome sighed with obvious relief that Pat's reaction probably wouldn't go beyond the room.

"Does this mean we can't be friends anymore?" Jerome then asked with sincerity, more a plea than question.

"Not at all, Jerome. You've got the best music around here. I'm not ready to give that up!"

Pat remembered fearing that Jerome's false move could make continuing their friendship less likely, but it didn't. In their remaining years together at Trinity until Jerome's ordination, Pat and Jerome remained friends, a bit wary of each other, and for Pat, perhaps, a little less inclined to drop in on Jerome to listen together to music. One time, however, after Jerome had invited him to hear some new music he had, Pat spent a few hours with him and another seminarian, Jacob Fedora, who Pat didn't know well but seemed friendly and was obviously close to Jerome. As Pat stood to leave, Jerome asked him to stay a minute while Jacob left, and then he reached to a shelf over his bed and handed him a book with the title *Notes of a Native Son* by James Baldwin, an author Pat didn't know. "This is for you, Pat. It's by a great author who really speaks to me. It's a bunch of essays. As a friend, I just ask you to read them, maybe get an idea about me you don't see. Anyway, you can keep it as it's a copy I got just for you."

"Thank you," responded Pat, a little perplexed but curious about this James Baldwin writer he didn't know. Later, Pat understood. With frank eloquence, Baldwin's essays talked about being black, about sexuality, and about life in a mostly white society. Having read this, Pat even more treasured his friendship with Jerome and the trust he felt in this gift to him, as he knew it came from the heart.

Even though Pat roomed with Luke, the two didn't become close. But to Pat, Luke seemed a good soul even if, perhaps, not a perfect fit for the vocation they all espoused. Even though Luke sometimes seemed frivolous, Pat thought he had a kindness about him, as, for example, when he tried to help other students who were struggling, or how well he led others in song while he played his guitar. Little did he know.

In his last year before ordination, Pat volunteered twice a week in the afternoons at the state penitentiary in Suffolk, about thirty-five miles distant in a rural corner of the state. Suffolk was a large facility, housing men in maximum-, moderate-, and minimum-security wings; a segregation unit; and another for those pending execution. It took Pat almost an hour to get to Suffolk— a trek. But to him this work seemed a natural sequel to his earlier time at the MacDonald Juvenile Detention Center, which had honed his desire to focus his ministry on those whose lives had gone astray. And he was lucky his Nonno Deluca had decided, when buying a new car, to give his old Ford Falcon to him. It was a boon to have this car, even nearly ten years old because it had relatively low mileage and his grandpa had well maintained it. Pat smiled as he thought about that clunker. It had lasted him through ordination until one day it choked its last smoky breath. Pat recalled with amusement that the towing charge matched almost to a dollar what he was paid at the salvage yard, leaving little left over to purchase his next ride of similar vintage.

Pat remembered his first impression of Suffolk. The massive and sprawling granite building was daunting, probably the architect's intent. The entrance gate was surrounded by high fencing, topped with razor wire, guard towers in the corners, creating a foreboding cage. Once Pat had been checked in, he was met by Jake Newson, a lead corrections officer, who said he had been detailed to give Pat a tour. When

Pat was first shown the general population area, he kept his reaction to himself. Only once before, at the March on Washington, had he seen so many black men in one place. How can it be, Pat wondered, in a state with a small African American population, that most men here are people of color? Something to learn about later; he decided not to ask his guide. Later, when he met with Warden James Tucker, he broached the question. Tucker, he later learned, had worked his way up the ranks, starting as a guard after a stint in the Army and, over time, wending his way up the ladder to the top. Now in his late fifties, Pat guessed, Tucker looked like a man who took seriously the need to keep in shape. With an angular face and sinewy body, he appeared fit for any eventuality. But his physical appearance belied his friendliness. When Pat was ushered into his office, he warmly welcomed Pat to the house.

"Happy to have you here, Padre. We surely could use some Godliness around here. If you ever have any questions or needs, please know my door is always open."

"Thanks for that, Warden. Just one at the moment. In my quick walk-around, I noticed so many more men of color than I see on the outside. Why is that so?"

"Well, Padre, the simple answer is that men of color commit more crimes per capita than their representation in the general population, but that's too facile. To really get to your question, we'd have to talk about racism, economic and social deprivations, and, most of all, the lack of opportunities or any horizons. But that's a lecture for another time. Get to know the men, Padre, and I think you'll begin to be able to answer your very good question." Pat's first meeting with the warden presaged many to come.

As the State's only place of incarceration for men, Suffolk housed adults who had been sentenced to terms ranging from a few months to death. There were nine inmates on death row, having been convicted of especially heinous crimes, some of them more than thirty years ago. Although the state hadn't executed anyone for decades due to a combination of seemingly endless appeals and a lack of urgency in leadership to actually carry out a death sentence, the mere possibility of an execution caused the condemned to be separately housed in a wing dubbed by the inmates and correctional officers as the Lost Corridor. For Pat, new to prison experience, thinking about the death row inmates was particularly painful because he believed that execution by the State was immoral no matter how terrible the crimes the condemned men had committed. Pat's initial thought would be to extend his hand in grace and forgiveness to any of these inmates who might ask to see him.

As he thought about it now, his first experience on the Lost Corridor had altered those untutored notions. A condemned inmate named Richard Brand had asked to see Pat soon after he started to volunteer. His memory now of that first trip to the corridor remained vivid and disheartening. When he was locked and unlocked through various checkpoints, Pat first noticed that the walls of the corridor were painted green and the cells, on either side of the corridor, were old-style, open barred so a passerby could look in, violating even a semblance of privacy.

Pat couldn't help glancing from side to side as he was led down the corridor. In almost every cell, he saw men sitting on the sides of their beds, most staring at nothing Pat could see, expressionless, a few gazing his way as he and the dark-skinned guard passed by on the way to Brand's cell. He made a mental note to ask the warden later whether these men were medicated as that was the impression their demeanors gave him. When they got to Brand's cell, he found a large white man, with close-cropped hair and wearing a sleeveless, wife-beater shirt standing close to the front of his cell, grinning at him.

"What's up, Padre?" was Brand's welcome as the corrections officer barked at him to back to the rear of the cell as he placed a stool for Pat to sit, just outside the bars. The corrections officer then backed away, saying: "Don't worry, Padre, we won't be far away, but we want to give you some privacy. And Brand, stay the hell on your bed. Don't approach these bars."

Pat was confused. "Shouldn't he and I be able to speak in private?" he asked.

"Not this fella, Padre. You'll see." Pat then turned to Brand, still seated.

"Welcome to my home, Padre. Hope you like it here."

"How can I help you, Mr. Brand?" were Pat's opening words.

"Oh, I don't know, Padre. I just wanted to see what you look like, and to have some company. It's pretty boring in here."

As Brand spoke, Pat's eyes were drawn to the man's neck and arms. From his hands to his face, Brand's body was inked in an assortment of designs, shapes, and numbers. Pat didn't know what any of these meant but he made a mental note to ask the warden about the dragon's head, the triangles enmeshed in one another, an Irish Cross with symbols next to it, an eagle superimposed on a circle and dots on his knuckles.... There were so many. This guy looks like a walking tattoo parlor, Pat mused to himself. Looking at this man as he now glowered back at him with hollow eyes, Pat sensed he was in the presence of evil.

"Mr. Brand, I'd like to help you in any reasonable way I can. What can I do for you today?"

"Nothing," sneered Brand. "I don't believe in any of the shit your kind is peddling. I just wanted to make sure you're a Christian and white, not like that last jigaboo, not one of them spades like a bunch of the people around here. At least that much is good. Here, let me show you my dick," he said as he reached for his pants.

Pat did not need to hear anymore to realize that Brand only wanted him there for his entertainment.

"I think we're done here, Mr. Brand. I'd like to help you if that's what you want, but, if not, there's no point in my being here."

Pat signaled to the officer that he was ready to leave. As he did so, Brand chortled, "Afraid of me, eh, Padre? Well, you ought to be, but I won't hurt you today. I thought you might like some of this, though," nodding to his groin.

"But you're not really my type. Anyway, even if I thought you were, I'll leave it to one of my boys out there in gen-pop to take care of you. I don't need any hassle from the nigger guards in here."

Immediately, Pat could hear rattling from other men's cells and yelling back and forth. "You cracker. Good thing we can't get to you. We'd do the State's job real quick," and the like with Brand yelling back, now with even more strident racism.

Pat was unnerved. How, he wondered, could Brand get a message out of this place? Something he'd have to ask the warden.

As Brand spewed more venom, the corrections officer quickly came to the cell door.

"Shut the fuck up and go sit on your bed, asshole. Light rations for you for a while if you don't simmer down. And the rest of you clowns," the guard shouted down the corridor, "quiet down. You know this cracker's just trying to rile you up. Don't let him."

"*Thought* it wouldn't take long," the dark-skinned guard said to Pat.

The guard then took Pat's arm while forcefully saying, "Let's get out of here, Padre, before this gets any worse." Pat accompanied the guard in a quick walk back down the corridor away from its odor of despair and odium. Pat was shaken and relieved to be gone from there, unsure if he'd ever return. When later he spoke with Warden Tucker, he confirmed that Brand was a white supremacist of the worst type, a thug who deserved the needle awaiting him someday and, as a white man, a minority on the row that was dominated by African Americans.

"I probably should have warned you, son, as it made no sense to me that this goon would actually want your help with anything spiritual. I think he's pure evil. He attacked and killed an entire black family in their home, raping the wife before setting it ablaze, he later claimed, because he didn't like their uppity ways in the small rural community."

Pat replied, "He told me he was going to get a message to the inmates in general population to 'take care of me' and he said that in a menacing way. Do I need to be worried?"

"Well, Pat, sometimes these guy get to a guard, particularly if he's in the Brotherhood. It can be a problem. We try to weed bigots out in the vetting process when they first come to work here, but sometimes we miss. I suppose there are guards who will do favors for the likes of him. I'm afraid we'll never completely stop that sort of thing, but, I wouldn't be too worried about Brand. He was probably just trying to scare you for the fun of it."

For Pat, this early experience on the Lost Corridor was eye-opening as he had never encountered such a dark soul. In spite of this experience and maybe a little bit because of it, Pat's thought that someday he could be a real chaplain was undiminished.

From time to time, Pat talked with Jack Stanley, the senior counselor at the prison. Stanley, in his late fifties, blond hair turning white, was a big man with the frame of a former football player. Now overweight but with a hint of his former self, he carried himself with an off-putting mien when among the inmates. But, he was friendly enough toward Pat to be an occasional resource on issues related to inmate behavior. After his visit to the Lost Corridor, Pat sought out Stanley.

"Jack, my one experience visiting a death row inmate, Brand is his name, was frightening and dispiriting. Are they all like that?"

"No, Padre. Some of those men are, in fact, pretty docile. Of course, many are heavily medicated, but a few of them, including the guy you saw, are pure evil; their rage is unrelenting."

"But Jack, my teaching is that man is not evil. Men sin, of course, but man is essentially good. This guy challenges that tenet."

"Oh yes," responded Stanley. "This guy defies any claim that man is essentially good. I read Rousseau in political science, the notion that men are inherently good, but I don't buy it."

Pat was surprised. "The teaching of my tradition is that man tends to be good—natural law, you know, that we innately strive to seek the common good. That comes from Aquinas and Locke too."

"Oh, I know those writings, Padre, but they're not for me. I'm Hobbes all the way. Studied political science and history in college. I think we're all born selfish, built to look out for ourselves. We need rules to make an orderly society. Guys like Brand just live outside those controls. They run amok right from the start and don't stop until they're caged."

"That's a pretty pessimistic view of life, Jack. Is there any room for God in that view?"

"Sorry, Padre, but you'll find me a pretty hard case. How can there be a God with evil all around us? Surely a beneficent God wouldn't permit such chaos."

"Well, Jack, I'm just a volunteer here but I'm hoping that someday I may return as a real chaplain. If that happens, I promise I'll go to work on you," Pat smiled. "But for now, I'll just say that God gave us free will, so we have the ability to do both good and bad. God's not somewhere pulling the strings of our behavior. I don't think he made us evil. Yes, we do sin, we even do evil acts, but God forgives us and brings grace into our lives if we seek His goodness. I guess that's a much longer conversation for us to have someday. One last thing, Jack, with your views about evil, what brought you to this place?"

"Well, as I said, I studied liberal arts in college but what could I do with that background? So, I decided to get a master's in criminal justice, and here I am. This job was available at the right time. And, I actually like working with the inmates. Oh, I don't have much hope for many of them but I don't mind trying to make their life here a little more bearable, if that helps bring some order to the place. Mostly, I just try to keep them in line. Without people like me around here, this would be an even more dangerous place."

While Pat was sobered by his conversations with Stanley, he found them challenging too. He remembered another time when they talked about the notions of forgiveness, mercy, and punishment, and their inter-relationship. Stanley had said, "Son, I am sure you're being taught in seminary that these concepts are not incompatible. We can have mercy for those we punish, sometimes even forgive them, if they're contrite, but don't fool yourself; this place mostly is about punishment."

"I can sense that," said Pat, "and certainly the banishment that prison represents is a form of punishment, but we're taught, as well, that forgiveness comes to those who repent even as we punish them. Think about how parents deal with kids. And, you know, sinners don't live in Godless space. Stories in the New Testament tell us that Christ spent his time on earth in the company of sinners and not kings and queens, today's equivalent of A-listers. The lesson for me is that prison work could be just the place for me, a Christ-like path to follow, I think, working with people who have sinned but for whom there is redemption."

Stanley responded, "Of course, Padre, I studied the Bible as well as a kid, but putting those ideas to work in a place like this isn't going to be easy for you. You'll see evildoings all the time here. You just got a taste of it with Brand. For me, I find it difficult to forgive what some of these guys have done."

"Oh, no doubt, Jack, that will be a challenge. The path to goodness is rocky but that just makes it more fertile for the Lord's work."

"Well, your energy and commitment is refreshing, Padre. I just hope you don't lose your faith if you come back here as our chaplain. It's a pretty Godless place."

Pat smiled to himself now as he thought about these early conversations with Stanley. On one hand, he thought the counselor showed wisdom borne of his experience, but everything he said had seemed tinged with cynicism and a sense of hopelessness. He did not want to adopt that attitude toward the diocese in his current dilemma.

Thinking about those early days at Suffolk, his mind roamed to George McNally, an inmate who was serving a thirty-year sentence for manslaughter but who had engaged Pat early in his work at Suffolk.

"Come sit, Deacon Pat, and I'll tell you all you need to know about this place," the lanky, wrinkly faced African American man had beckoned on Pat's first volunteer afternoon. Pat remembered that he responded by inviting McNally to join him in a game of checkers. To his surprise, McNally beat him in quick order. But when Pat couldn't hide his surprise McNally only said, "That's what comes from being here for nearly thirty years, Padre, expertise in checkers and TV game shows." Pat remembered being drawn in by McNally and taking the opportunity to visit with him whenever he had the time while at Suffolk. He also asked the warden about him.

His response gave him some insight into McNally. "For the first ten years of his imprisonment, McNally was held in maximum security, but, in time, we allowed him into the general population because the captain thought he was no longer a threat to safety. Once there, he settled into a routine of working in the prison machine shop and, when not working, mixing in general population. Maybe he's just worn down after all these years; I know he hasn't been a problem for years."

Without telling McNally that he had asked about him, the inmate confirmed the warden's insight in his own way.

"Years ago," McNally told Pat, "I made my bones with other inmates so now nobody bothers me. "In fact," he proudly boasted, "a lot of the men come to me for advice about how to get along in this place."

Having soundly trounced Pat in checkers the first several times they played, McNally next suggested that Pat try his luck with him at chess, a game McNally boasted he had also mastered at Suffolk.

Overall, Warden Tucker and the rest of the prison leadership welcomed Pat's visits to the prison. They found that he had a calming influence with inmates and correctional officers alike. For Pat, being a sounding board and companion, at times offering the hope of inner peace to inmates through his kindness toward them, whetted his appetite to deepen his knowledge of the concepts of punishment and forgiveness and their correlation, if any, to Christian concepts of grace and mercy.

He tried to continue talking about this with Jack Stanley whenever they were free, but Stanley was a hard case.

In one conversation, he remembered asking him, "If you think this place is just a cauldron of evil, what's the point in your being here? Why should the state pay money for these men to have counselors, or even people like me if they are just society's throwaways?"

Stanley replied, "Well, Pat, maybe that's right. In the main, I don't think my job is to make these men feel better about themselves, to settle some inner turmoil they may have. As I see it, my job is to help keep control, to prevent this place from running amok. Without strong controls, that's just what would happen. So, we're just not in the forgiveness and mercy business. We leave that to people like you."

Pat remembered thinking to himself: *I hope I never become so jaded. Surely, Christian values of forgiveness and human worth are woven into our ethos. Why else would our Constitution forbid cruel and unusual punishment? Or why even have a Bill or Rights to protect individuals against the power of the state? Why do prisons even have chaplains if society doesn't care about the individuals? Can't we be caring for people even as they are being punished?* These thoughts percolated with Pat throughout his formation and they continued as his life unfolded. As to Jack Stanley, Pat decided that either the old counselor was burnt out or he just had a very dim view of humanity. He thought this man might need some intervention but doubted he was up to it.

Pat decided that, if permitted by his superiors, he'd continue his formal education in order to grasp an understanding of penology and the relevance of God's message of peace and forgiveness to the men he hoped to serve beyond his ordination. For Pat, his days at Suffolk were often the high points of his weeks and months as he neared ordination. As he now thought about it, even though his prison work was always instructive and sometimes searing, none of it prepared him for the challenge he would soon face helping these young victims against the might of Mother Church.

X

EARLY PRIESTHOOD

Ordination had been a glorious event. Pat's family attended as well as close family friends from Duncan's Cove, and, of course, Father Mike, his early mentor and now friend. His parents flew in from Florida just for the event. The ritual was presided over by Cardinal Joseph Dunman, the state's highest prelate, along with the bishops representing the three dioceses the seventy newly ordained priests would serve. During the ritual, the bishops took turns leading prayers as the holy rite proceeded in the manner no doubt prescribed long ago, reflecting the gravity and majesty of the moment.

Pat thought his early years as a priest, in the main, had been the realization of his expectations. For the first few years, he was assigned to St. Joseph's in Rockville, a small town inland from Duncan's Cove but different in many ways. There, Pat was challenged to serve a mixed congregation, not like Holy Family, which served primarily families with Irish or Italian backgrounds. At St. Joseph, the congregation reflected the ebb and flow of the town's population. There were families whose predecessors had come from Puerto Rico, Haiti, and other Caribbean islands, who had originally arrived in the area to harvest tobacco and then stayed to work in factories. They had intermarried and some had children with their white farm bosses, creating a medley of nationalities and cultures that, in the dominant culture, lumped them into the general category of being Negro, now denoted African American, even though that general term hardly described their separate heritages. There were also families of immigrants from Poland and Eastern Europe who had fled to America in the early part of the twentieth century to seek freedom and opportunity. Serving this heterogeneous community was a new challenge. Pat enjoyed this experience as it widened the perspectives on race and ethnic diversity he had first gained in Washington, later deepened while interning at the MacDonald Juvenile Detention Center and Suffolk Penitentiary.

The two other priests assigned to the parish were companionable. While the rector, Monsignor Allen, was reserved, his younger cohort, Father Juan Hernandez, was the opposite. Short and stocky, Pat's new compadre was a font of wisdom and jocularity. Soon after Pat had arrived, Father Juan took him to his favorite Mexican restaurant. "Even though my family is from Guatemala, Pat, this food is pretty good, and I like that the wait staff speak Spanish," Juan had explained. During dinner, he briefly described how he had come from the warm to the cold. "My family," he said, "were land owners but they wound up on the wrong side of political changes so they fled, kids in tow, first to Mexico and then to the United States. Actually, we're not really Hispanics, I don't think, because we are mostly Mayan with a little Spanish mixed in. So, whatever that makes me, that's what I am," Juan said with joviality. "Now my parents work hard for everything they can get. My father owns a cab company and my mother works in the office. They do okay and they're very happy about me being a priest. How about you, Pat?"

"Compared to you, Juan, I'm pure vanilla. Local boy, never far from home. So happy to be here, to see what I can learn. This restaurant's a good beginning!" And so, they exchanged stories and began a friendship sealed with the clinking of lemon-ringed Mexican beer mugs.

Pat found that Juan did not have a dogmatic view of his faith; he was not didactic about the truths of the Church, which had been etched into them in seminary; he was a pragmatist, more interested in living a Christian life and being an activist for the good than in proselytizing. Pat remembered Juan once saying, "What a person does in life, the kind of life he leads, the example he sets, is so much more important than what he professes to believe." For Pat, this approach to the priesthood was enlightening. Seeing Juan in action with the parishioners, delivering homilies, making visits to the hospital, or working in the parish soup kitchen, it was clear to Pat that Juan was revered in the community for his kindness and caring— illuminating experiences for Pat, and relevant to his present conflict.

What you do, Pat now considered, is more important than what you profess. A good life is measured by one's acts, by the example they set. Adherence to rules, yielding to authority for the sake of obedience, seemed a distant second place as Pat now thought about his priorities.

After a few years, Pat was reassigned to St. Cecelia's in Kingston, a large industrialized town in the southern part of the state, and another experience with diversity. The town, which Pat barely knew, was on the rebound from decades of deterioration, but now, according to local wisdom, it was on the mend. Buildings were being rehabbed and hiring was on the upswing because the town leadership had found ways to attract new small businesses with tax incentives and an ad campaign selling Kingston as a family-friendly place to live. It had been more promise than reality but a successful sales pitch probably because of the town's strategic location on the New England seaboard. At St. Cecelia's most of the parishioners were black, at least in appearance, with a growing number of Hispanics from Mexico and Central America and only a scattering of white families. On his first day, Pat was surprised and happy to be greeted by his seminary friend, Father Jerome Robinson. He knew from chatting with Jerome at his ordination that he had been sent to St. Cecelia's directly from ordination and that he loved being there. When they sat to have coffee, Jerome said he'd welcome Pat's assistance in the youth program he had created consisting of sports activities, soccer and basketball, for any kids who wanted to come, Catholic or not, boy and girl, and afterschool catechism for Catholic students who were not attending parochial school. Pat happily accepted the challenge.

For Pat, this had been his first time working with girls. On weekends, when he could get a day off after sports on Saturday mornings, he'd often go home and seek advice from either of his sisters when they were around. Susan would say, "Just go with it, treat the girls just as you do boys; expect no less from them on the soccer pitch or the basketball court; show by example and encouragement."

Ruth, on the other hand, counselled, "Act kindly toward the girls. They'll probably be intimidated by you; many of them might not have positive male role models in their lives. Don't try to be their friend. Stay in your role as teacher and, of course, as a priest."

Pat remembered that early in this assignment to St. Cecelia's, Jerome had invited him to dinner, just the two of them. It was a Thai place, Jerome said was his new favorite, but alien to Pat, even though his tastes in food had broadened at the prodding of Juan Hernandez.

Once through the usual chitchat of a renewed friendship, the conversation took on a more serious tone. "Jerome, let's talk about you. How are you handling your vocation? Any potholes along the way?" He remembered Jerome smiling. "You mean the gay thing, Pat, is that what you're asking me about?"

"Well, I guess so, Jerome, but I don't mean to intrude, as your personal life is your business."

Jerome chided, "You're right about that, Pat. It is totally my business. Let me just say that my sexual orientation has not changed. I don't think that's something you can just turn off and on like a light switch, but I am under control, Pat. In the main, I believe I have been reasonably faithful to my vows, and when not, I have avoided even a hint of scandal in the community. Does that answer your question?" Jerome posed, his expression showing he was just a bit put off by Pat's questioning his personal life.

"I'm sorry, Jerome, I didn't mean my questions to intrude but I guess they do and I can see why. My concern is that you are so obviously a minister to the people here, an important figure in the community, at the center of so much important activity, I would hate to see if all crashing down on you. That's really where my concern comes from and not from any moral assessment of your life. Judging is not mine to do."

"I'll take it as that," Jerome responded. "And thanks, Pat, for not trying to size me up. I do enough self-reflection myself, but I think I'm good, and I love the opportunity this vocation has provided me to serve God's people. I will do nothing to imperil that."

"So happy to be with you, Jerome. I hope we can stay in touch once I move on to graduate school, if that's in my future. You are a dear person to me." And with that, they clinked glasses as their conversation quieted. Pat recalled that in his time at St. Cecelia's the subject of Jerome's sexual orientation never again came up. And that was fine with him.

One evening, after dinner at the rectory, Jerome approached Pat with an idea. As Pat recalled it, Jerome started, "I believe the clergy of Kinston, the churches, synagogues, and the mosque, if we banned together, could become a force for good in the community. My ideas aren't crystalized just yet, but I think it might be worthwhile for the parish to host a meeting of clergy to see if, together, whoever shows up could come up with ways in which the group could use its combined strength to alleviate some of the hardships we've all witnessed in this beleaguered town."

Pat remembered loving the idea but feeling clueless about how to proceed. Jerome, however, who had lived in the parish longer than Pat, and who had grown up amidst poverty, had concrete ideas about how to proceed. He also had met other clergy over time at interfaith services sponsored, from time to time, by St. David's Episcopal Church in town. Pat was eager for the idea. "If you know how to get started, Jerome, I'm with you. Just lead the way."

The venture began. Jerome's first call was to Father Mark Stevenson from Grace Church whose response was immediately enthusiastic; between them, they developed a list of others to invite to an initial meeting.

On a warm September day, Jerome and Pat hosted an interfaith lunch at the parish rectory with Father Mark, Rabbi Douglas Shuman from Temple Emanuel, Pastor Mary Hall of the 1st Baptist Church, Iman Elon Khaled of the Islamic Center, Pastor Richard Stevens from Faith Tabernacle, and Pastor Elizabeth Meyer of the 1st Congregational Church, the oldest church in the community. To Pat's surprise, Jerome opened the meeting by asking each participant, in turn, to offer a blessing for the success of their undertaking. "A blind request," one of them joked, "as we're not sure why we're here!" But around the table they went, one by one, most in English but one Pat assumed was in Hebrew and another likely in Arabic. A moving start.

Pat remembered being in awe as Jerome began, "I don't mean to be presumptuous but I believe all of us in this room share the common goal of bringing comfort and hope to the communities we serve. Could I ask each of you, in turn, to talk about your particular congregations and to identify the greatest unmet needs you see?"

As each person spoke, the common theme emerged: inadequate housing provided by absentee landlords, unemployment, substance abuse, and the lack of child care, which prevented some parents from even seeking employment. They mentioned as well their concerns that children often were unprotected and malnourished, and that the town's schools were inadequate in the provision of teaching tools, even books, for the students. Going around the table, eliciting this downpour of woes was exhausting for everybody, except for Jerome, who seemed energized by this litany of unmet needs.

"All right," Pat remembered him saying, "please look around the table. Is it too much to say that we are a caring group, clerics on a mission to our faithful, to bring them closer to God but, along the way, to ease their journey, make their lives more tolerable, lift their spirits? Each of us, I think, tries to do that in our individual way. Imagine what we, in combination, might be able to accomplish. But, no, don't just imagine; what if we could collectively act? For example, take the housing issue. Together our voices in harmony have more force with landlords, with the powers-to-be in Town Hall, than any tenant does or even any one of us. I've asked you here to talk about working together to make life better for our entire community. Sorry, end of speech."

Pat looked back at that first meeting with satisfaction and joy. From Jerome's initial inkling that the clergy, together, could be a force for good in Kingston came a nonprofit organization dedicated to housing betterment. And in two of the churches and Temple Emanuel, interfaith after school programs were developed where kids from anywhere could be tutored or engaged in useful activities, all without cost and staffed from volunteers solicited from the various congregations. Members of the group went to their congregations' lay organizations and were pleased by the generosity of the responses. Monies were raised, specifically, for school supplies and books, which were then turned over to the town's neediest. Overall, the seed of Jerome's notion of a joint religious effort to tackle some of the city's most intractable problems took root. To Pat, it was an amazing lesson in the power of one's convictions put into practical action. Action mirroring God's grace.

Things were looking up in Kingston when Pat received notification that his request to attend graduate school had been granted. He left Kingston with mixed emotions, happy to be on his way to graduate school but sorry to leave such a beehive of beneficial activity.

Pat enrolled in a master's program in clinical social work at Concordia University in Lawrenceville, an industrial town now at an ebb because of failed or departed manufacturing businesses. But in its midst also was Concordia, a seventy-five-year-old university of excellence known for its strength in liberal arts. It seemed odd and yet pleasant for Pat to now be attending the same college that both his sisters had attended: Susan in journalism, a study that led to her present occupation as a newspaper journalist, and Ruth in a cognitive therapy program, which prepared her for her present job in a rehab center. How life circles back, Pat remembered, thinking about following the tracts of his younger sisters.

Pat enrolled at Concordia because it was touted as having a master's in social work program with an emphasis on counseling. Through his graduate studies, Pat sought to enhance his suitability for assignment to a pastoral position at Suffolk Penitentiary, a goal he had formulated while volunteering there as a seminarian.

Knowing that Suffolk was not located in his home diocese, Pat had hoped that Bishop Ryan might be willing to "lend" him to the prison because he had done so well there as a deacon and because the request of a priest for an out-of-diocese assignment was not unusual since each year there was an adequate supply of newly ordained priests available for assignment to parish work. He had learned, as well, that the position of prison chaplain was provided for in the prison's budget, a feature that would relieve the diocese of paying his already minimal wage but a fact, nonetheless, he correctly thought would be attractive to the chancellery.

Once Pat received his master's degree, he was delighted to be assigned full-time to Suffolk as the prison's chaplain while still residing at St. Teresa's. His prison work now was a greater challenge as he was expected to respond to the spiritual needs of inmates of all religions as well as those of no particular faith. Pat eagerly embraced this opportunity by embarking on a course of self-directed study, to better understand the tenets of Islam, to learn more about African American history, and he boned up on the Scriptures, all of which, combined with studying Spanish, he thought would give him a more informed understanding of the inmates who sought his counsel. He had realized from his earliest experience with youngsters at the MacDonald Detention Center and then confirmed at Suffolk that the inmate population did not mirror, in either racial composition or educational achievement, the population of the state but that, in prison, there were a disproportionate number of African American and Hispanic inmates. Now immersed in this micro-culture, Pat realized how much he had to learn about lives unfamiliar to his own and the causes of criminal conduct in order to more effectively serve this diverse population.

In the main, Pat had been attracted to the inmates and not put off by the knowledge they had been incarcerated for criminal behavior, some of it violent and awful. For Pat, the concepts of absolution and forgiveness were core tenets of the Church etched into him during his seminary years, but his prison experience broadened his sense of "parish." In seminary, he had been taught that his primary focus as a priest would be on the Catholic faithful. How narrow, he now thought. His prison ministry had opened his heart to all who sought God's blessing. He believed that God's grace came to all who repented for their sins, and that through atonement, any inmate could unburden himself of his misdoings and perhaps gain a glimmer of inner peace.

XI

THE TRIALS

One bright afternoon as Pat rested on Sean's bench, looking out at the harbor as the fishing fleet returned and jockeyed for position at the coop, he saw Maggie approaching, her stride purposeful.

"What's up, Maggie? You look winded. Is anything wrong?"

"No, I don't think so, Pat. It's just that someone from the prosecutor's office called and it sounds important. She asked that you get right back to her." Pat hurried back down Fish Trap Hill to return the lawyer's call and to learn that the criminal trials against the priests were about to begin.

The trials occurred, one by one, in the same courthouse.. The print media, including Susan, were in full force; there were television cameras outside the courthouses catching witnesses as they came and went—especially the priests, who were the greatest interest. The prosecutor, Phillip Dodge, was able to have the children and their families escorted by court officers through a rear entrance, but the priest defendants had to withstand the jeers as they entered through the main entrance.

The trials followed a similar pattern. In each case, the child victim testified that he had been abused by the defendant priest and, with coaxing from the prosecution, the victim recited the details of the abuse. While Pat could not be in the courtroom for this testimony because he was slated to testify, he heard from the prosecutor that giving testimony seemed very difficult for the victims but also maybe, the prosecutor thought, there was some cathartic value for the youngsters being able to publicly relate their stories and confront their abusers. Pat wasn't reassured as he knew how tremulous the boys had been when first recounting the horrors of their abuse to him.

When Pat was called as a witness in each case, he confirmed that the young victim had reported the abuse to him and he detailed the account as it had been related to him as far as the law permitted. Beforehand, he had received the okay from the boys and their parents to repeat their accounts in court in spite of his earlier promise of confidentiality. He knew that his testimony would likely be helpful because the prosecutors had told him that evidence that the boys had reported their assaults to him would help prove that their claims were not newly fashioned even though they were reported to the police well after the abusive events took place.

In each case—in addition to Pat, the child victims, and one or more of their parents—the prosecution called Doctor Elizabeth Porter, a child psychologist. She testified as an expert regarding child sexual abuse. Doctor Porter explained that, typically, adults who sexually abuse children are authority figures in the children's lives. She said that often before the actual physical abuse takes place, the abuser will endear himself to the child with special attention, favors, or some other kind of behavior that may soften up the child for the ultimate abuse. This process, she stated, is called grooming, and happens in most instances.

She talked, as well, about the phenomena of late reporting, the fact that often child sexual assault victims don't immediately report the occurrence to anyone. This, she said, has many reasons but often it's because the victim has feelings of shame, guilt, and fear of retaliation by the abuser or not being believed by others. In such cases, Dr. Porter continued, the child often goes dark, becomes less communicative, sullen, perhaps unexplainably angry, often withdraws from activities, begins to fail in school, and spends an inordinate about of time in his or her room. The downward spiral, she explained, can lead to suicidal ideation, or self-harming, such as cutting.

On cross-examination in each case, the defense lawyer was able to point out by questioning that the psychologist could not offer any opinion about whether any abuse had actually happened as alleged or whether the victim, now testifying at trial, was telling the truth about the claimed events. In response, however, the prosecution brought out through further examination that the reason the doctor wasn't able to offer an opinion as to the credibility of the child claimant or the child's credibility as a witness was that the law prohibited her from doing so. Through this exchange, it became clear that Dr. Porter's silence on the credibility of each child was not borne of any doubt or uncertainty but driven by the evidentiary rules of court.

In each case, the defense presented no evidence; none of the priest defendants testified. Rather, the defense lawyers, in similar fashion, relied on their attempts to show through cross-examination of the boys that they were either mistaken in their memory or they were fabricating their stories for some ulterior reason. None of that worked. In all cases, the priests were convicted and given prison terms to be served at the Suffolk penitentiary. As a consequence of their convictions, they were separated from the Church, no longer priests. To his surprise, Pat felt only relief and no sympathy for these former priests.

Not long after the verdicts in the criminal cases, Pat received a call from Attorney Baker reporting that the civil suits, delayed by the pendency of the criminal cases and by pretrial requests for documents from the diocese, were now ready to proceed. Baker asked Pat to assist in the presentation of these claims. Pat readily agreed. "Let's remember, as we represent these victims, that there's another one no longer with us. We couldn't help his slide into self-destruction, Jed, but let Lawrence's memory be extra motivation for your success."

"Amen, to that, Padre. That boy's never far from mind. He was failed in so many ways. Too bad I can't add him to these suits, but it wouldn't work, particularly because that priest was found not guilty. But I'm with you in motivation."

Pat had been told by Baker that on behalf of the three victims, he had intended to bring a civil suit for money damages against the diocese on the basis that the diocese had known that the three priests had preyed on the children and yet had not reported their abuse to the civil authorities. Instead, Baker claimed in his court filings, whenever the diocese heard of any complaints against these priests, they were quickly relocated to other parishes to towns away from the scene of their predations and without providing any warning to the rectors of the parishes to which they had been reassigned.

Before trial, Baker had filed a motion with the court asking that the diocese be required to turn over to him the personnel files of the named priests in order for him to be able to document that; indeed, the diocese had done what he claimed. This discovery request, as it's called, caused a furor with the defense and much public interest. On behalf of the *Gazette*, Pat's sister Susan had covered the oral argument in court and reported the happenings in detail.

The motion was heard before Judge Robert Faulkner, a small, graying man with a pencil mustache and sharp blue eyes, an azure blue bowtie peeking from the top of his robes. He was a jurist known for his even temperament and wisdom and, occasionally, his jocularity from the bench. This time his demeanor was somber, humorless—all business. The diocese was represented by a lawyer from New York City, Robert Peckham, tall and imposing in pinstripes, white-starched collar, and a striped tie of some undetermined college provenance. He was reported to be representing other Catholic dioceses in similar claims, which were now becoming more prevalent as the scourge of clergy child abuse was now being widely reported and cases were finding their way into the courts.

Baker, representing the boys and their families, was, as usual for him, dressed less formally in a blazer and slacks, and his trademark Kelly green tie slightly askew, a less kept look that Pat knew was not feigned for the jury because that's how Baker generally appeared— approachable, and disarming. At the start of the argument concerning Baker's quest for the records of the diocese, he stated that he wished to see the priests' personnel files because they likely would shed light on the reasons for them being transferred from parish to parish and, if so, such evidence would support his central claim in this case regarding the culpability of the diocese. Attorney Peckham, without disputing that the files might contain damaging information, argued that the court did not have the right to make such an order as doing so would violate Article I of the United States Constitution protecting the freedom of religion. Peckham reminded the court of Thomas Jefferson's famous exhortation that there must be a wall of separation between church and state and that by acceding to Baker's request that wall could be breached.

"How so?" asked the judge. "That's a rather dramatic claim, counsel. If I grant this order, I don't know how that would interfere with the right of the Church to freely practice its faith."

Peckham argued back, "Judge, if the court can order Church records to be exposed to the public, how far behind can it be that the courts could make orders regulating the administration of the Church, which would be a clear violation of the First Amendment protection of the free exercise of religion.

"Fair enough," responded the judge. "But I don't think that allowing the plaintiffs' counsel to review the records should, in any way, dampen the right of the Church to preach its faith, but just to be sure, I am going to order that the records be turned over to me for my private review in chambers. If I see anything in there that goes to your point, I'll protect it from disclosure."

Shortly after that hearing, and before the judge had made any ruling, Attorney Peckham called Attorney Baker and suggested they discuss the possibility of settlement. A few days later, they met in Baker's office.

"Listen, Jed," Peckham began with feigned friendship, "I don't know how this judge is going to rule, but if it goes against us, the diocese has made it clear we need to appeal. They really don't want their files made public, and I've told them they have a decent argument based on the free exercise of religion. That said, I think this may be the best time to get this matter settled and I'm prepared to make an offer, if you're interested."

"Well, John..." Baker could play the phony friend game as well as anyone. "I don't know if my clients want to settle. I think they more likely look forward to a public disclosure of the diocese's backroom maneuvering in this whole scandal. They're pretty angry at the people in charge, the bishop and his vicar in particular. But, of course, if you have an offer, I am duty-bound to take it to them. What do you have in mind?"

"Well, to cut to the chase—I can see you are not much for foreplay—I believe the diocese would be willing to pay $750,000 to end this matter. That's $250,000 a family, a lot of money. But to do that, my client would insist on complete secrecy. The files would be returned to the diocese, unsealed. The terms of the settlement would be private and could not be disclosed by or to anyone. And, Jed—this is important—it's all or none. The diocese will only pay this amount if all three families agree. There's no point in paying one family only to have to defend against the other two with the risk that the diocesan files will become public. It's the avoidance of trial and, frankly, the maintenance of the diocese's privacy in how it conducts its affairs that makes this offer tolerable to the bishop."

"So, for $250,000 a family, that's the price you'll pay to buy their silence. Is that pretty much it?"

"That's a pretty crass way to put it, Jed, but, in essence, yes. When can you let me know?"

"I'll get my clients in here within the week and will get back to you. Thanks for coming over." And, with that, the meeting ended.

When Attorney Baker met with the families a few days later, the unexpected happened. Their response was not united, creating a conflict Baker had not anticipated. Two of the families, the Fallons and the Colsens, had no interest in settling. They wanted to charge ahead. But Mrs. Davidson, Michael's mother, was interested. "Do you think they'd pay any more than that offer, Attorney Baker?" she asked. The lawyer thought for a minute, then responded, "I'm not really sure, Mrs. Davidson, but I think that if we go to trial we could get more than that, maybe a lot more."

"But if that happens, we'd have to go to court. Michael and the other boys would have to testify, to relive their experiences all over again, with the hope that we could get more than what's now being offered."

"That, and a public disclosure of what the diocese has been up to," chimed in John Fallon. "To me, that's worth more than a lousy $250,000 to open the window on this travesty."

Seeing that a resolution would not be immediate, Attorney Baker suggested they end the meeting to think some more and then resume in a few days so they could further discuss it. And with that, the meeting ended.

Once the families were gone, Baker began to ponder the conflict he now faced. He went into the office of his new intern, Jennifer Chou, from Mathis Law School, who was with him for a semester as part of the school's work-study program and with whom Baker had discussed the cases. She was a challenging addition for Baker. Born in China, Chou had immigrated very young with her parents whose technical skills landed them jobs in the engineering world. A bright student, Chou had quickly mastered English and breezed through school, leading her to her present studies at Mathis. Short and thin with straight black hair and knowing eyes, Jennifer was both a puzzle and a joy for Baker. "Jennifer," he began, "as you know, I have three clients, the victims and their families, all suing the same defendant, but now they appear to be diverging. The diocese has made an all or nothing settlement offer, but two of the families want nothing to do with it while Mrs. Davidson does. Do you think that means I need to get out of this case? Do I have a legal conflict here?"

"I don't think so, Mr. Baker, although that would be a pretty good ethics question for the bar exam. Here, you have three clients whose interests, of course, could diverge, as maybe it has, but there's more to it. I don't think there's really a legal conflict because the diocese has made this an all or nothing offer. As you told it to me, this New York lawyer, Peckham, made it very clear that a partial settlement won't work. So, no legal conflict, but maybe a moral one. You once told me that Mrs. Davidson is a single parent and struggling. So she may really need the money. I can imagine how an infusion of money would be very enticing, but unless all three agree, that's not going to happen, at least by settlement. This reminds me of a course I took in conflict resolution. Maybe you need to think of yourself as a mediator among our own clients."

"That's pretty mature advice, Jennifer. I knew there was a reason you are in the top ten in your class," he smiled.

As he walked from Chou's office, his own phone rang. It was Father Pat asking how the case was coming and what Baker might expect of him in the coming trial. The call gave Baker an idea.

"Father Pat, could I come to see you? I have a sort of dilemma, maybe a moral one, that I'd like to run by you."

They met the next morning for breakfast at an out-of-the-way place on a small inlet just north of Duncan's Cove. They both knew it for its good coffee, omelets, and homemade muffins. Baker brought along Chou. "Father, this is my intern, Jennifer Chou, who's with me for a semester. I asked her to join us because, maybe, being young, and in law school, she might have a different perspective on this. And, I'm kind of hoping she might consider coming to work here after graduation."

"Whoa," responded Jennifer, "I know we talked about that once in pretty vague terms, but I'm nowhere ready to begin thinking about life after school. Anyway, I think I might really stand out around here. I know I told you I was interested in seeing what life in a small New England coastal town would be like, but I didn't mean like forever! I come from far away and this is so different to me."

Pat smiled to himself and wondered whether her obvious hesitation about looking different, fitting in, might just be well founded.

"No matter," said Baker. "There's plenty of time to talk about that as you get used to this place and our work. Let's talk about what's in front of us right now." Baker then laid out the problem for Pat. His response, like Jed's, was to question whether this presented a legal conflict. "I'm no lawyer, Jed, but it seems your clients have different positions in this matter and you're in the middle. Isn't that what's called a legal conflict?"

"That was my gut reaction too, Padre, but on thinking about it and talking with Jennifer, perhaps my problem is more moral than legal. Let me explain. The deal on the table does not permit conflicting responses from my clients. It's an all or nothing. The diocese won't settle with just one or two families. So, I really don't have a conflict among my clients. Legally, they can't go separate ways. If I had that kind of a conflict I think I'd be consulting with another lawyer, but I'm pretty sure my issue is a moral one and that's why we're here, sharing these wonderful blueberry muffins," he half smiled.

Pat listened while he ate, one eye out the sea-facing window, a distant boat motoring from the harbor, always a centering vista for him. "Look at those boats, Jennifer," he pointed. "That's common fare around here, and a pretty wonderful sight to see."

"Oh, no," coyly replied Chou. "Don't tell me, Father, that Mr. Baker has enlisted you too. I do like the view, though, I must say. Nothing like that where I'm from."

Pat then turned to the lawyer. "Jed, I have an idea," he finally said. "Do you think the case is worth more than $750,000 if you go to trial?"

"Oh, yes, Father, a lot more, but I can never be sure. The problem of clergy sex abuse is just now coming to the fore in the media. I saw these kids testify in the criminal trials. They were compelling. I think a lot of people would be very upset to learn that these priests were moved from parish to parish with no outreach to their victims or warnings to the new parishes, and some of those people are likely to be our jurors. And although it's difficult to monetize that, my sense is that the diocese could be in for a much bigger hit than what's on the table. But even if I could push the offer up, I don't think I could get this case settled with a non-disclosure agreement. And you know, Father, I really don't want to. I'd like to see what a jury will do here."

"Well, I think I may have an idea," Jennifer interrupted. "I know I'm just a student but this is a little like a class I took in conflict resolution last term from a prof who's the dean of the business school. She told us at the start of the class that every year since becoming dean, she tries to teach one course per semester somewhere in the university other than the business school, and we were the lucky beneficiaries this year. She preached the notion of finding solutions that meet all the warring parties' underlying interests. The idea is that disputes can be resolved with more elegant solutions than your typical zero-sum transactions in which whatever one party gains the other one loses. While the prof gave some hypotheticals, it never really struck me, perhaps because, after all, I'm just a student and you're adults, but what the prof said may have some applicability here. You just need to figure out something that could satisfy all three families without anyone of them having to give up something of importance to them."

Pat responded, "I think you're onto something, Jennifer. Kudos to you." He then turned to Baker. "You believe that, if tried, the case has value greater than the present offer. What if you could get your clients to agree that Mrs. Davidson and Michael would be entitled to the first $250,000 of any verdict the jury may render. That way, if the verdict is less than $750,000, say, $500,000 total, she and Michael would receive $250,000 and the other families would split the remaining $250,000. If they're really more interested in disclosure of the diocese's secrets, they might be willing to do this as they'd get that plus some money, although less than the Davidsons. Of course, if the verdict is over $750,000, the families would divide the entire amount evenly."

"How brilliant, Father," Baker and Chou said almost simultaneously. Chou added, "Father, are you sure you didn't go to law school along the way?"

"Thank you both," Pat smiled. "But I'm not sure lawyers have the market on creative reasoning. As I think you said, Jennifer, the professor who taught that course was actually from the business school."

"Well, I'll be." Baker came back smiling. "Practicing law without a license, both of you!"

"But you're welcome for the idea," smiled Pat. "Just a way of thinking outside the box, I think, an idea that came to me when Jennifer talked about her class in dispute resolution. I studied that a bit in my master's program, and it came back to me as Jennifer was talking. I'll be anxious to see if it works."

And it did. When Baker met with the families two days later, he invited Chou to sit in as he wanted her to have the experience of dealing directly with clients. He laid out the proposal just as he, Pat, and Jennifer had discussed. He did so without immediately urging it upon the families, as he wasn't sure they would be confident of his loyalty and impartiality if he pressed this outcome.

But, they were all very satisfied with it. While Mrs. Davidson would still have preferred that they settle, once she realized that the diocese would not settle with her alone, she became more willing to go to trial. Baker dutifully, and with a bit of glee, phoned his defense counterpart the next day and told him that the families were unwilling to settle at any price if it required a nondisclosure agreement.

Soon after the court hearing on Baker's discovery request, the media reported the dispute, bringing it to evening television news and the front pages of the state's two largest papers with a lead article by Susan, now a popular *Gazette* figure with a following created by her excellent reporting on the criminal trials.

Three weeks after oral argument, the court issued a written order, granting Baker's motion requiring the diocese to disclose its personnel files regarding the three priests whose misconduct was at the heart of the case. In his decision, Judge Faulkner stated that he had read the records, reviewed the law, and had seen nothing in the materials that needed to be protected by the Constitution. At trial they turned out to be a treasure trove. The records disclosed that complaints had been made about all three priests before their assignments that had brought them into contact with the plaintiff victims. Soon after one such a complaint, Father Reagan had been sent directly to Robbie's parish from a distant parish in the diocese. The other two priests had been moved more than once after the diocese had received complaints about them before alighting on the parishes where they had abused Michael Davidson and Carl Colsen. These reports were damning.

During the trial, Baker also had subpoenaed Monsignor O'Brien, the bishop's vicar. After a repeat skirmish from Attorney Peckham based on the First Amendment, Baker was able to question O'Brien about the transfers of each priest and whether there was any evidence in any of the diocesan files that the receiving parishes had been forewarned of claims made against any of the priests in connection with their reassignments. The vicar's stammering admissions of a failure to disclose such information shut the door on any possible defense of ignorance.

Before the trial, Attorney Baker had asked Pat to be a witness. Unlike his role in the criminal trials, Pat was going to be asked in this civil claim for money damages, what he observed to be the effect of the abuse on the three boys with whom he met. Based on his experience and education, he would also be asked about his views on the effect of adult sexual abuse on children of this age.

Soon after Pat agreed with Attorney Baker's request, and once Pat's name had been provided to the defense as the rules required, Pat was summoned once again to the chancellery, this time to meet with Monsignor O'Brien. He was as abrupt as the bishop had been. "We've had our eye on you, Father Keefe, in your support of these families with their terrible claims." Pat didn't bother to remind him that each priest had already been convicted and sentenced. He just stood mute. "Any further participation by you in any cases involving claims of clerical abuse and in any litigation against the diocese will be viewed by the bishop as an act of disloyalty—do you understand me?"

Pat at first just nodded but then remembered something Jed Baker had told him. "Respectfully, Monsignor, you might want to speak with the diocesan attorney and have him explain to you the law as it relates to witness tampering. I don't think you want to be threatening me right now."

O'Brien was unperturbed. "You understand, Father Keefe, that when you were ordained, you took a vow of obedience. Don't forget that. The bishop will view any participation by you in this scurrilous litigation as a breach of your vow and that would have grave consequences for your future as a priest. Now, please go." And with that, Pat's meeting with the vicar ended as abruptly as it had started.

Pat surmised from this meeting that the bishop's gloves were off, perhaps because the damning files had already been disclosed. To Pat, this seemed more like a threat of vengeance than any reasonable defense ploy. Undaunted, and perhaps emboldened by his conviction of the morality of his support for the victims, Pat resolved to be of whatever assistance was needed by Attorney Baker.

When he returned home that weekend, he decided to talk with Maggie about the tension he felt between his desire to assist Jed Baker and the warning he had received from the chancellery. He was surprised by the frankness of her reaction.

"The bishop's in a bind of his own making, Pat," she said. "If he had been watching the store, none of this would have happened. As a person of the cloth, his first duty is to those children and it's only by protecting them, by cherishing them. Frankly, only by atoning for his role in this tragedy can the diocese survive as a beacon of holy authority. The idea that the Church has to be protected because it's been around so long is foolishly egocentric. The value of the Church comes from the good it does, in the holiness it inspires."

She continued, "You are the only bright light in these kids' lives since they bared themselves to you. Don't you feel that it's your obligation to follow through with them, to aid their recovery? Their journey through the justice system, outweighs some general notions of obedience you may have to a misguided order."

Pat expected direct advice from Maggie, but he hadn't been prepared for her insistence and strength of conviction. When Maggie saw how startled he appeared to be, she commented: "I don't mean this in a harsh way, Pat, and I know how much you have loved your priesthood and that it must torture you to be at odds with the bishop, but you don't have children so maybe it's hard for you to internalize how pained these children must be. As a parent, I grieve for these kids, and I would want to do everything possible to comfort and validate them."

Maggie's response was an awakening for Pat. Nothing like Father Stan's somewhat philosophical, more scholarly approach to problem solving. Direct and undeniable. While he knew his duty, it had come from his head. Maggie, the widow and mother, had reached his soul as no one in the chancellery even approached. He resolved not to back away from assisting the child victims in the prosecution of the civil case.

When called to testify, Pat shared the children's tales of horror and the upheaval their experiences appeared to have brought to their senses of well-being and security. When asked his view as a priest of the typical relationship between a priest and the children in his charge, he reiterated that's it's normally one of authority, of trust, and of reliance for safety. He was able to offer his opinion based on his experience and education that when this relationship is broken, the results for a child can be heartbreaking, with lingering repercussions in a child's life as he or she grows older.

When the media learned that the offending priests had been relocated from parish to parish each time a complaint had been made to the Church, the community was aghast. Pat took no satisfaction in participating in the trial except to gain the sense that some form of justice would be done, even if it would only be manifest in a large financial award against the diocese. And for sure, the jury awarded each family the sum of $500,000 for a total verdict of $1.5 million, an amount that immediately grabbed headlines and evening news stories in the media.

Once theses verdicts exploded in the media, Pat dreaded the anticipated blowback from the bishop toward him. But none came. It was although he had become a ghost, a non-entity to the chancellery, an outcome that relieved and puzzled him.

While the guilty verdicts against the priests and the subsequent financial awards against the diocese gave Pat some sense of satisfaction, he remained anxious for the untold number of victims still suffering in silence and he was uneasy in his new conflict with the diocese. For all of his life, the Church had been his spiritual home, and now, for the first time, he was at odds with Church leadership. It was disorienting for Pat to be in this confrontational relationship, but he resolved not to lose grip of his deep faith; the Lord would shepherd him.

A week after the jury's verdict, Jed Baker called Pat and asked if they could meet for lunch. "For sure, Jed. You deserve a bit of celebrating, if that's what you have in mind."

"Well, partially that, Padre, but I have some news for you as well."

Two days later they met at The Claw. They warmly embraced, now veterans in an unseen war just emerging from the darkness. Jed got right to it.

"Padre, as you might not know, I will receive a rather large legal fee for my work on the case against the diocese as my arrangement was what's called a contingency fee agreement. In short, if we lost, I would earn nothing, but if we won, as we did, I would receive a percentage of the total verdict. It's done on a sliding scale—the greater the amount, the smaller the percentage—but it's still a lot. Of course, it won't happen until the expected appeal is decided, but I'm confident of the outcome. The judge did it by the numbers. I think the verdict is unassailable. So, when the money is disbursed, I have decided to donate $75,000 to a fund to be established at the Jefferson boy's high school in his honor.

"My idea is that the fund would make an annual award to a graduating senior whose generosity to the community has been particularly noteworthy. I have spoken with the current head of school and he is delighted. Once this happens, the school will publicize the existence of the plan in the hope that additional donations will be made. And yes, if you're wondering, I have spoken with the Jeffersons. They are very pleased. In fact, they have committed an additional $25,000 to the fund once it is established. Apparently this is money they had set aside toward Lawrence's college education."

Pat was awestruck and nearly in tears. "Jed, this is so generous and goodhearted. I don't know what to say."

"First, Padre, my donation is just part of my fee. I will not go wanting. Maybe this is just an insurance policy for me when my time comes." He now was grinning widely.

"I'm not done telling you everything yet, Padre. Legally, a fund will have to be established and a board to oversee it as it grows and then makes awards. Would you please consider chairing this board, Pat? I can think of no one more fitting for this task and I know the school will agree in a heartbeat."

"Of course, my dear friend. I would be honored." Pat was still choked with emotions as the waitperson came over to take their orders.

"Lobster salad for two," stated Jed without consultation.

XII

RETURN TO PRISON

At home with Maggie and Chris, with the trials completed and without the diversion of fishing, Pat decided to resume his duties at Suffolk. Emboldened by the bishop's apparent indifference to him, and missing his prison ministry, Pat returned to the prison without notifying the diocese, or, in any way, formally ending his leave of absence. Pat reasoned that the bishop would probably be relieved by his absence from the diocese and submergence into the relatively unseen world of prison life. Knowing this, Pat asked Warden Tucker if he could live at the prison in rooms utilized by the former chaplain and now vacant. He also suggested to the warden that, as the prison chaplain, he could become a prison employee instead of an outside contractor. He proposed that he be put on the payroll with associated benefits, an idea that the warden welcomed.

"You're a substantial asset around here, Padre. It's not going to cost much to harbor you here, if that's what you'd like, and the rest is minimal. So, certainly, we'll do that." Though curious, he didn't ask whether Pat was, in fact, starting to distance himself from the Church. From Pat's perspective, he didn't think about it that way. No action had been taken against him by the diocese. Though now only loosely connected to his superiors, he didn't feel alienated from the Church itself. For the time, he just embraced the bromide that out of sight is out of mind, and he welcomed the notion of not being in the bishop's sights.

Making his arrangement with the prison more permanent appealed to Pat for personal reasons. Since Suffolk was only about seventy miles from Duncan's Cove, he reasoned that he could return to Maggie's home on weekends to be with family and continue to shepherd any incoming additional victims of priest abuse. Also, he thought, perhaps he'd get a chance to go lobstering once in a while if the opportunity arose.

Once Pat and the warden cemented the new arrangement, Pat notified the financial officer in the diocese that it no longer needed to keep him on the diocese's group health insurance as the prison had agreed to enroll him in its plan. The financial officer, not a priest, expressed neither alarm nor curiosity. Indifference, Pat surmised. He received no confirmation from the diocese except a notice from the group insurance carrier that his membership had been terminated.

When Pat first returned to the prison, he went into the general population area to reacclimate himself. He was surprised at how many men came up to him, some silently slapping his back, others with a loud "Way to go, Padre," or the like. When he asked one of the men why they were cheering him he was told, "Because you helped put away those pervs, monsters who weren't fit to call themselves priests or even to live." Later, Pat asked the warden about this unusual response. "Why would inmates be so pleased that I had played a role in getting men convicted of crimes?" he wondered.

"Well, Padre, there are crimes and there are crimes. There's a sort of pecking order here, murder being at the top and molesting kids at the bottom. People who sexually assault kids are reviled around here. That's why we have to keep them apart from the rest of the population. Those former priests are in our segregation unit, and that's where they'll stay so long as they're with us. If we let them into general population, they wouldn't last a day." For Pat, this was a stark reintroduction into prison society.

Once settled into his new quarters—small living room, bedroom, and a bath; comfortable enough, Pat thought—he resumed his chaplaincy work. He found he was immediately in great demand either as a confessor for the Catholic inmates or just someone to talk to about personal issues, and there were lots of them in the population. He learned that Jack Stanley had taken an early retirement—no disappointment to Pat as he had concluded that Stanley's dark views of human nature were probably not well suited for his task.

He also received more requests for visits from other Lost Corridor inmates, which he was careful to scrutinize. He did not want to repeat his first experience with the white supremacist, but there were others, he found, who genuinely sought his solace. Even if he just gave these condemned men an opportunity to talk about themselves, their fears, their families, he thought his visits were worthwhile. Once, when talking with Warden Tucker, he expressed his hope that the penalty would never be used and perhaps actually abolished. "Amen to that, Padre," Tucker replied. "I'd do it because it's part of the job, and I guess I believe that since we have a penalty on the books, it's not my place to question it."

He found his old friend, George McNally, who brought him up to date on happenings and rumors in the prison; and, of course, McNally challenged his abilities on the board. All was well until, one day, Pat saw Luke Reardon clad in a blood-red prison jumpsuit, cuffed and shackled, being guided by two corrections officers toward the segregation unit. Pat saw that he was hunched over, shuffling his feet, no energy. Until that day, Pat had not heard that Luke had been arrested and convicted for child molestation. Seeing Luke was disorienting. Did that mean that Luke's victims were now receiving the counseling and were on their way to recovery? Pat could not adequately capture his feelings. Was he happy that Luke had been imprisoned? If so, was that charitable? What should he do about Luke now being part of his ministry? These questions puzzled Pat but, overall, he admitted to himself that he was relieved that Luke's spree of malevolence had probably come to an end.

Not long after Pat saw Luke, and while Pat was mingling in general population congenially talking with one or another about the latest sports news, he was suddenly attacked by an inmate who punched him in the face and kicked him to the ground. As soon as other inmates saw what was happening, they jumped on the assailant and wrestled him away from Pat, all while yelling to him that he had no call to attack the chaplain. "Oh yeah?" responded the assailant, now firmly in the grasps of corrections officers. "Go ask Luke Reardon. He'll tell you something different. This guy lied to the cops about Reardon, accusing him of diddling little kids, which got him arrested and then convicted by a jury, who believed the kids just because they were young and little and looked harmless. Reardon will tell you this guy is a no-good liar."

Although gripped in pain, Pat was stunned by this accusation. He was fearful too, for how this accusation might affect the other inmates if they believed it. Visibly bruised and shaken, Pat was taken to the infirmary, where it was discovered that he had no serious wounds and would be left only with aches and pains as the attacking inmate had been wrestled away before he could do any real harm. Nevertheless, Pat was devastated by this development. He decided that he needed to meet face to face with Luke to challenge this claim and to try to quell its spread.

A few days later, with the warden's permission, he arranged for a one-on-one session with Luke. It did not go well. Luke snarled at Pat, accusing him of violating the seal of confession and reporting him to the police. He was sure Pat was the reason he had been apprehended. He threated Pat that he better watch his back in the prison, as he had told everybody on the prison van that Pat had wrongly accused him of the crime that got him convicted. When Pat insisted that he had kept secret Luke's confession, Luke just scoffed. He reddened with rage when Pat suggested that by claiming that Pat had falsely accused him he was just deepening his moral abyss.

Luke huffed: "I don't care, Keefe. I'm a lost soul. Now, I just want you hurt as I know you told on me. If they think I was falsely accused, all the better for me. Guys in here don't like rats. They'll do my dirty work for me." At that point, Luke raised his voice, shouting that Pat had put him here by lying about him. His rant was loud enough to cause the guard to take Luke back to his cell. Thankfully for Pat, the segregation area was far enough from the general population area that Luke could not be heard throughout the prison.

To Pat, saddened and somewhat fearful, Luke was an anomaly. Either directly or indirectly, Luke still presented a physical threat to him. He had no doubt that Luke's false claims would leech out from the segregation unit into the rest of the prison. He worried also that a general belief in the population that he had falsely accused Luke could negate any goodwill he had established with the men. He was challenged, as well, to reach Luke's long-troubled soul. For the time, Pat decided not to try to further interact with Luke and to give him time to gather and orient himself in his new and adverse surroundings.

Luke did not go quietly. Whenever a guard came to his cell in segregation, he railed that he was innocent and that the so-called chaplain had lied about him because he didn't like him. Luke's accusations against Pat, of course, were eventually retold by guards to others and, in no time, were known throughout the prison.

Pat's concerns were mostly unfounded. Luke's claims were discredited by the lifers and other long-timers whose trust Pat had already gained. They, in turn, told the newer inmates that Pat was solid. In the main, Luke was thought of as a child abuser, just another con who wouldn't admit his guilt, his crime the lowest of the low. And if Pat had somehow turned him in, that was fine with them.

Pat also had lingering concern for the man who had assaulted him. His name, Pat learned, was Hector Richards, a twenty-two-year-old probation violator who had arrived on the same prison van as Luke. Pat was uncertain how to deal with him. On one hand, he recognized that Richards had committed an assault against him for which he deserved to be punished. Pat knew from his general familiarity with the prison rules that if convicted, Richards could be sentenced to serve additional prison time beyond his present sentence and would be segregated from general population because of his dangerous and violent act. Pat did not believe that such outcomes would be unjust. Still, he felt some concern that Richards had attacked him out of a mistaken loyalty to another inmate who had conned him.

In the prison, Pat knew, it was commonly accepted that people who falsely accused others cannot be tolerated. From this perspective, Pat sensed that he could forgive Richards if he could own up to his responsibility. How to reach him, though, presented a difficulty. When Pat asked about seeing Richards, he was told that he had been placed in a special segregation unit reserved for those who had been violent in the prison, mostly gang members, and, consequently, he was not allowed visitors. Pat responded with surprising vigor that as prison chaplain he should have the same access to this man as he had to other inmates in segregation and to the death row inmates. After more give and take, Warden Tucker intervened and told Pat he could see Richards, but under close watch in a controlled setting. When they met, Richards was perplexed. "What are you doing here?" he asked, "What do you want of me, after you put me in this hole?"

While Richards was clearly agitated, Pat was comforted by the realization that he was in restraints, no longer a physical threat to him. "Mr. Richards, I'm not here to ask you any questions or to double down on the charges against you. I just want to explain to you that I did not falsely accuse Luke of anything. As a Catholic priest, I strongly believe that such a serious false accusation would be a terrible sin, one that could even risk my being a priest."

The inmate interrupted. "Oh, so you just want me to believe that this guy Luke made it up from nothing, that you don't even know him?"

Pat remained calm. "No, that's not what I'm saying. I do know Luke. We trained as priests together. I haven't seen him much in recent years. We're not close, but I certainly know him."

Looking Richards directly into his dark, menacing eyes, Pat continued, "I didn't know he had been arrested until I saw him here a couple of days ago. I did help some youngsters who had been abused by priests, but as far as I know, none of the kids had been molested by Luke Reardon. They were other priests. Maybe Luke just assumed that I reported whatever he did to the police because he knew I had helped some other kids. But Luke is wrong about me. I haven't accused him of anything to anybody. Probably a child or children he molested went to the police and then he got arrested and convicted. But that has nothing to do with me. Maybe Luke just doesn't want to own up to his crime because he knows that could make life dangerous for him here."

As Pat spoke silently, he continued to face Richards, eyes upon eyes, speaking as though to his heart. Richards' eyes seemed to soften and his tension visibly eased. The mood in the room became less electric. Sitting back now, Richards said, "When we were on the van coming to prison, me and Luke and some others, he was saying that he had only been arrested because a priest he knew and didn't like had lied about him to the police. Sounded right to me," Richards continued. "It was pretty obvious that this guy Luke wanted revenge against this priest, who he knew was the prison chaplain. Reardon offered to pay anyone who would help him. Later in the ride when I spoke alone with him—we were seated next to each other—he offered to pay me $100 if I'd give you a beatdown and I agreed. He said that jumping you would be right because you're the reason he was on his way here. He wanted revenge against you." Pat just silently listened.

"So, I agreed. He gave me fifty bucks right there and said I'd get the rest later, but I never got it."

"What happened to the money you did get?" asked Pat, more out of curiosity than concern.

"Oh, they put that into my account when we got here. I'll use it to buy stuff. Reardon was real convincing, so I decided that making a few bucks getting even for him would be okay and maybe make me popular. I believed the guy," he confessed. "I guess I just bought the whole story and, yeah, the money was pretty good. And now that you've come to see me, you didn't have to do that, and I think your story sounds true. I know I'm going to get punished for what I did to you, Father. Do you think you could forgive me? I guess I really screwed up."

When Pat asked Richards if he was religious, he indicated that he had converted to Islam when he was first in prison for dealing drugs. "I'm back here because as soon as I got out I went right back to the street. I got caught, in a drug raid at the bar where I hung out and sometimes scored crack." In response to Richards' question about forgiveness, Pat asked Richards if he had studied the Koran when he converted. "A little," he said. "It was a kind of a prison thing but then I found it pretty interesting. I don't know much, though. It was just something I did."

Pat responded, "Even though I'm a Catholic priest, I have studied the Koran somewhat because I know there are believers in Islam here. I have learned that in Islam, truthfulness, confession, and forgiveness are important concepts. Most importantly, Islam holds that those who repent their sins, and who seek to atone for straying from the good, may be forgiven."

Now with more strength than trepidation in his voice, Pat assured Richards that while he knew he was likely to be punished for assaulting him, he appreciated his truthfulness. "I know, Mr. Richards, from the little I've learned about your faith, that forgiveness comes to those who are truly sorry for their bad acts, who repent their sins, who are determined not to repeat their sins, and who compensate those against whom they have sinned."

Richards' face turned in questioning. "Are you saying, Father, that you want me to pay you, give you some money? I don't have nothing."

"No," smiled Pat. "Not in this instance. I know from the Koran there are instances where that happens but not in this situation. I don't want or need anything material from you except the understanding, the belief, that I have done no harm to Luke Reardon."

Richards was surprised and seemed reassured by Pat's knowledge of Islam. He quickly asked Pat for his forgiveness, promising that he would not repeat such behavior against him or anyone else in the prison. "But," he asked, "how could I give you anything since I'm broke?"

"Well," Pat considered, "as I said, I don't want any compensation from you, but there is something you could do that would be sort of like compensation. Once you get out of segregation and go back into general population, you could make it known that you had been mistaken, that you had no reason to believe that I had wronged this man. And, you can tell others that you have, in fact, spoken with me and you think I'm okay. Make sure you also tell them that I have forgiven you and don't want you punished by any of the men who think of themselves as my allies." In saying this, Pat was reflecting on one of the truths he had learned about prison ethos: "If you're not my friend, you're my enemy." Prison is a nearly impossible place to be just a neutral onlooker.

Pat then moved closer to Richards, enough to stir the watchful guard. "To be clear, Hector, I do forgive you for harming me. I believe you are sincere and, as far as I'm concerned, you and I are now all evened up." With that, Pat offered him a blessing. He was a man, Pat sensed, who was humbled by his kindness toward him. Before they parted, Pat sought Richards' permission to tell the warden that he had repented to him, and that, in turn, he had forgiven Richards and hoped the prison would take that into consideration in determining his punishment.

When Pat later met with the warden, Tucker said that while some form of punishment was warranted because the assault had been flagrant and unprovoked, he would take into consideration that Richards appeared contrite to Pat. In the end, the warden decided not to refer Richards to the police. Instead he was disciplined by a period of segregation and deprivation of visits before being allowed into general population. He told Pat he was thinking, also, of taking the money from Richard's account.

"Warden, do you think that's necessary?" Pat asked.

"Not really, Padre, but the idea that he can keep the money just isn't right, no matter how little it is. He can earn some once he's out of segregation. Don't you think that's just?"

"Yes, I suppose going without for a while never killed anyone. Seems right, I guess." Thus ended an unhappy episode in Pat's prison ministry.

XIII

FALL FROM GRACE

In addition to his prison duties, Pat had been recruited to be the Catholic chaplain at James College, a small, coed private school in Palmerton, only about ten minutes from the prison. For Pat, James College seemed a quiet and protective enclave of study for students whose families could afford the steep price tag. Their ivied residence halls, study buildings, and library were separated by a large, tree-lined rectangular quad. At one end was a student center, and a performing arts building fronted with a wondrous mural of a dancing pair. Facing it across an expanse of lawn was a sports complex housing a swimming pool and basketball and racquetball courts. Just beyond the perimeter of this quad were sports fields and a small stadium, where soccer matches and football games were played—an idyllic setting for a refined education away from the main thoroughfares of life.

Pat's overall impression of this four-year college was that it probably provided an adequate liberal arts education in an environment shut off from its urban surroundings, isolating students from lives different from theirs in places their elders didn't want them to go. His interactions with students was a stark contrast to his prison ministry. Being around these young collegians challenged him not to minimize their need for counseling and the sacraments. He found that he enjoyed the campus for its serenity, but, oddly, felt more challenged in the more turbulent setting of the prison where the men's lives often were struggles from birth to confinement. He knew that his view of this college scene was probably skewed by its juxtaposition with the prison environment, and he monitored his attitude in order to be fully available to the students who sought his counsel, and to bring the liturgy of the Church to them.

Also, he found that he was attracted to a young assistant professor of art, Elizabeth Dawkins, with whom he had only fleetingly spoken a few times at the student union while queued for coffee. She had an allure that unsettled him. Whenever he had seen her either running from class to class or snacking in the uni, as it was called, he had been taken by this blue-eyed, shapely brunette. One day, she attended a lecture he was giving at the campus' Newman Center on goodness as a form of holiness. Afterward, she asked if they could further discuss the topic. She said she found troublesome the notion of being kind to unlikeable people. Pat leapt at the opportunity.

"What brought you here, today? I don't remember seeing you ever at the Masses I offer at the Interfaith Chapel on Tuesday and Thursday afternoons."

"Oh, no, Father, I'm not Catholic," she smiled. "I saw a flyer on the community activity board at the uni and decided to come over because your topic intrigues me."

Pat quickly invited Elizabeth to have a coffee and soon they were having a conversation on the notion of goodness.

"Do you think goodness is an absolute or is it just something each one of us defines according to how we think?" Elizabeth posed almost as soon as they sat.

"Oh, not so subjective, I think," Pat instinctively responded. "Christian teaching is that goodness is a reflection of God's presence in us. It's an absolute, and not just anybody's version of what that person thinks may be good for him or her," Pat continued, rising to the bait. There followed a fairly deep discussion, unusual for strangers but one that gave them windows into each other. To Pat, it appeared that this engaging woman might be more humanist than true believer and that appeals to logic rather than scripture might be more meaningful for her. Not long after they began talking, Elizabeth looked at her watch and jumped up, exclaiming, "Oh my, I have to get to class. Time flies." And off she went. Their initial meeting made Pat hungry for more.

After their first meeting, Pat and Elizabeth occasionally got together on campus for coffee at the uni, later brief walks, which in a few weeks evolved into more personal conversation. Their discussions went from safe and impersonal to intimate in a smooth reflection of their growing attraction to each other. Elizabeth was fascinated by Pat's accounts of his life with inmates at the prison and was impressed by his insights from interacting with them. Pat, in turn, began to learn about Elizabeth. She was the only child of college professors who lived and taught in Iowa. After high school, she had attended Oberlin College in Ohio, initially to study literature to follow in her mother's footsteps. But, at Oberlin, she had taken an elective class in art history then taught by a highly esteemed professor, popular for her teaching manner. For Elizabeth, as she told it, that class was the beginning of a lifelong study of art, its history, and its many manifestations. She talked rapturously about ancient art, of hieroglyphics, Greek and Roman art, particularly sculpture, of the Renaissance, of the impressionist movement started in Europe and transplanted to the United States, and of her particular love of the works of Wyeth and Homer Winslow.

To Pat, Elizabeth was an encyclopedia of the world of beauty well beyond his ken. Through her, Pat felt his world expanding. Growing up, his parents hardly ever took them to a museum or art gallery except for one trip to Boston where they had spent a whirlwind weekend, visiting colonial sights and, for a few hours, the Museum of Fine Arts. While he had gained some appreciation for Greek and Roman art, and medieval religious art during his seminary studies, the gamut of art from cave drawings to the modern expression that Elizabeth opened to him was dazzling. Although the school's art gallery was limited, Elizabeth was able to situate its holdings for Pat in a way that sparked a new appreciation for the creative mind.

They dared, on one occasion, to drive together to Catskill, New York, to visit nearby Olana, the home of Frederick and Isabel Church on the edge of the Hudson River built in the nineteenth century. Elizabeth had explained that Church had been a driving force in the Hudson River School of painting where the beauty of seascapes was celebrated. She explained that the architecture of Olana, complete with a bell tower, and its contents reflected what Frederic and Isabel had learned and enjoyed on their lengthy trip to Europe and the Near East, a distinct and unique presentation. One significant feature of Olana, explained by Elizabeth, was that every window in the home presented a vista of the Hudson and its surrounding shores, vivid and expressive landscapes.

Pat was enthralled with this gem and, more so, by Elizabeth's patience in interpreting all they saw to him. In addition to their foray to Olana, Elizabeth also liked to talk about poetry to Pat. She had minored in literature while at Oberlin and had a particular fondness for the poetry of Dickinson, Frost, Whitman, and, lately, Maya Angelou. From time to time, as they strolled around the campus lake, keeping a respectful distance, Elizabeth would read aloud portions of some of her favorite prose or poetry and talk about how descriptive writing captured her. Pat was struck particularly by Thoreau as his work echoed his own love of nature but in words eloquent in their simplicity. He related, as well, to the sense of solitude of Dickinson's poetry, works first introduced to him in Father Nolan's class, which seemed now from a different world.

One late afternoon, Pat and Elizabeth went to her on-campus apartment where she had prepared wine and cheese for them. And, in this intimate setting, one touch, one nodding smile, led to more. Elizabeth was eager and Pat was enthralled as they wound up in the bedroom having sexual intercourse, frantic at first but then gentle. Unlike his only other experience when he was a young teen, this time Pat was an avid participant. He had feelings for Elizabeth, and an appetite to spend more time because intimacy with her, physical and spiritual, seemed a fulfillment of what previously had been absent from his life.

It was not all bliss, however. At the same time as he grew more attached to Elizabeth, Pat was tortured by the guilty knowledge that he had broken his vow of chastity. He was conflicted and he was aware. Nevertheless, his increasing yearnings for Elizabeth, for the feel of her in his arms and the physical consummation of his budding love, were magnets beyond his capacity to resist in his present state of mind and heart. Yet always, Pat felt an innermost sense that he had veered dangerously far from his calling.

On their last occasion together, they visited New York City and stayed at the Plaza on the south edge of Central Park. Pat signed the register as Mr. Patrick Keefe, identifying Elizabeth as his spouse in perhaps his first written betrayal of his vows. In the morning, they walked along Fifth Avenue to the Metropolitan Museum of Art, where Elizabeth capably shepherded Pat through centuries of creative works by artists whose names he only vaguely recognized.

Being with Elizabeth expanded Pat's world intellectually, and his growing fondness for her enlivened him emotionally. Never before had he ever felt such a close connection to another person. Surely, with Father Stan, he had an intellectual connection, and he felt a special kinship to some of his colleagues, particularly Father Jerome, and, of course, he loved all his family, but this was different; harder to explain. Elizabeth had become a unique and unexplainable presence for Pat.

After they spent a few hours at the museum with Elizabeth as Pat's informal docent, they had a brief lunch at a small café, then continued walking back down Fifth Avenue en route to Rockefeller Center. Elizabeth expressed a desire to see the skating oval and the small shops along the ice's edges. As they approached, Elizabeth saw the towering spires of St. Patrick's Cathedral across the way, and she suggested they visit the church before going to the Center. Pat agreed, but as they neared the large brass front doors, about to enter, he suddenly hesitated, backed away, and said he needed to sit down.

Head in hand, he sunk into a deep reverie, a flashback to when he had last been in this place. It was when he was seven or eight on a school day class trip led by Sister Agnes Marie, one of the teachers at Holy Family. A group of them had taken the train, supervised by Sister Agnes and a parent whose name Pat couldn't remember. But his recollection of the cathedral was instant, vivid, and now searing.

He remembered the ornate brass doors, the explanations about them by the docent—an old woman, Pat thought, but kind and responsive to their questions. And he remembered looking up at the spires, thinking that they must have touched heaven. Inside, he had been awed first by the immensity of the church and then, when pointed out, the beauty of the stained glass windows, particularly the rose one. As they had walked along the side aisles, hand in hand as ordered by Sister Agnes and in hushed reverence, the docent explained the depictions of the stations of the cross.

Remembering all of this jolted Pat, and soon he was sobbing. When Elizabeth asked him what was wrong, he stammered, "I remember being on this very spot as a boy and that maybe this was where I first thought about being a priest." Tearfully, he turned to Elizabeth and dolefully murmured, "I just can't do this." When she responded that they didn't have to go into the cathedral, he answered, "No, I don't mean the church. I mean us." She understood immediately.

As he rose, he told Elizabeth they needed to return to the hotel and then go home. Elizabeth took his arm and silently they walked back, retrieved their bags and car, and began the trip back home, now quiet in their own thoughts. When they got back to Elizabeth's apartment, Pat made no gesture to open his door. As Elizabeth got out of the car, he simply said good night from his seat and that he needed to be alone for a while, apologizing to her for his sudden change in manner. Gently, Elizabeth reached through the open window to kiss him on the cheek while saying she thought she understood. In that manner, they parted for the night.

On the next day, Pat called on Elizabeth and asked if they could walk together, and she agreed. He told her that going to the cathedral had brought back strong memories and that he was now questioning himself about their growing affection for each other. She, in turn, responded that she sensed Pat's turmoil, which caused her great pangs. A woman of depth as well as passion, Elizabeth had been baptized as a Christian but, as a child, her parents had not been religious with the result that she felt no particular affiliation to any church. She was sensitive, however, and empathetic.

Softly, she patted his arm, and said she did not want to be the cause of Pat's losing his priesthood as she sensed how committed he was to his calling. Now tearfully, she said she could not bear the notion that her growing affection and appetite for intimacy with Pat could be the cause of his failure as a priest. Ultimately, they both knew that their affair was doomed. Their shared guilt overwhelmed their brief romance, and after a few more walks together and many tears, they agreed it had to end with a complete severance.

Rather than stay in Elizabeth's presence, Pat resolved to minimize the risk of temptation. Accordingly, at the end of the semester, he gave up his post at the school so he could more fully concentrate on his prison ministry without the constant temptation of Elizabeth's proximity. At least, that's what he told himself.

Pat was hesitant to confess his affair but he knew he must. He made an appointment to see Father Mathews at the seminary. When Pat was a seminarian, Father Stan, as a philosophy and theology professor, had demonstrated his equal facility with Socrates, Plato, Thomas, and later thinkers such as Luther, and his lectures had revealed the depth of his grasp of scriptures and Church orthodoxy. Pat remembered liking it that Father Stan had not been flamboyant about his learning, but rather he was able to convey complex theories of thought and ethics in a plain talking manner, encouraging his students to see the relevance of great teachings to their coming challenges as priests. But most of all, Pat now had a thirst for Father Stan's special knack for combining spiritual counseling with practical wisdom.

Pat knew that his embryonic love for an unattainable Elizabeth conflicted with his vow of chastity and singular commitment to the priesthood. But he wasn't sure whether, by his violation of his vows, he had crossed a one-way bridge. In seeking out Father Stan, he hoped for the plainspoken insights and direction he sensed would come from this man of depth.

Once Pat got to Father Stan's chambers, now familiar to him, he took a seat across from the older man. "Well, what have you got yourself up to this time, my young colleague?" was Father Stan's welcoming.

"Not so good, this time, Father. I'm in need of confession and advice, if you can tolerate me."

"Of course, Pat. Please be comfortable and tell me."

At that, Pat unburdened himself of his affair, part recitation, part apology. He asked his old mentor whether he had made himself unworthy to his priestly vocation.

"Not at all," quickly responded Father Stan. "That is, if you are resolved to continue your priesthood and to fight to be true to your vow of chastity. You are not the first priest to fall and you will not be the last. Take heart and recommit yourself to your ministry if that's the path you seek. The good Lord welcomes sinners to His table." They then talked in a manly exchange about the pressures of the vow of chastity and how treacherous it can be for a priest in the midst of his years of virility. Father Stan's frank but unscolding reaction to Pat's account of his affair relieved and energized him to recommit himself to God's service. He left Father Stan's rooms with a quickened step, his heart lightened by the knowledge that God's capacity for forgiveness is infinite.

XIV

EXECUTION

Pat's contact with the inmates on the Lost Corridor was minimal, a circumstance that suited him. Although he visited the corridor from time to time, he was always wary about going there because of the horrific experience he had with the inmate, Brand, the white supremacist who had just played with him to satisfy a perverse urge. One day, however, his attitude of reluctance was abruptly broken. The newly elected governor, Cyrus Powell, had campaigned, in part, on what he called a law and order agenda. This included a promise to be tough on violent crimes. Soon after he took office, Powell introduced new legislation for harsher penalties for repeat offenders and violent felons.

The state legislature decided to hold hearings on the governor's proposals, slowing the process in spite of the governor's request for swift action. As part of his crime-fighting program, the governor also promised during his campaign that, if elected, he would carry out long deferred death sentences for the state's worst criminals. Here, there was no roadblock except public opinion. The announcement of his intentions to restart executions caused editorials in both the state's leading dailies, the *Canton Gazette* and the *Daily Clarion* in Forester, with circulation in the southern part of the state. Susan had written the lead column in the *Gazette* expressing the paper's unconditional opposition to the death penalty, arguing that it was barbaric and that no civilized Western country other than the United States still had the death penalty. The *Clarion* was more circumspect, asserting that some who had been condemned may not, in fact, be guilty of their crimes, and urging the governor to exercise extreme caution in proceeding.

Powell was unmoved by media stirrings. He knew he had the support of the majority of voters in the state, however thin, and a strong core of solid supporters who avidly supported execution. To him, executing prisoners who had committed unspeakable atrocities was consistent with his campaign promise to restore law and order to the state.

The governor's public announcements had a tumultuous effect on the Lost Corridor, causing disquiet throughout the prison including among several of the corrections officers. Speculation reigned over who would be the first to be executed and whether, in fact, it was actually going to happen. And, sure enough, soon after the governor's announcement, he signed a death warrant for Leroy Small, a black man who had been convicted thirty-five years ago for a double murder—the shooting of a store clerk and a bystander in the course of a gunpoint robbery at a Kmart store in Forester. Small had exhausted all his federal and state appeals. Then, after losing his direct appeals, his lawyers filed a series of habeas corpus petitions to no avail alleging that Small's trial lawyer had been ineffective and later that the imposition of the death penalty itself was a violation of the federal constitutional prohibition against cruel and unusual punishment. Their writs had gone through both the state and federal court systems, ultimately ending up in the Supreme Court, which, just last year, had signaled its refusal to hear Small's pleas. Now, there was nothing between Small and the death chamber but a reprieve from the governor, which he feared would not be forthcoming. Faced with his imminent death, Small had asked to see the chaplain.

When Warden Tucker told Pat of Small's request, he agreed to see him but he wasn't sure what real comfort he could bring to him and he still had some trepidation about being on the corridor. While Pat had not thought much about the death penalty because it had not been an issue in the state for a long time, he was aware that the Church was opposed to it and he knew that members of the clergy of several faiths, including the Catholic Church, had voiced their opposition when the governor had made known his intention to restart the machinery of execution. Pat was also thinking of his only other experience on the Lost Corridor and did not want that repeated.

What can I do for this man? Pat wondered. *Is giving him solace enough when I'm so convinced that executing people is immoral?* Feeling off his spiritual axis, and unsure he was up to the task, Pat decided once again to seek guidance from Father Matthews back at the seminary. Pat regarded Father Stan as having not only great learning in scripture and philosophy but also as a font of wisdom. In seeking out Father Stan, Pat remembered from seminary days that the professor frequently lectured on the role of priests in living Christlike lives. He talked about people whose lives he admired—Gandhi was one Pat particularly remembered—and sometimes he'd sit with groups of students in the common room just talking about the struggles of being a priest true to his calling by throwing hypothetical scenarios at them to test their reactions. Socratic in his method, Pat had found Father Stan's approach to teaching challenging and inclusive. *No way to duck for cover* had been the common mantra about Father Stan's classes. Surely, he'd have some wisdom to help Pat decide how to deal with this plea from the Lost Corridor.

"What brings you here, Pat? Have you entangled yourself in some new dustup from which you can't extricate yourself?" Pat knew Father Stan often spoke in metaphors.

"Not sure. I feel trapped, Father, as much as a ship heaving from side to side in an unsettled sea. I'm just not sure which way to point the bow." Stan nodded as he invited Pat to sit in the well-worn leather chair across from him.

"Father Stan, as you know, our beloved governor has decided it's time to turn the switch back on death penalty executions, and the inmate first in line has asked me to come to him."

"They don't do the electric chair, do they?" gasped Father Stan.

"Oh, no, I didn't mean the term *switch* literally. They plan to give him a lethal injection, a process other states began using in 1977 after the Supreme Court's moratorium on the death penalty was lifted. It's supposed to be more humane, if you can imagine any state killing to be so."

"Then, what's your concern, Pat? Do you feel you shouldn't see this man for some reason or do you just not know how to deal with him?" queried Father Stan.

"Well, I know I should go see him—that's my job as the chaplain. I just don't know what to say to him, what good I can be to him. It seems so ironic to me that on one hand the State has decided to kill him but at the same time they want to provide a chaplain to him. Are those two notions compatible?"

"Well, a little background first, Pat," responded Father Stan, now sitting up, attentive. "Historically, the Church has not been against the death penalty so long as it is imposed for just reasons. Aquinas wrote that its imposition could be viewed as just under proper circumstances. And, you know that historically, the Church was in the death business. During the longstanding inquisitions, we executed people for heresy, or turned them over to civil authorities to carry out the ultimate punishments. Remember our studies of the Crusades. So, one way or another, killing people or having them killed for perceived sins against the Church was commonplace for several centuries.

In more modern times, earlier in the century, the United States Conference of Bishops in Washington, D.C., issued a statement, cautioning against the use of legal execution except in the most extreme cases, and most recently, Catholic scholars, including a great theologian, Cardinal Avery Dulles, the son of Alan Dulles of World War II fame, have argued against the death penalty on moral grounds. Dulles says that since the traditional reasons for imposing the penalty—retribution, deterrence, and reform—don't hold up under scrutiny, there is no moral reason for having the death penalty.

I agree with Dulles. Retribution is really another word for vengeance. The State has no business being vengeful. Supporters of the death penalty shy from espousing the public value of vengeance. They claim instead that it's a deterrence, but statistics contradict them. If they were correct, you'd think the states that most ardently use the death penalty would have the lowest rates of murder, but that's not the case. In fact, Texas and Florida, two states that routinely execute people, have higher murder rates than many of the states that don't have a death penalty. So, deterrence is out the window. That leaves reform and that term, as it's used in the criminal context, means to reform the wrongdoer. Well, I guess the proponents win on that one, Pat, since a dead man can no longer commit crimes. Sorry for the tirade but this subject brings bile to me. Anyway, what does that have to do with your going to this poor soul?"

"Father Stan, your vehemence about this comes across loud and clear and I'm on board with your thinking, totally. With no moral or legal justification, I think execution by the State is simply evil. So, when I meet with this man should I share those feelings, tell him I don't agree with what's about to happen to him? Do I owe him any honesty about that?"

"Pat, you came here for advice so here it is. This is not about you or your beliefs about capital punishment. I understand how you may feel off your pins right now, but it seems to me your way is clear. Your task simply is to minister to this man. It's not important to him that you think what's going to happen is an abomination as that won't bring any solace to him. Just be there for him. I'm sure you know, Pat, this poor devil deserves God's mercy in spite of whatever terrible crimes he committed. So, Pat, my counsel to you is that you should go to him, minister to him as you would any other sinner, and leave the big policy picture, if that's what you call it, to others. In short, Pat, whether or not this man is killed by the State is out of your hands. Others will fight that battle. You task now is less pubic, more intimate. Go administer to his soul."

Pat interrupted, "Is that enough, Father Stan? Shouldn't I try to do more?"

"Remember always, Pat, you are a priest and your task is to minister. This man, if he's sincere, seeks God's grace. This makes me think of a woman, Dorothy Day. Have you ever heard of her? I think I probably talked about her when you were a seminarian here."

"Yes, I'm pretty sure. Wasn't she a sort of radical, a convert to Catholicism who served the poor and founded something called the Catholic Worker Movement? What does she have to do with this, Father? I think she was very much an activist and you're suggesting I leave that to others in this instance."

"Well, she was, Pat, but she also had something to say about prayer and action. Beyond all her social activism, she was a deeply spiritual woman. I remember her saying someplace that love and ever more love is the only solution to any problem. There was also another great person whose writings I would strongly recommend you find. He was Thomas Merton, someone else you may remember from one of my lectures. Merton was a Trappist monk from a place called Gethsemane in Kentucky, a unique kind of monk because he didn't remain cloistered in his monastery. Rather, he traveled far. In fact, he died in an electrical accident not too long ago in Thailand. More importantly, he was an intensely spiritual man, a mystic and activist, if it's possible to combine the two, a poet and writer whose work has inspired men and women of many cultures and religions throughout the world.

Aptly for your dilemma, Pat, Merton once said that our job is to love others without stopping to inquire whether or not they are worthy. To put it in Merton's words, Pat, your task now is simply to love this man who is about to die. Giving him love will be your finest contribution to him in his last hours. That's your task and the challenge facing you. And remember, Pat, ministering to this man will bring spiritual peace to him. You are but an instrument. Try to keep yourself, your very human, deep-felt feelings, out of it. God's speed, Pat."

"I think I understand, Father Stan. Thank you for your direction. I knew you'd help me get my bearings. These waters are just uncharted for me. No matter how much I have prayed, I'm not sure I'm up to this task."

"On the nose, Pat. That's one of your great attributes: humility. I know you understand what you need to do."

"And, as for the big picture, I'll be there whenever they pick the date, and I'll have a van-full of like-minded seminarians. And, no doubt there will be a throng of protesters but that makes no difference to your responsibility. You belong with this man no matter how terrible his sins and how awful his fate to be."

Somberly, Pat thanked Father Stan for his advice. They embraced and Pat left, his step slow, his mood troubled, but at least he was resolved to minister to this man and put aside, for the time, his dark thoughts about the death penalty.

When Pat first went to Small's cell, he was struck first by how gray this black man was and how he appeared—small, gaunt, short-cropped white hair, and sad eyes. Unlike his experience with Brand, the guard simply asked Small to step to the rear of the cell so Pat could be admitted. The guard even brought a chair into the cell for Pat to sit on. Pat was confused but he asked no questions. As he sat, the guard left, saying he'd be within shouting distance if needed and added, "But I'm not worried about you, Leroy. Glad I could bring the padre to you. Hope you have a good visit."

Small immediately rose from his bed. "Oh, Father Keefe, I can't tell you how much I appreciate your coming to see me," he said as he took Pat's hand in both of his.

"Please make yourself as comfortable as you can, Father." Pat noted Small had only one visible tat, something indistinct on his arm, faded as though blurred with time, a surprise to Pat as he had become used to seeing extensive body art on many of the inmates. He remembered when thinking of his first impression of Small, how his sister Susan had so playfully shown him her ankle tat, colorful with flowers, in her first year of college. Strange juxtaposition of memory, he now thought.

"Well, Mr. Small, I'm pleased to meet you, obviously not under these circumstances, but I want to help you if I can."

"Please, Father, call me Leroy. Nobody around here calls me Mr. anything," he grinned. Small then immediately began his story. "First, Father, I want you to know that I did, in fact, shoot and kill two men when I was in my twenties. I so mourn those people, even more than the thought of my own coming death. Long ago, I prayed God's forgiveness for this sin right here, in this cell. But I know I need comfort now, Father, and I hope you can help me with that."

Pat responded quietly, "I want to do that, Leroy, if I can." Pat did not feel capable of this task. In spite of his talk with Father Stan, he still had reservations about his usefulness. Nevertheless, he decided that his personal misgivings could not block his availability to this condemned man. If he only could get out of thinking about himself, his own reactions, then maybe he could offer some solace to fortify Small as he confronted his looming demise. After having consulted with Father Stan, Pat was fortified in his awareness that his task was to minister; he would have to subordinate his own beliefs and his instinct to protest. Small didn't need to hear any of that. And, he knew as well that when he next visited Duncan's Cove, his whole family would be up in arms about the renewal of the death penalty and would have a lot of questions for him. He tried to get those thoughts out of his mind, to be in the moment, to help this man. Things were much clearer, he thought, when they were just classroom hypotheticals.

Before meeting with Small, Pat had asked to see his prison file. There, he learned that he had committed a robbery and double murder when he was twenty-two, an age where he had already had an adult-sized arrest sheet for drug possession, drug sales, and an attempted home robbery in which he had been scared off by the owner. For the drug-related offenses, Small had first received drug counseling as a juvenile, and when he returned to the system a year later, a suspended sentence, with substance abuse counseling and testing as requirements of his probation. And for the later home invasion, Small had served three years at Suffolk before being released on parole, which he later violated for drug usage, returning to Suffolk for an additional two years.

From this record, it was clear that Small was never compliant with the terms of his sentences and that, early in his prison stays, he often got into fights while in general population, earning him repeated confinement in segregation. From what Pat could infer from Small's history, there was no evidence that he had benefitted from his earlier incarcerations as it did not appear he had attended any Alcoholics Anonymous or Narcotics Anonymous meetings, nor had he obtained his GED. Reading his prison file from those early days saddened Pat because, in a way, those pages foretold Small's ultimate fate. It appeared to Pat that Small, still then young and angry, had been let loose back on society a few times without reform and ultimately returned for a final time as a condemned man barely an adult.

Pat learned that Small had been reared in a one-parent home and that his mother had her own major substance abuse issues, resulting in the loss to the State of two children who came along after Small. He saw, as well, that Small had repeatedly been physically abused by one boyfriend or another of his mother, likely shutting him down early in his adolescent years, and stoking the fires of his anger. Recapping Small's file in his mind, it appeared to Pat that Small had been on his own since he was twelve with no formal schooling after ninth grade and minus any parental guidance; generally no caring or direction from any stable adult in his formative years.

While to Pat, this history did not provide any excuse for the violence that brought Small to the Lost Corridor, it gave him some insight into the dysfunctional abyss of Small's early life. At the time of Small's sentencing for the capital murders and robbery, the probation officer noted that he had tested positive for opiates when apprehended a day after the shootings, a finding never disputed by Small. In fact, at his sentencing hearing, his lawyer had tried to utilize his substance dependency as mitigation, an effort rejected by the jury and the judge.

Pat also noticed in Small's file a copy of a petition for clemency that had been filed by his attorney with the governor. From it, Pat learned that Small appeared to have made a turnaround about five years into his sentence, a change the writer attributed to Small's interaction with Pastor Tyrone James, a Baptist minister who worked at Suffolk for more than two decades before retiring. Pat was fascinated by this mention of the pastor and had made a note to discuss him and his influence on Small when they met. In addition to the note about Pastor James in Small's file, Pat read that two wardens—James Tucker, the incumbent, and his predecessor, Neil Kelly—had made notes in Small's file, echoed in the lawyer's document, that since Small had arrived with a death sentence and after a few years of adjustment, he had quieted down, had become well mannered, never a bother.

Kelly had even noted that Small often talked with the correctional officers, who, for some reason, seemed to gravitate to him, even for personal advice. He appeared, both wardens had observed, to have found stability while in prison and, from his cell, seemed to be conducting some sort of ministry for all who would listen along the corridor. How odd, thought Pat, and what an irony. Pat concluded, with no basis, that if the governor had bothered to read this comprehensive and compelling clemency petition, it just might have softened his heart and his resolve to end Small's life.

Small continued, "I'm pretty sure I was baptized as a Christian when I was very young, and I'm pretty sure my grandma was a Baptist; I never really attended church as a kid and I don't have no particular feelings for a church except I am a Christian. I believe in Jesus, our Lord and Savior. That just happened after I got here, though. As a kid, I spent most of my time on weekends after I was about twelve at a bar operated by one of my mother's boyfriends. But now, in these many years here, I've read and reread portions of the Bible." At this Pat cocked his head. "Oh yes, Padre…can I call you that?" Pat nodded. "Yes, of course, Leroy, that's what pretty much everyone here calls me."

Small continued, "I believe in the goodness of God and that sinners who are sorry for their sins can be saved. That's my hope. There was another pastor here, Pastor James, who came to see me almost weekly for nearly all the time I've been here until he retired. We read the Bible together. See it right here. The good pastor left his Bible with me, God bless him, and I read some of it every day."

As Leroy held the Bible out to Pat, he took it, noticing it appeared well used. Small continued, "I find real comfort in the Gospels of Mathew and Luke, from the parables about the life of Jesus that sinners who repented were welcomed into his company even when the more powerful scorned him for spending time with them. That talks right to me." Small smiled. "After Pastor James retired, I missed seeing him, reading the Bible together. I'm hoping that you and I can talk some about Jesus in the time I have." Leroy then asked Pat if he would hear his confession. This proposition surprised Pat and momentarily tugged him in two directions.

He asked, "Leroy, why would you want me to hear your confession since you're not Catholic, and surely you must have discussed your sins with Pastor James?"

"Yes," Small smiled, "but I need all the help I can get. The more times the better, I'm thinking."

Pat knew that the sacrament of penance was intended for Catholics, those who believe that the Catholic Church is the only route to salvation. But his personal sense of Christ's teachings was different and shaped by his belief in a beneficent God. Even before ordination, Pat had come to the view, unspoken, that salvation was not reserved only for the few who happen to have the benefit of the formal teachings of Catholicism. He had concluded, instead, that union with God should be available to anybody who professes a belief in Christ and who truly atones for his or her sins. In having this view, Pat knew he was out of step with Catholic orthodoxy, but he was unbothered by this risk of heresy. He had concluded that only good could come of trying to redeem anyone of any faith so long as they believed in a divinity. Besides, thought Pat, what harm can come to him or to Small if he opens the sacrament of penance to him? And so he agreed.

Small's confession was jarring and breathtaking. His outpouring of his teen criminality exceeded the report in his prison file and stunned Pat for its scope and randomness, crimes committed apparently to support a substance abuse habit that had drowned him in dysfunction. Small had mugged innocent people on the street for whatever was in their wallets and for their jewelry. He had prostituted himself for drugs. His early life was one of complete degradation. In telling the story of his brief life out of prison, Small was quiet, even measured. To Pat, he spoke poignantly of his sorrow for the harms he had done, and his sincerity was evident as he sought absolution, which Pat eagerly gave him. "After hearing all that, Padre, are you sure you want to be with me?" Small asked with just a tad of a twinkle in his eye.

"Oh, more than ever, Leroy" was Pat's comeback. "Your history is right up God's alley." The two men smiled at each other.

After that first visit, Pat saw Leroy almost daily. He was impressed with Small's acceptance of his coming fate. At times when talking with Small, Pat wasn't sure who was consoling whom as his own discomfort with the death penalty was unhidden in spite of his resolve to keep his feelings to himself.

Towards the end of their first meeting, Pat had offered to Small that he would baptize him into the Catholic Church if he wished, but Small only smiled and said he couldn't do that. "Thank you, Father, but you know, that would just kill my grandma—that is, if she were still alive—to think that one of her offspring had become a papist." They had a good laugh about that. Foregoing the notion of a conversion to Catholicism, Pat gave Small his blessing and then, contrary to his seminary teachings that receiving communion is reserved for Catholics, he shared communion with Small, a moving event for both of them, and one of profound grace each time it occurred.

Small's acceptance of his coming death fortified Pat for the grizzly procedure ahead. Not only had Small clearly atoned for his horrible conduct, he appeared also to accept the state's response to his crimes even if delayed to the point that Small no longer represented a danger to anyone. For Pat, Small's acceptance was initially difficult to harmonize with his own beliefs, but after prayerful consideration, Pat began to embrace what he already knew, what he and Father Stan had discussed. Small's need for comfort in his last days mattered more than his own misgivings about the ghoulish process that was about to unfold. And so, he agreed with Small's request that he would stay with him in his final hours and then be present behind the window when Small was injected with the concoction of drugs that would end his life.

Before Small's scheduled execution date, Pat spent a three-day weekend in Duncan's Cove—perhaps, without knowing it, to steel himself for the execution and to be in the warmth of his family. It turned out not to be as comforting as Pat had anticipated. Maggie invited Pat's sisters, Ruth and Susan and her spouse, Bill Sweeney. Chris, of course, was on hand and eager to join in the heated talk about the death penalty. When Pat told them that he had met Small and had agreed to witness the execution, they were uniformly quiet. "You know, the *Gazette* has written a strong editorial against it," Susan said. "And I agree."

Pat smiled back. "False humility, Susan. I know that piece was your work. I was happy to see that your paper took that view."

Bill, an English teacher at Chatham Community College, chimed in, "No matter what this man Small had done. We are better people than this. We should not be revenge seekers." Ruth, who was now working in the rehabilitation department of the Charleston Hospital and whose personal life seemed no mystery to the rest of the family, said that her friend, Beth, had told her that states that utilize the death penalty have no lower rate of violent crimes or murders than states who do not put people to death. And, in a coup de grâce, Ruth pointed out the current stance of the Catholic Church against the death penalty. Maggie asked Pat what he thought about it.

Pat was measured in his response. "I agree with all of you who have spoken. What the State is about to do is an abomination, a public sin if there is such a thing. But my task as a priest is to lay aside those feelings, at least not to express them, in order to bring God's message of love to this man, who I am actually getting to admire, strange as that may seem."

"Wait a minute," Bill interrupted. "It's one thing to be opposed to the death penalty on moral grounds, but let's not go too far. This guy killed two people. He's a horrible person. I'm not sure he's worthy of God's grace."

"Ah, Bill," Pat quietly responded, "that's a hard stance to take. You know, Christ was the first to forgive sinners. There will be time for judgment for this man but, like any human being, he is entitled to forgiveness so long as he truly atones for what he has done. And that's my only focus, the only one I can have right now. And I will tell you that this man has great sorrow for the evil he did."

Pat loved his siblings and had welcomed Bill into the fold. Having thought about the likelihood of this confrontation, he was, at least, intellectually prepared for it.

He continued: "By consoling Leroy Small I am not condoning what he did and I'm surely not helping to carry out the State's sentence. My focus must be laser sharp. In fact, I should tell you that Small has asked me to be a witness to his execution so that he will know he is not alone in his final moments, and I intend to do that as unpleasant as I expect it to be. So, I ask you, what should my response to Small be? Should I refuse his plea for company in his last moments on the grounds that I abhor what he did or as a protest against the death penalty? Certainly not. If that was my attitude then I should seek another vocation."

"So, Uncle Pat," asked Chris, "if we all go to protest outside the prison, are you okay with that?"

"Absolutely," replied Pat, "and I wish I could be there with you. I hope there is a throng, a horde of people to raise their voices against this travesty. To be there with you would be the easiest thing for me to do. But my task as a priest in this instance is singular; my focus has to be on this condemned man. He deserves spiritual comfort at whatever cost to my own."

Pat's quiet words and demeanor seemed to win over his family. They said they pitied him for his duty. They wished him Godspeed in his task, and in return Pat—half in jest but more in faith—blessed them with the sign of the cross as he left their company.

Before Pat left, he asked Ruth to take a walk with him up to Sean's bench as he wanted to ask her about something. They walked astride, the diminutive Ruth quick-stepping to keep up. "Oh boy," Ruth feared, "here we go about the Church's view on lesbianism as he surely must have been thinking about that." But, to her satisfaction, Pat was not judgmental, just inquisitive.

"Tell me about Beth," Pat said as they walked in unison. "She seems interesting but I really don't know her."

"She's just wonderful," Ruth said as her eyes sparkled and her pace quickened. "We met at the Student Union at Concordia and immediately clicked and we've been inseparable ever since."

"As kids, I never knew you were gay," Pat responded. "When did you first know?"

"I can't pinpoint the date," Ruth answered, "but I think in my early high school years I realized that boys didn't attract me, but girls did. I kept those feelings under wraps, however. I was afraid what others, particularly Dad and you, would think, but when I got to college, away from family and the old ties, I felt freer and then it just happened when Beth and I met. I'm so in love, Pat, I hope you're not disappointed in me, as I know it's against the Church."

Pat did not respond immediately but suggested they continue walking together quietly and talk more when they got to the bench. As they went along, however, he put his arms around her, giving her an affectionate squeeze. Once they were seated and had a moment to drink in the scene of boats moving about the harbor, Pat turned to Ruth.

"First, dear sister, know that I'm happy for you that you've found love. I know the Church's position about homosexuality and I also know that there are good, holy priests who are homosexuals, so how have I dealt with that? Two things, Ruth. Personally, I have no problem with whom one chooses to love. We priests take a vow of chastity but we can be imperfect and still fulfill our mission as priests. I don't judge others and I don't want to. Each of us has to carry out our vocation as best we can. Frankly, I'm more interested in how caring any colleague is to the community than in his personal life so long as he's discrete and doesn't bring scandal to the Church. So, if I don't judge my brothers who are gay, that should give you an idea that I'm not bothered at all about your sexuality. Just be happy and good, dear Ruth, and take care of yourself."

187

"But what about child molesters, Pat? You know we're hearing more about that now and, of course, I know you were involved in those trials."

"That's a totally different thing, Ruth, and has nothing to do with love or caring. Abusing children is a monstrous act and should not be compared at all with a person's choice of a love mate. Please don't make the mistake of comparing them or of thinking of yourself in that way. That surely would be an undeserved torment."

"Well, I don't, Pat, as there's no abuse in my love for Beth. But it seems that others see both homosexuality and child abuse by adults as just two kinds of deviant behavior."

Pat now spoke with force. "We can't cure all ignorance, Ruth, but we can vigorously condemn the evil of child abuse while showing at the same time tolerance if not embrace for a form of love we may not fully understand, such as women loving women or men loving men."

Ruth jumped in. "Thank you for those words, Pat, but you know you can't say that aloud as it's not Church dogma. The Church views me as a sinner. That's why I don't go to confession or to Church anymore as I don't agree that what I'm doing is wrong."

"How sad," Pat softly said. "Ruth, precious little sister, I am not your judge. Yes, I cannot say publicly what I feel about this because it would get me crosswise with the higher-ups, but, on a personal basis, I just want you to know that I'm very happy for you and I hope to have the opportunity to spend time with you and Beth."

Ruth hugged Pat with tears as the two, holding hands, drank in the scene before them. They then strolled amiably back to Maggie's house, where they all said their goodbyes, and Pat left to return to his prison home.

All was set for Small's execution except for an answer from the governor to the pending petition for clemency until, one day, Pat received a visit from Joseph Haddox, a correctional officer he had come to know while mingling in general population. Now overweight and in his late fifties, the balding officer had begun working at the prison after an enlistment in the Army, where he had been trained as a military policeman. Pat sensed that Haddox was, in the main, an amiable officer who could be firm when the situation called for it but who, more generally, just got along with the inmates and appeared to be accepted as a decent guard, neither feared nor loathed as were some of the other officers, particularly among those of color. Haddox started speaking immediately, quickly, excitedly.

"Father, Warden Tucker has decided that the members of the execution team, the men who will escort Small from his cell to the death chamber and the men who will then strap him to a gurney, will be randomly selected from those scheduled to be on duty on the date and time of the execution. I've just been notified of my selection for this team. I'm supposed to strap the poor bastard to the gurney. Sorry, Father."

Tearfully and visibly shaking, Haddox continued. "I don't think I can do this. For years I've been privately opposed to the death penalty. I think it's immoral for the State to take another's life, but my personal beliefs, so far, have never interfered with my duties because no one has been executed in the twenty-three years I've been working here. But if I refuse, I'm afraid I could be fired for insubordination and then lose my pension. And I'm just a couple of years away from retiring. I don't know what to do. Hope you can help me find some way to avoid having to take part in this horrible act without having to sacrifice my career and all I have worked for."

The officer's plea presented a challenge to Pat. He respected Haddox's moral beliefs as he shared them. But he was on weaker ground in advising Haddox about acting on his beliefs. On one hand, Pat thought, if Haddox refused to participate, he should bear the consequences. But, Pat mused, how easy such advice would be for him to give since he, himself, would not have to suffer the consequences of

Haddox's choices. In the end, Pat came to the view that Haddox should not be punished for upholding a personal moral code and following his conscience even if it was not in sync with the community's judgment. He told Haddox he'd try to help him.

Pat said he'd talk with Warden Tucker on behalf of the troubled corrections officer, a plan for which Haddox was grateful. When Pat and the warden met, the warden's initial reaction was negative. "All correctional officers know that sooner or later they could be called upon to participate in an execution. I picked people by random instead of seeking volunteers because I know some of these guards have no use for the condemned people and would actually savor the opportunity to be part of the team, the justice team, some call it. I know there is sadism among some of the guards, and I don't want to give vent to it. I try to curb it whenever it see it, such as more harshly punishing inmates in segregation than is necessary to control their behavior, or separating inmates during recreation who are doing nothing more threatening than talking with each other. That's one of the reasons we carefully screen applicants for guard positions. On the other hand, there may well be officers who have been selected who feel the same as Haddox and I can't open the door to selective refusals."

Pat had an idea. "What if you reconstitute the team, this time indicating that you are going to recast the net for team members while noting that if a selected guard strongly opposes the death penalty, you will excuse that person." The warden didn't immediately reject the notion.

"In that way," Pat continued, "you could exempt those who truly oppose execution while not limiting yourself only to those who volunteer." After giving it some thought, the warden agreed that Pat's idea could work.

"Sometimes you're a pain in the neck, Padre, but I don't know what I'd do without your settling influence around here."

Shortly after their conversation, a new death team was formed of randomly selected guards, with just a few opting out on the basis of their opposition to the death penalty.

When the execution day arrived, Pat was summoned to Small's cell, a different one now closer to the end of the corridor. Leroy's lawyer was there but left after reporting that he had just received word from the governor's office rejecting their petition for clemency. When Pat was alone with Small, he was struck by his calmness. Small indicated that his faith was strong, that redemption could now be his, that he had fully atoned for his sins and had come to Jesus with Pat's help. He then asked Pat for his final blessing, which Pat gave with solemnity and kindness.

Pat knew, but did not say, that a vast crowd of protesters had gathered outside, completely covering the road leading to the prison, and that for the most part they were standing in silence, many with lit candles. Pat knew, as well, that the planned execution had been the subject of more newspaper articles and local television news as the date approached but, as with the crowd outside, Pat chose not to discuss these developments with Small because, to him, they seemed like distractions, clutter for this man who had already accepted this end to his life.

About thirty minutes before the scheduled execution time, Warden Tucker visited Pat and Small in his cell. He indicated that he had not heard from the governor beyond the advisement Small's lawyer had received and he was not hopeful of any reprieve. Small just looked at him and shrugged. The warden then went over the procedures, telling Small what to expect in the short time to come, and he made sure Small had no questions for him. Shortly later, two other guards came to the cell and Pat was told it was time for him to leave. He and Small embraced, both in tears.

As he left, Pat spoke softly, "Leroy, you have walked a righteous path in these so many years; now is the time for the Good Lord to receive you into His hands. Goodbye, my friend,

God be with you." As he was exiting the cell, he heard Small softly say, "Don't worry about me, Padre. I'll be okay. I think I know where I'm going, a good place to be free, and I'll be looking for you by and by."

Escorted by the warden, Pat could only pray that Leroy was right as he walked to the end of the corridor and through the door leading to the place of death and viewing room. There, he found himself in a hushed group of people, including members of the print and electronic media. Representing the victims Richard Cox and Robert Tukey were grandson Michael Cox and nephew James Tukey. Crammed into the back of the room were four other men in suits. Pat assumed, without giving it much thought, they were from the defense or prosecution teams or maybe from both.

When Small was brought into the execution room by three guards, he was placed on a gurney and strapped down while the curtain to the viewing room was still closed. Once it was opened, revealing Small prone and tethered to the gurney, tears welled in Pat's eyes. How could this be happening in a civilized society where we pretend to value life? It was breathtaking to Pat to see the efficiency, the starkness of what was about to happen. In a moment, the warden read aloud the death warrant and then he asked Small if he would like to say any last words. "Yes, Warden," Small responded, eyes wide open, head turned toward the spectators, voice tremulous but loud with determination.

"First, I want to apologize to the families of the victims. I have no excuse for the evil I did and I don't dare ask your forgiveness because it is not mine to ask. That can only come from your hearts and from whatever faith you may hold. But I cannot tell you how many times over all these years I have mourned your losses and I have prayed—yes, I do pray—for you. In the decades of my incarceration, I think I have become a different person. I have studied, I have read, and I have prayed. I am prepared to meet my fate, whatever God has in store for me. I thank Father Pat, who has prayed with me and consoled me these past days. And finally, Warden Tucker and staff, I forgive you for your role in this killing. I accept this punishment but we know, all of us, that it is wrong." Now his voice quieted in resignation as his body continued to shake against the restraints. "My evil deeds do not excuse this like response from the State. Thank you and may God be with you."

Small then closed his eyes as the warden signaled for the death serum to begin flowing into Small's veins. First came a sedative and then a killing drug with the expectation that life would ebb from Small quickly. But it didn't. After the first injection, Small appeared to doze off. But then he seemed roused after the second fluid was injected and, to the horror of all the onlookers, he began to pant and to writhe in obvious pain, his body jerking in spasms against the restraining straps, not going quiet until nearly fifteen minutes had passed. The spectators watched in stunned silence, some stirring uncomfortably, a few gasping, as life was wrenched from Small's life until his last ragged breath brought stillness to him. Pat watched in tears, prayer, and anger. Leroy Small's death, the brave way he faced it, and his botched execution seared Pat. He knew that the scars from that night would forever mark him.

Immediately after the execution, Pat fled the room to join the crowd outside. There, he found his sister, Susan, in the parking lot standing near a television truck as she had told Pat beforehand where she'd likely be. He knew she'd be there on behalf of the *Gazette* and he had promised her that he would briefly describe Leroy Small's last moments. Pat was awestruck by the size of the crowd, many carrying placards, some simply saying "no death penalty," others "Pray for Leroy," and a few "Condemn the Governor." But many just stood there in silent vigil, a shared sorrow in a large throng.

When Pat reached Susan she pointed to a van toward the rear of the crowd. "It has some kind of amplifier on its roof, Pat, and earlier it was playing music, like hymns, and so many people were humming along. It was moving; unifying."

Pat looked in the direction of the van, and through the thinning crowd he saw Father Stan and a group of younger men standing around the van. "No surprise," said Pat. "That's Father Stan Mathews from the seminary, Susan, a dear man, a mentor to me. He told me he'd be here, but I didn't know about the music. It's like him, though, to think of something that might make this crowd more a congregation than just a throng of protestors. God love him."

Susan smiled, quick to her job now. "Will you take me to him, Pat? I'd like to get his perspective."

"Of course, but let me tell you something first. I think it's important and should be known. Small's words at the end were moving, almost heroic. You should ask the warden for a copy of the tape as I know it was recorded. For what reason, I can't say, but it should be heard beyond that room. His courage, his contrition, his humanity in the face of his impending death was stunning. I can't explain it any other way. People who care about the death penalty should hear these final words. In that way, they will have to own a share of what happened to Leroy Small tonight. And, Susan, the execution was botched. Leroy died in great pain. That's not supposed to happen, but it did. And, once the effects of whatever concoction of drugs they used took effect, there was nothing anybody could do but watch."

"Oh my goodness," Susan reacted. "I'd better get back to the newsroom to get this out for tomorrow's paper."

Standing next to Susan was a man she had been interviewing before Pat walked over to her. "Father Pat, this is James Tukey, the grandson of one of Small's victims. Mr. Tukey, this is my brother, Father Pat Keefe. He's the prison chaplain and was present at the execution. He said it was botched. Did you see that as well?"

The grandson's response was surprising.

"Yes, I saw the whole thing. I don't know what an execution is supposed to look like but this was pretty gruesome. Of course, I'm sure my grandfather's was too. I'm personally opposed to the death penalty and, in fact, I wrote to the governor seeking clemency for Small at least five times because I know my grandfather, as well, abhorred the death penalty. But, in the end, I felt I needed to honor my family. And now, with this botched execution, I hope there will be momentum to put a halt to it. Death by the State is simply vengeance. Maybe now, it will stop."

And it did. Once the media reported the details of Small's last moments, how his body seemed to be wracked with pain, a public outcry pushed the state legislature into passing a moratorium at least until a more reasonable method of execution could be found. The governor did not have the votes to veto the legislature act and so he stewed, his thirst for justice as he saw it stymied.

Two weekends later, Pat returned to Duncan's Cove for the weekend. On Saturday, he was recounting to Maggie the final events of Small's life. He spoke of the irony of his growing fondness for this man who had done such evil. He talked too about the loneliness of life on the death corridor and wondered aloud whether despair must be part of a sentence of death. To Pat's surprise, Maggie asked him whether there were books available to the men on death row.

"Why no," replied Pat, "at least I didn't see any in Leroy's cell and I have never heard they were circulated beyond the general population. What would make you ask that question?"

"Well, just thinking about all the time they have with nothing to do but stew and fret. Giving them something to get their mind off their coming doom would be merciful. Isn't that good enough reason to try to get something to them?"

Pat's response was strong. "That's such a kind idea, Maggie, thank you for your consideration. It shows a compassion for these men not shared by many, I'm afraid I'm not sure how to make that happen but it's worth trying to pursue."

"Well, I have a friend, Maryann Anderson, who's a part-time librarian in town. We see each other once in a while for a glass of wine after work. She's divorced, and we enjoy each other's company. She asks about you once in a while. Last month when I was talking with her about your work at the prison, she asked whether inmates were allowed books and I told her I didn't know. Maybe she'd have some ideas about getting reading materials to those poor wretches."

"Interesting idea, Maggie. I know books from the State library are circulated in the general population but I don't think the condemned men get any."

"Well, maybe I can talk with Maryann. Would you like to meet with her to talk about it?" asked Maggie with just a bit of coyness to her voice.

"For sure," said Pat. "Maybe next weekend after I have a chance to talk with the warden about the idea."

"Good. I'll call her and maybe we can meet for a glass of wine Saturday afternoon."

On his way back to prison the next day, Pat thought about the idea of books for the condemned. He was concerned that the warden might not see any point in making books available to men whose lives might shortly end. He had some apprehension, too, that the warden, even though kind in many respects, might not have any interest in spending funds to improve the quality of lives of men who had committed such wickedness that they had been banished from life. But the answer was right there when Maggie asked how long these men had been in solitary confinement pending their execution. The more he thought about it in the following days, the more sense Maggie's suggestion made. His desire to talk with the warden was now firmly set. On Thursday, Pat spoke with Warden Tucker when he raised the question. The warden scoffed, "Why bother?" There's no point to it since they're all going to die sooner or later."

"So are we," responded Pat.

The warden rejoined: "Yes, Pat, but you and I, unlike the condemned inmates, have not forfeited our lives by egregious criminal conduct. Anyway, why coddle these men who are the worst of the worst?"

"Warden, I think I've gotten to know you since I've been here. To me, on the exterior you are by the book. You run a safe and correct prison but underneath, I've seen your goodness. You were kind to Small in his last moments in the way you spoke to him and the way your men treated him under your supervision. And, you took a chance in acceding to the wish of Haddox to be excused from a duty he thought was immoral. Giving these condemned men an opportunity to read, to learn, even to *imagine*, as a good read can make you do, isn't going to negate their coming executions. Maybe, though, through the insights gained from reading good literature, some of these men might come to some understanding of their own responsibility for their own fates. I know some will have no interest, and so be it, but for the few, what's the harm?"

"Well, maybe, Padre, but who's going to monitor what we give these guys to read? There's a lot of violent, even salacious stuff out there. I can't have these guys stirred up over some ideas they get from a book."

"I'll see to that, Warden, and I'll show you the proposed book lists once my plan is in place."

"It's a definite maybe, then," said the warden as he got up to leave. "Got to go, Padre. I have another meeting."

Pat was elated. He thought it pretty likely that once he was able to show the warden that giving death inmates the opportunity to read would not pose a security risk, the question would just become a matter of finances and logistics. He then spoke by phone with Maggie who promised to set up the Saturday afternoon meeting with her friend, Maryann.

They met at the Claw, now a favorite haunt whenever Pat was in town. With a large window, a bar running the length of the room with small tables to the side, and nautical bric a brac adorning the walls, it was a hospitable place for its sea-loving customers. Pat and Maggie arrived first and ordered beers and shortly later an attractive woman Pat vaguely recognized walked up to the table and took a chair. "Hi, Maggie and Pat. Oops, sorry, Father Pat, I mean. Long time no see. I'm Maryann Anderson, Maggie's friend forever." The trim, sandy-haired, blue-eyed woman took a seat next to Maggie.

"Do I know you, Maryann?" asked Pat. "And please, call me Pat. I'm a priest, of course, but this is home."

"Well, Pat," Maryann began, "I sort of knew you when you were at Saint Mary's Prep and your sisters and I were at the girls' reformatory nearby," she laughed, "and once in a while I'd come over to hang around with Maggie, as we sort of ran together."

"Oh, you were like that," Pat smiled back. "Well, let's get you something to drink," as he beckoned to a member of the wait staff.

Maryann's face then turned serious. "I know what you've just been through, Pat. God bless you for your kindness to that man. I read Susan's article, and I've talked with Maggie, here, about your experience."

"Thanks, Maryann, but of course it's not about me. I just hope we've seen the last of the execution chamber in this state. It's so grizzly and unproductive of any social good."

"Amen to that, Pat. Let's talk about your book idea."

Once Pat outlined his idea, he asked Maryann if she thought the local library could help. "There are only a few men there, Maryann, so I don't think setting something up for a revolving library loan system would be too heavy a lift, and I think I can help out financially if that's needed."

"Oh, are we now paying priests enough money so they can throw it away on reading matter for convicts? I think we can handle the money part, Pat, as having a small-scale lending library is nothing new for us. We do it with the hospital and with two senior citizens homes in town. What kind of books do you have in mind, Pat? I can't imagine your readership isn't particularly well educated."

"No, that's right, at least for most of them who come from impoverished circumstances with little formal education. So books easy to read and of course no violence or anything else that could overheat these men."

Maryann was enthusiastic. She said she'd have to run it by the librarian but didn't think they'd be any problem.

Thus began the Lost Corridor inmate library exchange. On a monthly basis, Maryann had her library selected ten books, fiction and nonfiction, which she then got to Pat, who in turn saw that they were offered to the inmates once the selections had been vetted by the warden. They were a collection of the classics and a mixture of current writings, books of drama, adventure, and heroism. This new venture was welcomed by some of the death inmates and rejected with derision by others. No harm done, thought Pat, and perhaps, for a few, a new avenue to self-understanding and, at least, a more humane way to idle time away while awaiting the force of the State.

On weekends, when he was home, Pat often dropped by the library to check on the lending program with Suffolk, each time also looking forward to the prospect of seeing and chatting with Maggie's friend Maryann. Her attraction, he told himself, was based merely on their shared interest in the humane treatment of inmates at Suffolk. He was resolved to stay true to his course and, yet, on each opportunity, he relished the opportunity to see her.

XV

GROUP SESSIONS

In the course of dealing with the inmates, Pat had learned that several had been victims of child sexual abuse. Some of these men were in prison because they, in turn, had abused children once they had grown out of childhood. Other inmates had been abused but had never recovered from its effects, leading them into dysfunctional lives, including the criminal conduct that resulted in their incarceration. Having seen the traumatic effect of abuse on the youngsters he had counseled, and realizing, generally, that child abuse can make an enduring imprint on the lives of its victims, Pat suspected that some of the inmates at Suffolk were likely abused as children. What did such men have in common, he pondered, except that they were either victims or perpetrators of child sexual abuse, or both?

While Pat understood these commonalities, his greatest concern was for the men who had been abused as children. They would become his priority. Was there something he could do, some intervention, that might be helpful to these men so that they would be less likely to re-offend upon release and so that the victims, all of them, could find hope that their lives could become peaceful and worthwhile?

Pat decided he wanted to find a way to directly deal with adult victims of child abuse. He entered this intervention slowly and carefully. First, he met alone with individuals who had confided in him that they had been victims of sex abuse as children and whose criminal offenses did not involve child sexual abuse. He knew, intuitively, that mixing abusers with the abused could be non-productive, even explosive. For that reason he eliminated from consideration those men who had been abused as children who, in turn, had become abusers as adults. Perhaps, in some other way, he thought, these men could also be helped but later, once he had the experience of working with those who were abused as children and who had not later become abusers. When he spoke with Warden Tucker about the idea of group sessions for these men, the warden was weary of setting too many inmates together on such an explosive subject. But he trusted Pat's instincts. After talking it out, the two agreed that Pat would start with a small number of men and the sessions would take place in a setting readily accessible to correctional officers should there be any outbursts.

Gradually, Pat introduced the notion to inmates he had come to know and whom he thought could benefit from the experience of telling and hearing each other's stories. "Why the hell should I do that; what would I get out of it?" was the most common reaction, together with "Why would I tell anybody about that?"

In response, Pat shared his belief that simply talking about these events could be helpful even years after they occurred and that sharing their experiences with one another in a safe setting could help each man know that he is not alone. He also suggested that coming to understand the source of feelings of unworthiness, anger, and alienation could be useful to each man as he tried to forge his life ahead. As to confidentiality, Pat acknowledged the risk that each inmate's personal story could become known and that only by building trust would the group be protected. He promised that he'd go slowly in asking each participant to share. His assurances were not enough for some but a few men agreed.

Pat started with a group of five, a manageable number, he thought, and he was happy with its apparent racial and ethnic diversity. In selecting these men, Pat was sure not to choose anyone who had demonstrated racial or ethnic animus. He checked their files with the warden in this regard as he wanted a reasonable chance for success, unburdened with participants who had acted with bigotry while in prison or whose background revealed race or ethnic-based animus. That said, Pat knew, from his own training and work in the prison, that for many people, inmates or not, prejudice seethed just under the veneer of civility, and that he would have to be mindful of any undercurrents as he worked with the group.

At their first meeting, Pat started slowly by discussing his understanding of the aims of the group. He expressed to the men that they all needed to be safe, and he asked each in turn to affirm his commitment to the safety of all members in the group. He asked them too to agree that their meetings would be confidential. This went well. Pat's introduction was an effort to seed a sense of group and also to bring to mind the need for self-control and trust. He told them that they had been asked to join the group because he had learned from them that each had been the victim of sexual abuse as a child and he indicated that each person in the group had assented to Pat reporting that to the group.

Pat then discussed, generally, his understanding of what can happen to a child who has been abused, how the experience can make one insecure, feel a sense of guilt and unworthiness, and that as the person grows older how it can affect the ability to form relationships, to trust and be trusted. He discussed, as well, the havoc sexual abuse can cause to a person's sense of sexuality, the ability to form close relationships, and lastly, the turn to self-destructive behavior and harm to others that often occurs. All of these consequences, Pat stated, are shared, to some degree, by victims of childhood sexual abuse. As he said this he looked around and saw men quietly nodding.

Pat then appeared to change the subject. He asked each man, in turn, to say something about himself that others might not know.

"Why the fuck should I do that?" asked Hector Lopez followed by "Oops, my bad, Padre." The wiry, diminutive, heavily tattooed man then slunk down into his chair.

Pat just smiled. "No rules in here about language so long as you don't use it against each other or me. Otherwise, you're all forgiven for your language ahead of time. Please just talk as you normally do with each other when you're just hanging around. Don't worry about me." Smiles all around.

"Well," Lopez continued, "I was a damn good runner. Had the fastest time in the 440 in my school. Coach thought I had a real chance of doing something with it but then it all went to shit because of what my fuckin' older brother did after he moved in with us. He was a lot older, really, from some other man my ma had. After that, I just lost all interest, then got into some crack and it was all over from there."

Lopez was quickly followed by tall, blond-haired Albert Peters, also in his young twenties. "My stuff's not like that but maybe sort of. I liked to mess with drums, even took lessons and really liked just messing around, making up riffs. My teacher thought I was pretty good. Even had a set at home, but after my grandfather started in on me, it all went to shit. I never went back to the drums. Still kinda miss it but that's not my life now. Bangin' heads is more me now," he laughed.

And so the stories went around the room, each in turn talking about some lost opportunity or hope. How interesting and sad, thought Pat. He had only asked each to mention something that others would not know as an icebreaker, but every one of the men talked about a loss.

Pat then asked if any of the men wished to add any effects to abuse to those he mentioned at the start of the session or to comment on those he had recited. And then the flood gates opened wide. One after the other, the men began to talk, some with great emotion in words that would cause a church crowd to blush. Light-skinned Melvin Stevens had been quiet but now he raised his large frame up from a slouch. "It was my mother's boyfriend, that fucker Rashad." He nearly yelled. "When I was about ten, he stayed at our house a lot, sat around boozing and drugging. My mother left me and my little brother and sisters with him sometimes when she'd go out in the evening for who knows what. Doin' crack probably. That's when it started. First he was nice to me, buying me stuff like ice cream and letting me watch television even when the other kids had to go to bed. But then, he started sitting next to me while he was drinking stuff. He even offered me some. I never knew what it was but it tasted off, hard to swallow. A couple of hits one time too.

"One night, when we were sitting together, he put his arms around me. At first I liked it, but then he took my hand and put it on his dick. I didn't know it but I guess he had opened his fly and his dick was sticking out straight like he was hot. He told me to rub it hard and I did until he came all over the place. When he was done, he got some towels and then told me I better not tell anyone. It would be just our secret. And, he said he'd keep giving me stuff and letting me stay up, but I couldn't tell my ma or any of the other kids. This went on for a while, a bunch of months, I guess, but I got tired of it and didn't like him no more so I just started going to bed early or sneaking out. I never told my ma until much later when Rashad stopped coming around."

As Stevens was telling this story, he was looking all around the room but not making eye contact. Then he looked directly at Pat. "This was only the third time I've ever told this story, man, and when I first told my ma, she just told me not to say such things and sent me off to bed. That's why I never said it again until I wound up telling a probation officer, who got it out of me somehow."

Then Brad chimed in. "My shit's just like that except it was my freakin' uncle, if you can believe that. It was just like you, Melvin; after my dad took off, he moved in. He treated me real nice and then wham, he started in on me and then he made me promise not to tell my ma because, he said, she'd be mad at me. So, after it happened, I stayed up in my room.

Sometimes, I sat on my bed and cut my legs and arms with a scissors, but then a friend at school told me to try some drugs he had been using and, for me, it was great. I was hooked and happy until the first time I got caught."

And so it continued, one man after another as though a dam had just burst. Pat nodded as each man spoke, occasionally thanking the man for his courage. "That took a lot; thanks for sharing," or words to that effect. The outpouring was so great that the flow was difficult to control, but in this first session, Pat decided to let it play out in the time set by the warden for their meeting. At the end of this first session, he thanked the four who had spoken out and said that next time he'd make sure that Angel, who hadn't spoken, would have the chance to tell his story if he wanted to. Garcia, the youngest in the group at nineteen, just looked at him in silence, then said, "Maybe, Padre. We'll see." Although robust in appearance, to Pat, this man Garcia seemed worth worrying about. *He doesn't seem good,* Pat said to himself. *Worth keeping an eye on as the group moves along. I hope he comes next time.*

Before ending the meeting, Pat promised that once each had an opportunity to speak freely of his own experiences, Pat would attempt to provide some feedback, a structure to their conversation that hopefully could allow them to talk about constructive ways to deal with the abuse they had endured as children.

These sessions continued on a weekly basis with surprisingly good attendance and animated discussions. There were rough spots, to be sure, mostly men speaking over each other, showing a lack of restraint, but in the main, Pat was pleased with the respect the men seemed to show for each other. From these sessions, Pat saw patterns emerging. In each case, the speaker had first been abused when he was pre-adolescent; or nine or ten or eleven. In some cases the abuse continued into early teen years, while in others it was short-lived because the abuser was not a constant presence in the child's life. In every case, the abuser was a person of some actual or perceived authority, an untouchable whom the men, as boys, would never have dared to accuse. Three of the men had confided in their mothers but in each case the mother said she didn't believe it had happened, said the kid was lying. When this first came up, Pat asked the men how it made them feel to be called liars.

"Really shitty, man, that your own mom doesn't believe you. Knocked the hell out of me" was Brad's response, others nodding. In these instances, the speaker said his denial was too much to handle.

Angel, who spoke up at the third meeting and revealed that his abuser had been his mother's boyfriend, added: "That just kind of ended it for me. If my mom didn't believe me, who would? So, what the hell? No point in trusting anybody. I knew I was on my own."

The consequences to the victims were sadly alike—a sense of hopelessness and loneliness, dejection and alienation, followed by anger and acting out. In some cases, the men said, they began to cut themselves out of frustration and self-hate, and in others they acted out in violence, sometimes against siblings, or school or neighborhood kids occasionally bad enough to get them in trouble with the juvenile authorities. For all but one, their first encounter with the criminal justice system came after the abuse. "Not me," said Hector. "My older brother got me ripping things, first just for food, and then other stuff, and we shared, got closer, and that's when it began, but by then I already had a juvie probation officer." Another said, "How come, Hector, you didn't tell none of them people?"

Others laughed. Juan chimed in. "Are you kidding, man. What makes you think someone like that would believe you? Nah, you just keep it quiet, live it."

As these stories unfolded, the group participants were braced by their too common experiences cutting against racial, ethnic, and economic lines. A couple of men in the group had grown up in financial comfort—compared to the rest, who had been reared in deprivation.

The commonalities cutting across the differences of the men's backgrounds was striking and unifying for them. Each had been abused by an older male who was, in some manner, an authority figure, most often a family member or boyfriend of a mother. In nearly every case, the abuser had attempted to develop a relationship with the victim by ingratiating himself with favors or other desirables and then by sitting with them—watching TV, playing video games, or sharing some other activity. In his studies for his master's, later amplified by the mental health experts with whom he had dealings, Pat had learned that this phenomenon is known as "grooming"—the process of gaining a child's trust so that his guard is let down.

As the meetings continued and trust grew, Pat gently nudged the men to talk about how they thought being abused had affected their lives. How being abused as adolescents, particularly by adults whom they trusted, had stripped their confidence and weakened their ability to form close relationships. Now responding with more ease, even vigor in some, the men talked about how their experiences had brought despair and a sense of worthlessness to them, feelings that, in turn, contributed to their failures in school, their anger sometimes becoming rage, and their distancing from others ultimately leading to the criminal conduct that caused their incarceration. Common to this group was self-abusive behavior—physical or excessive drinking or drugging at an early age, developing habits that turned into physical and emotional dependence.

When starting this group, it had been Pat's notion that if these men could hear what they had in common, he could reaffirm to them that the root cause of their adult dysfunction was, maybe to a large part, the abuse that they had endured. He hoped that with this realization, just maybe the men could begin to free themselves of the chains that had hobbled their lives. And, he encouraged the men, where appropriate, to participate in the prison's alcoholics anonymous and narcotics anonymous programs in the prison.

The group work was not without surprises. At one session, they started to talk about the priests who had arrived at the prison and were now in segregation. Brad blurted out, "If I ever see one of those queers in here, I'll give him a good whacking."

Pat's response was quick and unusually direct.

"By queer, do you mean a man who is attracted to other men?"

"Yeah, like my uncle who did me," responded Brad.

"No," Pat responded with an uncommon edge to his voice that made all look up. "All the research shows that there is no connection between homosexuality and child abuse, no evidence that men who are attracted to other men are likely to assault children. On one hand, we're talking about a love relationship between two adults. But abusing kids is not about love. It's about craving power. Some male sexual abusers prey on little girls as well as on boys. That doesn't make them heterosexual abusers. It just means that they are indiscriminate in their choice of victims. You should never confuse the notion of being gay or lesbian with the abuse of children. No matter how you might feel about homosexuality, please don't equate it with child abuse. One thing has nothing to do with the other."

"So, you're saying that these priests are not queers, Padre?"

"Right, Marvin, at least in the way I think you mean it. These men are here for sexually assaulting kids. If they were just queer, as you say, that would be against their vows as priests, but that's no crime, Marvin, and it's nothing like abuse. Please be sure to know the difference because a lot of good people are homosexual. It's really nothing like the same thing."

"Man, how can you say that, you being a priest?" Brad spoke up. "Ain't that against the Church rules?

"Yes, it is," acknowledged Pat. "But those are rules created by the Church. Abusing kids, that's an evil that goes beyond any Church rule. Let's just say it's God's rule. Nobody can change that."

This exchange caused more discussion in the group, but, generally trusting Pat, the men seemed to back off conflating child abuse with sexual preference. At least they stopped talking about it in that way.

In this group work, Pat saw sparks of recognition and surges of energy that lifted his spirits. In spite of his impotence to deal directly with the victims of Luke's abuse, he saw that he could have a positive effect on the well-being of these wounded inmates.

Participation in these sessions was fluid, as some inmates were released from prison while others, knowing about the meetings, asked Pat if they could join. Pleased that others wanted to be part of the group but wary of its size, Pat was careful to keep its numbers down. And before each inmate was able to join the group, Pat conducted several one-on-one sessions to gain comfort that the inmate could handle feedback from others, could be nudged to share his own experiences, and could display emotion without totally losing control.

Several months after his group work had started, Pat was approached by Maurice Jones, an inmate he thought had left the group when he was discharged from Suffolk. "Yeah," Jones said, "I got out but didn't last long. I smoked some dope just a couple of days after my release and then blew a urine test, so here I am, back again for two more years." Pat expressed his sorrow to Jones that he had slipped and that he was back in prison. Still, he welcomed him back to the group because he cared for him and thought he could still gain some benefit from group sessions. To Pat, giving up on this man was not an option.

Not long after Jones's return, while Pat was with Maggie and Chris in Duncan's Cove, Susan, who was visiting for dinner, asked him if he had read about the police shootout over in Rochelle, in the western part of the state.

"No," said Pat. "What happened?"

"Well, I just heard the story in the newsroom last night. It seems that a guy was trying to rob a convenience store but the manager wouldn't have any of it. He said he thought the guy looked high on something and when he pointed to the back of the store, the guy looked away, giving the manager enough time to grab his pistol from the shelf below him and he just blasted the guy, shooting him five times, killing him on the spot."

"That's awful," Maggie chimed in. "Who was the guy?"

"Somebody named Angel Garcia," Susan responded. Pat's heart sank.

"What else did they say about him?" he asked.

"Nothing much except he had just been released from Suffolk a couple of weeks beforehand. Did you know him, Pat?"

"I'm afraid I might" was all Pat could say.

Hearing that name and worried it was the man from his group, Pat needed to excuse himself, to walk around for a bit to gain his balance. He dreaded learning that it was the man he thought had made such progress in group. He paced quickly to Sean's bench, where he sat in quiet grief as the fading sun darkened the harbor below.

On Monday morning, when Pat stopped to see the warden, he confirmed that it was, indeed, the Angel Garcia who had been in the first group with Pat.

"This is the second guy from my group, Warden, who hasn't made it on the outside. Fortunately, the first one, Maurice Jones, was just a relapse, but with Garcia, he lost his life. Was it drugs?"

"It appears from the medical examiner's report that drugs played a role, Father," the warden replied. "His opiate level was very high."

"Why do you think this is happening, Warden?" asked Pat.

The warden's answer was measured. "Well, first I should tell you the bad news. We have a lot of return guests here, Padre. Probably around twenty-five percent of the people we discharge are back here within a year or two. And that's pretty much the national average."

"That's terrible," Pat reacted, now gaining some traction. "Can't we do something about that?"

"Easier said than done, Padre. We dump people on the street after they finish their sentences, even if they're on parole or probation. And then the supervision of these people is pretty marginal. In most cases, they go from structure here back to wherever they came from with all the old temptations just reignited. It's no surprise. It's mostly the young ones, not the long-timers. They're usually the guys here for offenses related to drugs or break-ins, that sort of crime."

"Isn't there anything we can do about that, Warden?"

"It's all about money, Pat, and focus. Here, our priority is to keep people safe—inmates and the rest of us. We don't have any real budget for preparing people to leave, and we're not about to get any money for that sort of thing. This governor's not interested in the prison problem, or even in recidivism as such, only if it makes the community unsafe. He's big on keeping people here longer and sending them right back even for minor violations of their terms of release. He wants them off the streets so he can taut his record for law and order. That's the unvarnished truth of it, Pat."

"What's the solution?" repeated Pat.

"Not sure, Padre, as this problem vexes even the pros. I think we need much more money and programming to help prepare these people for life after prison, and then once they're out, we need to give them some structure, some guidance." Pat thanked the warden as he slowly left his office, his mind churning.

XVI

GRACE HALL

Later that day, while strolling through the recreational area, chatting amiably with inmates and looking warily at some knotted in their gangs, Pat was thinking about the two members of his group who had failed shortly after release from Suffolk, one dying for it. A thought came to him. "What if I could get a transition house going, a different kind, one where we could offer counseling and support, and maybe get some businesses in the community willing to give these people a chance to work? I need to talk with someone about this," he thought aloud, and he knew just the person.

A week later, Pat visited his friend, Father Jerome from St. Cecelia's in Kingston, his second parish assignment. "Hey, Pat, long time no see" was Jerome's greeting, along with a hearty embrace from the even larger black man than Pat recalled as he opened the rectory door to Pat.

"Jerome, you look as good as you can get and maybe even a little more of you now," Pat joked back.

"Come on in, Pat. I'm sure you didn't drive to beautiful Kingston just to see my ugly face and my giant-sized physique. What brings you here?"

Now comfortable in a sitting room and after a little banter about music and sports, Pat asked Jerome how the interfaith effort was going in town. He was happy to hear that the group's work was alive and growing.

"We now have a housing program for families in need. We have convinced the town leadership to let us rehab a couple of old buildings, which we have turned into apartments. The town's been great and the group's congregations have been marvelous. We've been able to raise the needed funds and get a lot of donated labor from skilled volunteers. And, we have a great afterschool program going at two places, here and at St. David's, where kids from anywhere can come. We have volunteers who tutor them and also a sports program to keep the kids active. Lots of support here for what we're doing. You sound like you have something in mind, Pat. Can I help?"

"Yes, I hope so. In my work at the prison, I have learned a lot, with more to come, for sure, and I have seen goodness as well as evil. Most of these men live in despair, Jerome, just trying to get by, keeping their heads down to avoid trouble, looking forward to the day they will be free. But here's the problem. So many of them, when they are released, wind up back at Suffolk again within a year. The warden told me about twenty-five percent of the men don't make it; they come back."

"Why is that, Pat? Those are terrible numbers."

"Yes," frowned Pat, "I'm no expert, but from what I've read and learned firsthand from some of the men, their failures have many roots but there are also some factors that keep reappearing."

"Like what, and what can we do about that?" Jerome said with obvious interest, as Pat had hoped would be his reaction.

"Well, the common factors seem to be a lack of family and community support, no housing or jobs, and no caring attention or guidance to help them move forward and out of the ruts of their too familiar pasts. And, a big factor is the continuing pull of substance abuse."

"But don't they all have probation or parole officers?"

"Yes, but these people are overwhelmed with caseloads. So all they can really do is meet when the men are required to report, do urines to make sure they're not using, and if they are, and if it's not a repeat problem, to urge them to attend Narcotics Anonymous or some other form of counseling. But they don't have the manpower to do real follow-up, and these guys need much more. They need close, caring eyes, mentors, and door openers to give them some hope, a pathway ahead, to mitigate the risk that they'll just regress into their old ways."

"Okay, I get it, but why are you talking with me about this? I don't really know anything about prison, parole, or probation other than what I read in the paper or see on television. Or maybe happened to some kids when I was young. But I didn't know anything then other than that I had to get out."

"Fair enough, but I think you know more than you realize, even just by intuition as well as your insights about community life in general. When you and I were here, together, Jerome, we talked some about social ills, about community life. Ever since I've known you I've thought you had great social instincts. You certainly taught me a lot. I have a vision I'd like to share with you if that's okay."

"Shoot," said Jerome with a smile.

"Thanks, my pal. Here's what I'm thinking. I see a large building that houses maybe twelve to fifteen men; it has a couple of offices and a meeting room, a rec room, and all the other spaces that any residence has. There's a person living there who is similar to a college resident assistant, but with a more supervisory role, like a director. I see a counselor who comes to the home to meet with the men, to refer them to the particular assistance they need. The house director goes to businesses to find placement for these men and reaches out to the families of these guys to help reconnect them, carefully of course, if that's possible. Getting back into their kids' lives, acting as a parent, eventually taking some responsibility could be key to the stability of some of these men in the long run."

"Nice ideas, Pat, sort of utopian. How's anything like that going to happen? Are you thinking of leaving the prison, leaving us to take on this new thing? Are you the director you're describing?" Jerome asked, now with a tinge of trepidation in his voice.

"No, my friend, although I've had my moments of doubt about my vocation. I suppose many of us do. But I'm not ready to pack it in. I just think of this as an extension of what I've been trying to do as the prison chaplain. Not a sea change for me personally. At least I don't think so."

"Well, that's a relief, Pat. We can't afford to lose good priests, particularly with what's going on with these pedophiles. I was real proud to read about what you did for those kids. So, back to my question, what does this vision of yours have to do with me?"

"Well, Jerome, maybe it's too big a step, but I was thinking that's where your interfaith group might be able to play a leading role. I'm hoping to tap into the energy and strength of those good people you have gathered to uplift this community, now in an added way. These folks, with your leadership, have shown they know how to get things done."

"Okay, Pat, but here's the hard question. Why should they do this, or more crassly, why should they want to house a bunch of felons in this city that they are trying to rise up?"

"Fair question, Jerome, one I've thought about. As people of God, all of your leaders share a love of man and aspire to guide the fallen into more perfect lives."

"Nice rhetoric, Pat, but these people are pragmatists too."

"Yes, of course, and I apologize for the high horse. The reality is that people are returned to prison because they commit crimes that get them put back there. Drug selling, house burglaries, store robberies, and the list goes on. If we can help in redirecting some of these people onto better paths, a few at a time, then our homes, our convenience stores, our streets, will be safer places for us. That's the reason to get into this fight, Jerome, to provide a safer lane for these newly released men to travel and, in turn, a way to steer them away from the criminality that affects all of us.

"Okay," responded Jerome as he sat back, his voice now showing more energy, less doubt. "What's your plan?"

"Well, I'm hoping for your help in developing the details, but, in general, I propose another lunch meeting at St. Cecelia's and the same cast of characters. If he's willing, I'd bring along Warden Tucker from Suffolk as he's so much more knowledgeable about the problem of recidivism and its causes. My intent would be to present the concept I just laid out for you: a house for recently released inmates, a place of caring and correction, with a program of counseling, family reunification, job assistance, all geared to help these men make a successful transition into being viable and productive members of our communities, not necessarily Kingston in the long term, but wherever they may ultimately go.

"I see an intense period of residential adjustment, maybe around six months; I'm not sure as I don't know enough to fix a time period, but not a long stay, as we want to filter men through this program so we can help more than just a few, but a long-term project for sure. Generally, that's the vision I'd like to share with the group, and then, of course, I intend to seek their responses and, ultimately, their willingness to take the leadership in making this happen. What do you think, Jerome?"

Jerome smiled. "You knew you'd get me, Pat. Of course this is a great idea, and I'm happy to help bring it to the group. Let's pick a date."

And so they did, a Wednesday a month ahead to give Jerome time to contact the interfaith board members and for Pat to hone his plans. Once back at Suffolk, Pat went directly to the warden's office where he outlined his idea and he requested that the warden accompany him to the Interfaith meeting.

"But what's my role, Padre? I was raised Catholic but don't go to church anymore. Do you think I really belong in a room with a bunch of priests and ministers?"

"And a rabbi and an imam, to boot," smiled Pat. "Warden, there's no admissions test; no one's going to question your own religious beliefs, I can assure you of that, although I can't promise that I won't take a run at you someday," Pat responded in obvious jest.

"I'd like you to attend because you're a pro on the subject of what happens to these men when they're released and the sort of behavior that sends them back here. My goal is not for you to give a dissertation on the causes of recidivism, but I'm hoping you will just speak from your experience about these men, what you know about their lives and what you think, from what you've seen, they need to help them succeed once out of here."

"Okay, Pat, I think I can do that."

"We'll talk more, Warden, but for now, thank you, and please mark your calendar for the first Wednesday of next month. I'll drive."

Pat could think about little more as he kept mulling over the best approach to the interfaith board while also fine-tuning his ideas for a house. He decided it should be named "Angel's Place" in remembrance of the man killed in the convenience store robbery and, perhaps a grim warning as well to the home's residents of the possible consequences of failure in their new challenge. He was a little worried about the play on words, but naming need not be etched just yet, he realized.

Two weekends later, Pat returned to Duncan's Cove for a family get-together, this time at Susan and Joe's recently purchased home in a newer part of town: a simple ranch with an attractive front yard and gated backyard, perfect for their frisky Irish setter and, perhaps, a hint of a child's play yard to come. Maggie was there as well as Chris; so were Ruth and Beth, who had become a steady presence. As far as Pat could see, Ruth and Beth were now an accepted duo in family gatherings. While Pat hadn't sorted out his feelings about homosexuality, he was happy for Ruth and, in a way, proud that others were not outwardly judgmental about her choice of a love partner, showing, instead, an open acceptance.

Pat thought this was perhaps a family trait derived from their Deluca grandparents. He remembered their restaurant had seemed to attract characters from across the spectrum in appearance and mannerisms, making the place one of convivial hospitality for all comers. And Beth was not a shy member of the circle. Rather, she let her beliefs and feelings be known, sometimes clashing with Susan, who, once in a while, wrote an opinion piece in the *Gazette* reflecting her moderate thinking on political and social issues, certainly more in the center than Beth, who was a firebrand for her ideas. Chris was there as well, now solidly into his teenage years, a mostly joyful handful for Maggie as she tried to help him wend his way to manhood without Sean.

Susan and Tom had recently purchased a turkey smoker, which they had decided to try on their family, a brave and successful experiment enjoyed by all except for Ruth and Beth, who announced they had become vegans. They brought a huge veggie dish, enough for all, and to complement the largest turkey Tom could fit into his new toy.

Once at dinner, seated at a large, makeshift table, Chris, as the youngest, said grace at the urging and sometimes cajoling of his elders. Tom turned to Pat. "What's the mood at the prison now, Pat, after the botched execution?"

Pat responded, "Well, I'd say we're back to the normal miasma of anger, fear, dread, and depression, but other than that, things are great at Suffolk." Following the expected guffaws, Pat interjected, "But since you've given me the floor, I do have a notion I want to run by everybody as I'd like your reactions and also any thoughts you may have to improve on the idea."

"Go for it, Uncle Pat," Chris chimed. "You're always into something newsworthy. What's your newest?" Pat wasn't sure whether Chris's comment reflected cynicism, but he decided to ignore it for the moment and to dive in.

"Well, since being at Suffolk, I have become concerned about the number of inmates who are sent back to prison not long after they've been released. When I talked with the warden about it, he said it's a national problem and their statistics were about the norm. Around one in four inmates is back within just a year or so, and they're mostly the young men, the nonviolent offenders, whose crimes often stem from substance abuse. So, I'm thinking about trying to start a halfway house for recently released men but a different kind of one."

"In what way?" asked Ruth, clearly interested. "Are you quitting the prison, the priesthood?"

"No to both," Pat was quick to say. "My thought is that the plan should not take me away from my prison work, at least I don't think so. Let me explain. The residential living situation I envision would be for recently released inmates, a place to live together with a house director, and the assistance of a counselor who would be there either daily or several days a week, with an outreach effort to find places where these men could work. I envision also a program to reunite them with their families, particularly their children, in a protective setting where the bonds of kinship could hopefully be retied."

"What a marvelous idea," exclaimed Ruth, "but is it practical? Sounds like it could cost a lot of money, and what's going to be your role in this?"

"Well," responded Pat, "at this stage it's just an idea I've shared with a priest friend with whom I served at St. Cecelia's in Kingston, but he likes it and wants to help. You may remember I told some of you when I was there that Father Jerome and I started an interfaith community board to help with housing and daycare, a group led by minsters from several denominations and a rabbi and imam. When I met with Father Jerome just a few weeks ago, he told me the group was alive and well. I ran this idea by him as a new project for the group and he was all for it. So we have a meeting set for a week from Wednesday where I want to lay out a plan. What do you think?"

Several around the table answered together, "Where will the house be?" "Won't the neighbors mind?" "Where will you get the money to pay for the building and the program?" And, "What makes you think this can succeed when normal probation and parole officers can't keep these people in line?"

"Important questions, all," Pat quickly acknowledged, "but I think it's worth a try, and I'm willing to invest my efforts even to make a dent. If you could see the men who have been returned after unsuccessful releases, the desperation and despair in their faces and mannerisms, and if you knew of the harm caused by the criminal conduct of some of them who don't make it on the streets, I think you might think it's worth trying something different."

Then, nods all around. Susan offered, "Pat, once you're up and going, maybe I could interview some people, talk to some of the interfaith board members, help frame the program in a light that might take some of the edge off people's fears and natural resistance to the idea of having felons in their community."

"Great idea," Pat responded. "And thank you. But for now, can we just leave it at this table, as I don't want to get people's concerns up before we have a chance to develop our plans in a more concrete way?"

"You got it, Pat," quickly answered a smiling Susan.

"When I go to St. Cecilia's to meet with the interfaith group, I want to have a plan for how to make this happen. How about we go around the table and you give me your ideas in just a word or two and I'm going to take notes? That would be a big help as I prepare." And so they did, one by one, throwing out the possible steps, and from those together with the ideas he had already considered, Pat was able to put together an outline for his presentation to the interfaith group. "What a family," Pat later mused with satisfaction.

The interfaith group meeting went well. When Pat and Warden Tucker arrived, they were warmly greeted by the clergy who were milling about the large dining table in the priests' formal dining room.

"What have I gotten myself into?" mused Tucker to himself. "I haven't been in the same room with so many religious people since the public hearings on the botched execution." But as he surveyed the room, he sensed warmth, openness, perhaps a little scrutiny from a few, but if there was any antipathy toward him, it was well veiled. For Pat, the meeting was a sort of homecoming, a reunion with the founders of the interfaith group, all the same faces except one, Pastor Vicky Reed, who introduced herself as the minister of the First Congregational Church in Kingston.

What a collection of God's messengers, Pat thought to himself, *each praying in his and her own way but united in love for God and service to community. Surely Jesus is in the room,* Pat ruminated, and not just in the presence of his friend Jerome, in the spirit of all these good people. *Oh, the heresy,* Pat chucked to himself with a sense of contentment that surprised him.

"Brothers and sisters," Jerome started, "please serve yourselves from the sideboard where I hope we have put some food out for each of your tastes, and once you're back at the table, we can begin talking as soon as we have grace. Rabbi Shuman, would you do the honors for us?"

Oh my, thought Pat. *Jerome really has gotten into the ecumenical spirit. Well, good for him."*

Rabbi Shuman rose and, looking at the ensemble, said, with a twinkle, "Well, I usually do this after breaking bread, but I'm happy to do my part." That said, the rabbi intoned, in a deep basso voice and in Hebrew, words he then repeated in English: "Blessed are You, Lord our God, King of the Universe, by Whose word all things came to be," after which there were several "Amens" heard around the table. As the group took seats, Jerome pointed out the baklava on the side table, remarking, "Thank you, Iman Ihbram, for the generosity of your house."

"My pleasure," responded the Iman. "It's a gift from my wife, Abeer, who loves to bake and told me I couldn't go without bringing something, as to do elsewise might reveal my bad upbringing."

"I think your wife must be Jewish," the rabbi quipped with a twinkle to the smiles of all, and then Father Jerome spoke again.

"And please notice the Irish soda bread brought by Father Stevenson from St. David's Episcopal. I'm sure it will be good even if it's an Ulster recipe."

"Oh, I don't know," rejoined Pat. "I'll eat it anyway since my good father, bless his soul, is not around to chide me for consorting with the likes of the orange."

"And finally, as to gifts," Jerome chimed, "look at the wonderful fruit basket that arrived today in Rabbi Shuman's arms: pears, apples, figs, and dates; how gracious of all of you to complement our table."

And with that, the room turned to Jerome, who began to speak.

"Brothers and sister, as you will remember, our friend Father Pat was assigned here at St. Cecelia's for a few years before he continued his education to obtain a master's in social work, and then he became the full-time chaplain at the Suffolk Penitentiary. He is here today with Warden Tucker with an idea for which he seeks our help. There are no strings attached to partaking in our meager meal, my friends, just that you give him a good ear."

Taking his cue, Pat stood, thanked all for coming, and then launched into the reason for his presence.

He started, "My plan concerns the issue of recidivism, the phenomenon of inmates who are released from prison who then re-offend, often not long after being in the community, and wind up back in prison, their lives in tatters and, of course, with additions to their trail of victims. I'd like to find a way to block this revolving door, a few men at a time, with an innovative program that would include safe housing, mentoring, counseling, job opportunities, and, when possible, family reunions. Before I get into details, however, I'd like to ask Warden Tucker to speak for a few moments about the scope of the problem."

The warden rose. "Please feel free to speak from your chair, Warden," Jerome said. "Only the rabbi gets to stand when he invokes God's blessings on us!"

Oh my gracious, thought Pat, as others chuckled. *Jerome really has this down.*

The warden began, "In his time with us, Father Keefe has truly been a godsend to the entire prison community—the inmates, staff, and to me as well, not that there's any hope for me," the warden chuckled. "He has been a comfort to the men in their despair, a peacemaker in a place where confrontation is the norm. Padre Pat, as he is known, has consoled so many who feel lost in this place and, no doubt, within themselves. He has also suffered for his caring, as some of you may know. So, I guess the bottom line is that he's become an important part of what we do, a trusted member of our team, and an inspiration. When he came to me with this idea and asked me to accompany him today, I was happy to do so, even putting aside my trepidation of being around so many wiser spirits." Guffaws were heard all around.

"And," the warden added, this time with a more serious mien, "an inkling that this project could someday take him away from us."

Tucker continued, "Father Pat is right about recidivism. It's a terrible problem, not just for the men but, more importantly in my opinion, to the communities where they go and commit more crimes, which get them locked up again. Let me tell you something about these men. Typically, they are young, nonviolent offenders. The great majority of them came to us with some level of substance abuse, if not outright addiction. For the most part the long-termers, including some of the killers, kidnappers, and rapists, are less of a threat to come back when they are eventually released. That's probably because they're so much older when they finally finish their long sentences. In my world, we refer to that as aging out of crime. Of course, there are exceptions, as we all know from reports of serial rapists and child predators, some of whom go right back at it, the pathologically ill and demented, but I'm talking more generally about the typical returnee. Young and nonviolent. Substance abuser. Poorly educated and from dysfunctional families. That's the general profile." With that, the warden turned back to Pat.

"Let me speak from the heart," Pat began. "At the prison, I run a group counseling session for men who, as children, were sexually abused. The long-term impact of child sexual abuse is something I care deeply about, because so many of these victims' lives are horribly altered by the experience of having been abused as youngsters. In my group, which always averages about five or so men, we have no adult predators. Their only common trait is that they were victims as children, but what got them into prison varies. A lot of drug-related offenses, selling for sure, but burglaries and larcenies as well as some more violent crimes.

"In the short time I have led this group, we've lost two members, one to recidivism and the other was killed. The first man was released on parole but was back in prison within weeks because he was caught in a drug raid. So now he has to complete the portion of his sentence that had been suspended. The second man, also released on parole, was shot by a store owner he was trying to rob to get money in order to buy drugs. At least that's what his girlfriend said when the police later talked with her. She said that when he was released from prison, he tried to stay straight, even went to Narcotics Anonymous a few times, but when he couldn't get a job, he just grew despondent and, soon enough, he went back to drugs."

"These sad stories," Pat related, "they caused me to talk with the warden about what kind of aftercare is available to men who are released from prison, and what the warden told me did not paint a pretty picture. While Warden Tucker here was sympathetic, you can gather that from his presence with us today, he acknowledged that the corrections department has no real program for transition back to the street because the department's budget is consumed in providing safety and security for the inmates and officers who guard them. And, when I spoke with probation and parole, I learned they are so swamped; they can't do any more than routine visits and substance abuse checks."

"So let me get to the point," Pat continued. "I propose that the Interfaith Group sponsor a transition house for men who have been discharged from Suffolk. If you are willing to consider the idea, we'd have to find a suitable building, maybe an old mansion in disrepair or an unused factory building, nothing new. If each of you thinks about your own flock, maybe you'll think of a person who has or knows of someone with a building they'd like to donate and perhaps get a tax break instead of just holding on to a hulk they have no interest in keeping.

"Once we find a building, we'd then need different kinds of help. We'd need a lawyer to search the title, to find out about zoning, and see what licensing will be needed to overhaul a building into a residence. We'll need someone, maybe a few people, to develop a plan for community relations. Lots of people, particularly if the building is near other people's homes, will be resistant to the idea of a group of felons living nearby. Developing this plan will take strategies, insights from people who know how to marshal community support. Once we have a building in mind, we then have to create a fundraising plan, assign tasks, develop a building and social program budget. Lots of work here but I believe it's doable if you think it's worthwhile and within your mission."

Quiet now around the room. "What I have in mind," Pat resumed, "is not simply a transition home. That's been done with some short-term successes. What I want to try to do is to create an opportunity for these men to re-integrate into their communities with hope and prospects for solid citizenship. That means we'll have to offer individual and group counseling to include substance abuse issues, interview training for jobs, all of that, and we'll have to make contacts with future employers. And a big part of this, I want us to find a way to help reunite these men with their families. Many have kids they hardly know and don't support. That's no good for anybody. If they can work, they can support. And if they can find a productive way to be involved in their kids' lives, that's a plus all around.

"This is a big, ambitious undertaking I'm suggesting, and I come to you with the knowledge that you're already doing so much for this community. I hope you don't find my suggestion to be brazen or presumptuous. And, thanks for listening."

For a few minutes, the room was quiet. Deep breaths could be heard but no voices until Father Stevenson from St. David's Episcopal spoke out. "This will be the most difficult challenge we've faced, but I, for one, think it's extremely worthwhile, particularly if we can develop a program that might be cloned elsewhere," he said. "What we do here, if we succeed, could have a ripple effect. From what Father Pat and the warden have said, we have a big problem here that affects our communities and also, by the way, the families of these men. If there's some way we can help to encourage their productivity and to safely reunite them with their children then we will be indirectly helping to save the next generation from errant pathways. I'm in."

"Amen," intoned Pastor Stevens from Faith Tabernacle.

"That's twice now," cracked the rabbi in response, then more cautiously: "I think this might be something my congregation could be interested in supporting. I'm not sure."

Jerome interjected. "Perhaps the best way is to go around the table with any questions and comments and then see if we have a consensus one way or another. And, of course, no final decisions have to be made today as I bet we can get Father Pat back here. But, if you have questions for the warden, maybe now would be the good time to ask."

"That's fine," said the warden. "But if you need me back, say for a community meeting or to talk with the town's governance, I'm happy to do so. As you might have guessed, I'm a fan of Father Pat, even if the birth of this program may someday take him from us."

With that, the meeting broke up. Pat had little chance to get caught up with Jerome, but as they parted, they agreed to be in touch by phone. And, sure enough, in about a month's time, Jerome called.

"I have good news, Pat. A couple weeks after the meeting, I started hearing from the others. I'm so happy to tell you that everyone thinks it's a great idea: a must, actually. For my part, I spoke with the rector, Monsignor Cunningham, who's fine with it. He's close to retirement and just doesn't want us to bring any bad attention to the parish, but I've assured him it would only be for the good. With his blessing, I spoke with the parish council and they're all in. Others have said the same. Those who had to go to their congregation's leadership have done so and the response is universally positive."

"Any catches?" asked Pat.

"Actually, Pat, only one. Nobody wants any sexual predators involved. No rapists; no child molesters. Other than that I haven't heard of any other bars to going ahead."

"That's great," Pat responded. "I have been thinking about the sexual offenders, and while I would like to see some program to rehabilitate those men, I agree that trying to fit them into the program I envision could bring the whole thing down. I can live with that restriction. In fact, I agree with it, sadly. So what's next?"

"Well, Pat, I have one more piece of really great news. Pastor Reed of the Congregational Church called and told me that one of her parishioners, no name given, but someone she talked with about this project, told her he has an office building he's trying to unload. Apparently, it's in a business part of town. He said that when he built the building on spec about twenty years ago, he had a firm under contract to lease it but at the last minute they backed out and then filed for bankruptcy. And, he said, although he's had parts of the building rented from time to time, managing it has become a chore as he ages. He said he thought that he might be willing to give us the building, as is, if his accountant tells him he could get a decent tax break for making it a donation. I'm waiting to hear back from him."

"That sounds promising, Jerome. What do you know about the building?" "Well, after the pastor told me about it, she and I and the potential donor drove to it and I was surprised by how good it looks. Of course, it's an office building, two stories, around 30,000 feet, I think. On each floor there are several offices, and then a larger area with work stations scattered about, a lunch room, and a few other rooms for, I guess, mail and copying and the like. There's an elevator that still works."

"Too good to be true, Jerome," exclaimed Pat.

"Maybe so, Pat. God is good. Let's see what happens before we get too excited."

In another two months' time, Jerome called Pat again to say that they should have another meeting of the group because the building deal was looking positive. And in short order, the group reconvened. This time, promise was in the air. "We have a building," Pastor Reed announced. "It's in a good location and can be ours whenever we can close."

"How exciting," Rabbi Shuman responded, "but aren't we getting ahead of ourselves? Don't we need more planning before we own a building?"

"For sure," Pastor Stevens chimed in. "Is there any pressure to get this building right away?"

"No," responded Pastor Reed, "but I think we should be willing to indicate to the donor that we're very interested and think we could close before the end of the year as he's looking to capture the tax benefits in this calendar year."

"Fair enough," said the imam. "Let's talk about what we need to do to make this happen."

Pat was ready with a list he handed out. It was well organized and covered, in detail, with a timeline for renovating the building and obtaining the necessary permitting. Pat's list also included a piece on public relations, reflecting the need to assure the community on any safety issues, although, in that regard, he noted that risk might be minimized because the building was in a business district with few apartment buildings or homes within walking distance.

After some discussion, it was agreed that the chairperson of the Interfaith Group, Pastor Mary Hall, would write a letter to the potential donor signaling the interest of the group in taking title to the building. All other tasks were then divvied up so that by the late afternoon after a three-hour meeting, a plan was in place to proceed. Pat left that day tired and exhilarated, two senses he didn't know he could simultaneously experience.

XVII

PLANS AFOOT

While Pat was energized with the exciting prospects in Kingston, his work continued at the prison, meeting with inmates to discuss their issues or hear their confessions, mingling with them for easy rapport, and, of course, an occasional game of chess. In time, he had become more adept, but he knew he was a long way from being a master.

Pat and Jerome spoke on a weekly basis. Plans for the transition house were moving apace, Jerome reported. Once, after Jerome's description of the house was finished, he asked Pat, "Does that interest you, Pat, the idea of being the director, living in this house? Could I be witnessing your defection into lay life?"

Although Jerome was chuckling when he asked this question, Pat sensed a hint of concern in it.

"No, Jerome. Didn't you ask me this once before?"

"Just checking, Pat. I know dealing with all that clergy abuse and then being part of the execution had to be impossibly hard" was all Jerome said, and then the call ended.

Pat wondered, *Was Jerome sensing something in him that he didn't recognize?* No, he decided. Jerome's just leaping to conclusions.

In several more weeks, Jerome was able to report that the group's fundraising committee had reached out to the congregations represented by the clerics on the board and that the board had been successful in procuring a grant from the Community Foundation. Jerome reported as well that an article in the *Gazette* by Susan had raised the profile of the project in the community in mostly positive ways. Pat had seen the article and was grateful that Susan had focused on the promise that an integrative approach to the men's rehabilitation would benefit the community. Jerome said as well that concerns from some members of the community had been quelled by a couple of public meetings led by members of the board. All in all, Jerome reported, the project was well underway with physical renovations scheduled to begin once all the permits were in place.

All that was now needed, according to Jerome, was program content, connections to potential employers, finding a suitable counselor for the house, and, most of all, selecting a director. This news elated Pat as he continued his prison ministry, occasionally visiting the building site to see for himself the physical manifestation of his idea.

XVIII

A SAD ENDING

Pat was floored one day when Luke sent a message through a guard that he'd like to speak with him. Pat knew that Luke was being housed in the segregated part of the prison as were the other convict priests. In Suffolk, Pat had learned that child molesters were viewed as the worst of the worst by the rest of the prison population and, accordingly, they were constantly at risk of being attacked, if not killed. With some apprehension, Pat agreed to a meeting. Once there, Pat was surprised at Luke's disheveled appearance and ragged demeanor.

"This place is like a dungeon, Pat. Do something to get me out of here. I know you have clout with the warden" were the first words from Luke. No greeting, no thank you for the visit. "The guards in here are bums, treat me like dirt," he complained. Contrary to his normal instincts, Pat did not feel sympathy for Luke.

"I'm sorry for your circumstances, Luke, in spite of what you did to put yourself here, but I don't think it helps for you to try to blame others or to complain. Maybe this is a time for introspection" was all Pat could say.

Luke's response was as cold as Pat was feeling. "I didn't ask you here to lecture me, Pat. I don't need that from you."

Pat's compassion for Luke was tested by his surly and unrepentant demeanor.

"I don't think feeling sorry for yourself is going to make you any more comfortable, Luke. Please tell me why you asked to see me."

Pat wasn't ready for his response. "I hear you're conducting group sessions for abuse survivors. That's something I'd like to do, Pat. Do you think I could get into the group?" Pat's instinctive reaction was negative.

"Why should I permit you to join this group of victims when you are an abuser, a person who wreaked the kind of havoc on kids that so clearly played a role in the dysfunctional lives these men led as they turned into adults?"

"Because," replied Luke, "I too am a victim of child sexual abuse." This declaration disarmed and quieted Pat.

"Look," said Luke, "I have been defrocked and excommunicated from the Church. I have nothing to live with except my guilt. And, I now realize that it wasn't you who got me arrested. In fact, I got a letter from the father of one of the kids; it was a hateful letter, full of anger, but I learned, at least, the complaint didn't come from you. This guy said he had gone to the police and was happy I'm here, and that all those other kids had come out of the woodwork once I had been arrested. So, Pat, you're off the hook with me."

Pat was unmoved. "Luke, thanks for nothing. I guess you must feel bad too about paying that man to assault me. Or do you want me just to forget about that since you've now come to your senses and realized I had nothing to do with your being here?" Pat was surprised at the anger in his voice and decided he should curb himself. No point in getting frustrated by this guy all over again, he mused to himself.

Luke went on, "Plus, I think if I could be part of this group and apologize for what I have done—maybe that would be useful to the other men." Pat was taken aback by Luke's hubris, but rather than cause an eruption, he tersely said that he'd discuss it with the men in the group. As victims, the shared experiences of the men in the group had created a bond and given them a common enemy. Luke, if he was telling the truth, was both victim and abuser, a phenomenon that Pat knew from his studies was not uncommon, as disheartening as it was. Research into this subject was incomplete but there seemed to be a suggestion that in some twisted way the adult abuser was acting out his anger by taking it out on children. Pat told Luke that he'd get back to him.

Luke replied "fine" and said he was tired and wanted to sleep. Pat left, a feeling of emptiness heavy on him.

At their next session, Pat broached the subject with the group. He told them that another inmate, a man who had been convicted of molesting young boys but who claimed to have been abused himself as a kid, wanted to join the group. Pat said he had his own opinion but wanted the men to have a chance to decide. Their reactions were swift and insistent. "No," they adamantly responded in chorus. Brad added, "Why the hell would we want to sit around with a guy who did to kids the same crap that screwed up our own lives? The guy you're talking about is a fucking perv—sorry for talking like that, Padre, sometimes I forget. This guy probably just wants to get out of seg once in a while because he's bored." Looking at the others, Pat saw passion in their agreement.

"Okay, okay, I thought so," Pat quickly came back. "It's your decision, one I expected and, frankly, my own view as well, but I wanted you to have the chance to make the decision because this is your group. I'm just here to help the conversation along." Pat was braced by the vehemence of the group's reaction, but he respected it. For him, it was, in part, an intellectual exercise as to whether someone who was both victim and perpetrator could sit with others who had not been perpetrators, but to the men the reaction was visceral, instant, and personal. That was a lesson for Pat—to heed his heart when in conflict. Sometimes, he concluded, our inner voices speak truths more clearly than classroom teaching.

While he had been somewhat intrigued by the notion of giving an abuser the opportunity to apologize to a group of adult survivors and to give them the satisfaction to tell the abuser, firsthand, the lasting effects of his depravity, he understood he needed to prioritize the needs of the men in the group over the wishes of Luke for forgiveness, and over his own curiosity about whether it could work. At the end of this difficult discussion, Pat thanked the men for their honesty and he told them he fully concurred with their determination to keep the group limited only to adult survivors who had not themselves become perpetrators.

His subsequent conversation with Luke was depressing and it confirmed the instincts of the group. "Yeah, these guys just don't have the guts to deal with me" was his reaction. "They're so selfish." To Pat, Luke's unpinned reaction made him think back to his basic course in psychology when the class studied the traits of a sociopath. Luke fit the bill. Pat surmised that Luke, as a serial abuser, was probably not like some other offenders whose offenses were singular, not repetitive. He concluded that Luke was far from the point of atonement, and he had foreboding he'd never get there without significant mental health intervention. For now, Pat decided, Luke will have to stew in his own guilt. Maybe, he thought, he'd be willing to meet privately with Luke, even hear his confession again, if he could get a sense of genuine remorse from him. But he did not expect that to happen.

Approximately three months after Pat met with Luke, he learned from the warden that Luke had been killed in the prison laundry. Warden Tucker indicated that Luke had convinced the correctional officer in charge of the segregation unit to let him work two afternoons a week in the laundry room, which was adjacent to the unit. The guard, mistakenly, had thought Luke would be safe there as the laundry work crew was small and well supervised. But Luke's body had been found in a laundry cart bloodied by a fatal stab wound to his neck. Pinned to his shirt was a typed note, large letters, bold face: "CHILD RAPIST."

Tucker indicated to Pat that an investigation was underway and they were confident of finding the assailant. However, he surmised, it was probably a lifer more interested in the satisfaction of taking out a child molester than about whatever extra punishment might ensue. When the warden spoke with Pat, he reported that officers had found a variety of shanks and shivs in inmates' cells, but, as yet, they had not been able to tie any of their trove to Luke's killing.

Thus ended Luke's sad and harmful life. The aftershocks stayed with Pat. He was troubled by his coldness toward Luke and failure to make any further efforts to bring any spiritual comfort to him. And, now, he felt only a hint of remorse over Luke's death. Was he satisfied in some perverse way that Luke had suffered a violent death? Was his murder just? *Shouldn't I feel pity for the person whose life ended in tragedy?* he silently wondered. No ready answer came. He concluded that only prayer and quiet reflection would help him find his moral bearings, to gentle his anger at least enough to allow room to pray for Luke's soul.

He started by deciding to conduct a funeral rite in the prison chapel. Because Luke had no relatives who were willing to claim his body, there would otherwise be no spiritual sendoff. Pat thought that was the least he could do. In spite of a prison rule that permitted inmates in general population to attend chapel services, only the warden and Pat's first chess partner, George McNally, attended. Pat went through the ritual, even sprinkling holy water on the casket, doubtful of its beneficial effect. Not every call to duty comes from a welcomed voice, Pat had concluded in resolving to conduct this service. Later, Luke's body was interred in the prison cemetery, the final resting place for those inmates who die without families willing to claim them.

XIX

A STARTLING ADMISSION

A few days after the funeral, while Pat was in his office awaiting visits from inmates during his regularly scheduled hours, there was a knock on his door.

"Come on in," Pat responded, and once the man entered, "What can I do for you today?"

"Padre Pat, my name is Felix Guerra. You probably don't remember me, but you talked to me once for maybe joining the group of men who had been abused as kids."

Pat tried to recall the man from his looks. Short-cropped dark hair, brown skinned, a paunch, and, of course, the ever-present tattoos traversing his arms and marking his face. *Maybe,* Pat thought to himself, *but I really don't think I know this man.*

"I'm sorry, Mr. Guerra, I don't remember, but I guess you must have decided not to come."

"Yeah, Padre, I was messed with as a kid but I wasn't ready to sit around and talk about it with a bunch of hombres like me, so I said no. I'm sorry now I didn't take the chance."

"Well, it's never too late. Men come in and go when it's their time. Are you here for long?"

"Oh, yeah, I'm here for dealing, Father. Actually I had a big crack operation going, so I got mucho because it wasn't my first bust. So, yeah, I'm here for a long bit."

"Well, Mr. Guerra, what can I do for you today? Please have a seat."

"May I close the door, Padre? And call me Felix, if that's okay with you."

"Certainly, Felix."

Pat could tell this man was tense. Of course, it wasn't unusual for someone to ask that the door be closed. That's where he heard confessions. But this was different. Guerra had an edge Pat couldn't read. At that moment, he was glad for the alarm button on the wall behind his desk. Sounding it would have a corrections officer in the room in seconds.

Guerra began. "Well, Padre, I'm here because I want you to hear my confession. I was born Catolico but haven't been to church for a long time. But now I think I need God. I don't really know what to do." He spoke quickly, excitedly, jumbling his words, some Spanish here and there. *This man is really troubled,* thought Pat. *I'd better go easy.*

"You are safe with me, Felix, and, of course, I'd be happy to hear your confession. You know, God's not here just for the ones who are faithful. Scriptures teaches us that God takes great joy in welcoming sinners back into the fold. So, anyway you think about it, I'm ready to hear what you have to say."

"Is it true, Padre, that whatever I tell you stays in this room, that you can't report me to anyone else?"

"Absolutely, Felix, so long as it's about something you did in the past. If you tell me you intend to do something bad in the future, that's no secret. I will report that, so the secrecy is just for past sins."

"Okay, then, Padre, I'm the guy who killed that child rapist, Reardon. I stuck a shank in his neck, right into the side where I must have hit an artery 'cause he bled right away. I had to jump back to avoid getting blood all over me."

Pat took a deep breath. He had heard other inmates confess violence, but this was close to home. He sat back, looked at the man before him.

"Well, Felix, how do you feel about what you did? Are you here just because you want to get this off your mind or are you sorry for what you did?"

"Both, Padre. I'm not usually a violent man. Oh, I've sold lots of drugs, done other stuff, but I've never hurt anyone, at least directly, until I did that guy."

"And, if I may ask, Felix, why do you think you did that?"

"I've been thinking about that, Padre, ever since I did it and got back to my cell with nobody nabbing me. At least not yet. All my life, at least since I was a muchacho, I stuffed some things way down, deep I mean, trying not to think about them. I've always just tried to do my thing, but something about this guy brought all that back up again, and maybe I just wanted someone to pay for what had happened to me. That's the only way I can explain it, Padre."

"Well, Felix, let me ask you a very important question. How do you feel, now, about what you did? Are you glad you killed him or are you sorry?"

"At first I felt kind of relieved, like something had been made right, but when I thought some more about it, I began to think that maybe I had just snapped. I'm no killer, Padre. So, yeah, I'm real sorry for doing that. That's why I'm here. I want to ask God to forgive me. I don't plan on telling anyone I did it and I don't think they'll ever be able to pin it on me, but I'll take my chances there. Not with God, though. If I ever learned anything, it was from mi madre. She said never stop believing in God. I've sinned lots, Padre, but never like this before. Please bring me God's forgiveness. I know priests can do that."

Once the man calmed down, he then knelt, said the sign of the cross in Spanish, and began his litany of a life of crime culminating in the killing of Luke. He shook as he spoke, his sentences were part recitation, part plea for forgiveness, alternating between English and Spanish. Pat was convinced of his contriteness. He blessed him and granted God's absolution to him. Much relieved, Guerra stood, then embraced Pat before hurrying away. "Mil gracias, Padre. Deo gracias!"

A week later, Warden Tucker stopped by to chat, as he sometimes did in the afternoon. "You know, Padre, we haven't yet found the guy who killed the priest, Reardon; funny, because the grapevine usually yields up someone pretty quickly. Around here, killing a child molester could make someone's mark. This guy must be different, not a bragger. If you hear anything, please let me know; we really want to catch this guy. We can't let this kind of thing go, you know."

Pat was quick to respond, "You know, Warden, I can't do that. If I am ever seen by the inmates as a snitch, that would be the end of my usefulness in this place. Please don't ever ask me to be a detective for you."

With that the warden just looked at Pat, stood up, said, "Roger that," and left.

XX

CROSSROADS

On a gray morning in January, Pat was deep into losing a chess game to Leroy Whitaker, another one of his habitual partners. Whitaker had been sentenced to life for murder thirty-five years earlier and he was now the kitchen chef. Of medium stature, Leroy had a neatly trimmed beard, knotty white hair, and a few distinctive tattoos on his arms and right hand. On his left upper arm was an image of Christ transfixed by a cross, and on his right elbow, spreading outward to his upper and lower arm, was a spider. He also had five dots inked on his hand between his thumb and forefinger.

Pat was no expert on the various kinds of prison tats, but he had been told that the cobweb and the five dots were typically worn by inmates with life sentences. Crudely inked prison tats, Pat thought, but marks of status in the prison community. Pat had learned from the prison vine that in spite of these somewhat off-putting marks inked into his body in his earlier years of confinement, Leroy was nearly a master-level chess player, based on learning the game fifteen years earlier from another inmate. Pat enjoyed trying his skills on Leroy and didn't mind losing, as he routinely did, as he enjoyed the patter between moves. He knew Leroy often bated him about religion, the nature of good and evil, and, as often as not, he willingly fell into Leroy's traps, leading from time to time to more serious discussions that transcended their setting. Leroy liked to talk about big topics. In a place that featured an inordinate amount of downtime, this fellow, Pat concluded, had used it to think and to learn.

One time, Leroy asked Pat to talk about the nature of good and evil, how God could allow such evilness to take place. Pat responded, "Well, Leroy, those are big questions. I think there's such a thing as the natural order, the way we get along; it is in our nature to be good, to exist together in harmony, but I know, also, that people do evil. God created us with free will, the ability to choose. While I think it's more natural to choose the good, many don't. So I think, in a way, evil is just the absence of good."

"I don't know, Padre. Some of those dudes I knew on the street, here too, they're just pure evil."

"Well, Leroy, I don't think I'd put it that way. We all have the capacity for good and evil. The people you're talking about, the ones who may have done really bad things, they too have the ability to do good. We're all God's children. They have just lost their way."

"So, Padre, are you saying you have some evil in you," Leroy rejoined, "but you just have more of the good?"

"Not quite, Leroy, and maybe I've lived in a safer environment, where the choices have not been so hard. My teaching is that the potential for evil is in each of us. We can choose but in the nature of things, I believe we are good. And that's why society generally works too."

"That's easy for you to say, Padre," Leroy responded. "You didn't grow up hard, nothing but people scratching and clawing, jumping over each other, just to live. Doing evil just to get by."

Leroy often talked about his life as an adolescent and teenager, what he had learned on the street and about his change since coming to Suffolk.

"I was angry, man, reckless and impulsive, doing just what came into my head. That's how come I killed that guy in a card game just for cheating. I got really mad at him and popped him, 'cause I was always carrying. Couldn't afford to go nowhere without protection. Here, I'm calmer, less driven. Maybe it's just because I'm older. I accept my guilt and I'm sorry for what I did. Nothing I can do about it but at least I can try to be decent to people around me. That's what I do," he smiled.

To Pat, Leroy seemed to have practical wisdom, not book-learned, but honed by his years of coping, first on the street and now in prison. Pat appreciated Leroy's insights and his humor. Sometimes he was self-deprecating but usually just reflective in the way he saw himself in relation to his environment. In some way this man, imprisoned for decades, seemed free, an enigma that intrigued Pat. Deep in thought, Pat was unprepared when Leroy suddenly sat back and said, "Father Pat, can I talk with you about something serious?"

"More serious than the nature of good and evil? Really, Leroy? Please do." Pat smiled. "Of course, Leroy, I think I know: Are you going to tell me my game is hopeless and we need to try, maybe, cribbage or I need to go back to checkers?"

"Nah, Padre, this is something real serious. You know I'm here for life, but when I was sentenced, they didn't take away the possibility of parole and now I'm actually eligible. The warden says he thinks I have a chance because my sheet here has been clean for the past twenty years and they got too many people locked up. I guess they might think this old man ain't no danger no more."

"That's wonderful, Leroy. Let me know if I can help."

"Well, Padre, that's the point. I think maybe you can. If I get out of this place, I got nowhere to go, got no family anymore, least no one who wants to claim me. I haven't had any visitors for years. Everybody's moved on, I guess, even my kids who are now getting on and have their own families. So, I'm kind of scared about what I'll do, but I have an idea."

"What's that, Leroy? You know I'm here for you and, Leroy, I'm sorry to know you're family's all fallen away. You and I have never talked about that. It must be hard."

"Oh yeah," replied Leroy. "But you know, Father, I did wrong and they had their own lives to lead. It's just part of the whole deal, what happens in life, so now it's just me."

"I guess I understand, Leroy. So what's your idea?"

"Well, Padre, I know what you're doing in Kingston. I saw the article in the *Gazette*, and that got me to thinking. You're going to need a cook to feed them men and that's what I do. What if, when I get out, if I do, I come to live in that house, not just for a while as a transition, but as a permanent resident as the chef? I could probably help out in discussions too because I think I've learned a thing or two over the years. If I could do that, I wouldn't need much money, just pocket change because I'd have a place to stay and food to eat, and maybe that's something that might work for you too."

Pat was surprised, first that Leroy might get out and then he was intrigued by his idea. *I guess it makes sense for Leroy,* Pat thought, *since he'd have no other place to live and doesn't know any work except being a chef, and getting a job in a restaurant could be hard with his record.*

"I need to think about that, Leroy. I know you're a really good chef as you've figured out how to prepare wholesome meals for the men on a limited budget, and you've shown some creativity, too. I've been the beneficiary of that. And, one thought I've been mulling over: We're going to have a pretty big kitchen. Perhaps we could cook for more than the men living in the house. Prepare food for shelters, or other places where they don't have facilities. And, maybe something for the homeless."

"Oh man," exclaimed Leroy. "You really are a thinker, Father Pat. I'd really love to be part of doing something like that out there. I'd feel real good about that."

"Let's talk some more about it, Leroy, and I'll discuss the idea with the board back in Kingston. Meanwhile, good luck with the parole board. When's your hearing?"

"Next month, Padre."

"Okay, Leroy, but let's get back to the game. I think I'm about to mate you."

"That's what you think, Padre. Just watch this move." And so the game continued until Tim Gates, a corrections officer who had walked over to watch the game, interrupted. "I just got a call on my handheld, Padre. There's a phone call for you in the warden's office. It's from a Bishop Turner."

Pat was perplexed. He knew that a new bishop had been appointed to serve in the diocese where he was ordained, but why would the bishop want to speak with him? And certainly the caller was not the bishop himself, he mused. When he got to the phone and said hello, he heard, "Good morning, Pat, this is Brad Turner. Could you come see me at your earliest convenience?"

"Of course, Your Excellency," responded Pat. "I can come tomorrow morning."

"Ten o'clock, then," responded the bishop. "I look forward to seeing you." And he hung up. Dumbfounded, Pat wondered whether it was a prank. *Yes, that's the name of the new bishop, but what bishop would make his own phone calls and what bishop would ever speak with such informality and familiarity? And, if that is the new bishop, what does he want with me?* Pat decided he'd call the chancellery later in the day just to see if the call had actually come from Bishop Turner. And sure enough, when Pat reached out to the chancellery that afternoon to "confirm" his appointment, the bishop's secretary initially said he knew nothing about it but after checking the bishop's schedule on his desktop computer, he saw the name "Pat Keefe" was keyed in at 10 a.m.

Pat was perplexed. Who is this man who acts in this unusual way, makes his own calls, refers to himself in such an informal way? Pat had never met him. He knew that Bishop Ryan had abruptly announced his retirement after the criminal trials and the large judgment against the diocese, and that, in an unusually short time, Turner had shown up as the new bishop. Pat had attended the investiture presided over by

Archbishop Slate, new himself to the state. Pat sat with many of the priests of the diocese, but he had skipped the reception afterward, having no interest in meeting the new prelate or hobnobbing with anyone else.

As a prison chaplain, living at the prison and with no financial connection to his diocese, he didn't want to linger or to comingle with the clerical hoy ploy. *How did this new man even know about him?* he wondered. Maybe he was going to pick up the ball dropped by his predecessor and send him to some godforsaken place in a faraway part of the diocese from where it would be impossible to get back to Duncan's Cove on weekends. The idea of being found on the radar perplexed and concerned him.

Promptly at 10 a.m. the next day, Pat presented himself at the chancellery and was immediately ushered into the bishop's office. "Good morning, Pat, I'm Brad Turner. Thank you for coming."

"Your Excellency," Pat began to respond as he took in the tall, angular, graying at the temples man with the mien of a former athlete. "It's Bishop Turner," he interrupted, "or when we're alone, Brad will be fine unless I am presuming too much familiarity as, after all, we have just met. You now, Christ wasn't crazy about the authorities. If the Good Lord wasn't, then why should we celebrate high-toned titles?"

Pat was thrown off his pins. *What bishop acts like this?* As he sat down, he began to take in the office. Gone from the walls were the certificates, diplomas, and other accolades, signifying the importance of this man's predecessor. Gone too were paintings and other objects of fine art he had seen in his unhappy meeting with Bishop Ryan. The office he now saw was relatively bare, containing a simple desk and a couple of comfortable chairs fronted by a table on which sat a globe of the world. In place of his predecessor's trappings of the office, Turner had displayed a few photographs, one as a young priest with an older couple, perhaps his parents, and another, a grouping of youngsters, mostly African American, in a

246

semicircle with Turner flanked by two other adults, both women of color. Also on a bookshelf was a picture of a baseball team whose members were wearing a logo unfamiliar to Pat.

"I see you're looking at my sports memorabilia," remarked the bishop. "That's from when I was a pitcher with the Catnats, a Double A minor league team in Philipstown, PA. I lasted only two seasons until I was injured but, if I might say without feigned humility, I was pretty good and thought maybe I had a shot at the big leagues until my arm quit. What you see here are gifts from the team for my one no-hit game. Quite the memory for me. Have a seat, please, Pat, and I'll tell you why I called.

"First, please let me you the story of how I got here, as I think it relates to why I asked you here today. After my brief stint in the minors, I went to college in Youngstown, Ohio, and during my sophomore year, I decided I wanted to become a priest. I'll give you the short story and the rest maybe sometime when we're having a beer. I was accepted into St. Joseph's Seminary in Pittstown, PA, and ultimately ordained in 1975. After a couple of assignments in suburban parishes, I was sent to Holy Child, a parish in a very poor part of Pittstown. I loved it there. The people had nothing by way of material goods. Nearly all were on some form of government assistance because there was no employment. For many, the promise of factory work had lured their predecessors north but, in time, as one by one the factories closed, those people lost their incomes and, for many, despondency set in.

"We had a lot of alcoholism and other forms of drug dependency, a legacy that seemed to infect families well beyond the users. A lot of single-family homes there too, the remaining parent, almost always the mother, often found the struggle overwhelming, resulting in drug abuse and the attendant failures in childcare. So often these good people fell into irreversible despair, which, in turn, so tragically affected their lives and their young ones. As you might guess, this was not a coveted assignment, but for me it was a learning opportunity and a chance to put in use much of what we learn by studying the parables.

"For the first time as a priest, I felt I had been called. Perhaps that sounds egotistical, but I don't know any other way to explain the feelings I had once I got my traction in this community. In time, I was able to see beyond the despair, the pervasive scent of hopelessness, and I resolved to find ways to raise the spirits of these good people, to try to ease the hardship of their lives. I started a youth program where we invited kids of any faith or none to come to the parish hall to play basketball and discuss whatever was on their minds. We provided meals on a daily basis in the soup kitchen, breakfast and soup and sandwiches for lunch in a tent I was able to rent for free, right in the church parking lot. That took some politicking with the rector but it worked.

"Of course, we had to do our own fundraising but we had a few guardian angels. There were a couple of guys from the ball team who had made it big we were able to enlist, and then there were parishioners from the suburban churches where I had served before I got to Holy Child. The generosity of people is truly a grace. Whether it comes from a sense of community, or a feeling of guilt for being blessed with financial success, or just unvarnished charity, we were the beneficiaries of many generous people and, in time, a few foundations decided our work was worthwhile. Enough, in fact, to allow us to purchase and renovate a rundown factory building where we now have a shelter, a kitchen, and a clothing distribution center.

"If I do say so, Pat, it was quite a success, and I loved every bit of it, particularly as I got to meet and work with so many people of this outwardly gloomy place. And then one day, I got a call to come to the chancellery to meet with the bishop. Probably like you today, I was anxious to know what the call was all about as, like you, I had ruffled a few feathers along the way. Certainly, I didn't expect what happened next. As I entered his room, Bishop VanBuren rose from his chair, extended his hand, and said, "Congratulations, Bishop Turner." Was I taken aback! Van Buren explained to me that he had recommended me for a bishopric to the cardinal nuncio, who you know resides in Washington, D.C., and is the Pope's representative to the country. Nobody in the United States gets elevated in the Church without his blessing.

"At any rate, the nuncio apparently passed my name on to Rome and, what do you know, here I am. One last part, I suppose. After I went to Rome and met with the cardinal in charge of the agency that makes recommendations to the pope for new bishops and cardinals, I was summoned to meet the pontiff. I guess that's unusual, at least historically. But, there I was, in the company of the pope. Our conversation was brief. His Holiness stressed to me his intentions to appoint a new cadre of bishops, people who are more interested in service than status. He shared his awareness that bishops typically come from the ranks of the Church bureaucracy, those who have served in some administrative capacity or other important places, men who typically have not spent a lot of time in the trenches, so to speak. He told me he intends to change that as much as he can in the time God gives him in Rome. And with that, the pope gave me his blessing and bade me bon voyage, a salutation I did not take as referring to my plane ride back home. So, that's my story, Pat. No, I am not going to tell you that the pope has made you a bishop, at least not yet, but I do have a request to make of you.

"First, let me tell you I've read your file. Sort of skimpy, actually. It tracks your seminary days, your early parish assignments, your work at St. Cecelia's helping to create an interfaith organization in an effort to tackle some of that community's problems, and now your assignment to the prison at Suffolk. Then your file contains notes of how you helped victims of child sexual abuse by some of our fallen brethren. I see too that you had some unpleasantness with my predecessor but then you seem to have gone off the grid, at least as far as the diocese is concerned, because apparently you have closeted yourself in your prison ministry."

"Well," responded Pat, now somewhat emboldened by Turner's casual demeanor, "I really didn't so much hide myself from the chancellery as I tried to lower my profile. Early on, I had decided that I could best serve the Lord in a ministry to those most forsaken, at a prison and not in a parish setting, and I was hoping nothing would change that in spite of my rocky relationship with Bishop Ryan."

"Yes," replied Turner. "Well, that's all over, Pat. You're safe with me. In some ways, you and I have similarities, at least in the way we have fashioned our priesthoods, I guess until this happened," the bishop said as he waved his arms about the room.

"But then," asked Pat, "how did I come to your attention, Bishop? I thought I had pretty much made myself invisible to this place."

Turner laughed in responding, "Yes, for sure you tried, but you were not totally successful. You see, Father Stan Mathews is an old friend of mine. We met once at a convocation of priests in Elmira, New York, and we immediately hit it off. Oh yes, strange bedfellows you might think, but we both enjoy a good read and, from time to time, a taste of the Irish, so we have made it our business to communicate by mail and to try to see one another once in a while. Not too hard because Stan had family in the Midwest, now unfortunately gone. Well, when I first got here of course I went right over to the seminary to see Stan, whose getting more physically infirm but still has a crackerjack mind that seems to pierce the fog that sometimes envelopes others his age. Aside from reminiscing with him, I sought his input as to what he thought the diocese's greatest needs might be. And that's when your name came up.

"Stan told me that the two of you had frequent contact during your seminary days and that he sees you from time to time, even now that you've tucked yourself away. To tell you the truth, he couldn't stop raving about you. He thinks you're smart, as your seminary record shows. But, more importantly, he believes you're a man of goodness with a firm sense of God's way. Stan thinks there is a dispirit in the air as a result of those priests being exposed for their despicable conduct, and he senses that's not the end of the story as more and more of this is becoming known here and abroad. From Stan's perspective, and I think I agree with this, he thinks we need to revamp our seminary process from A to Z, and that's where your name popped up. He thinks that you could play a significant role in helping us.

"Oh, I know you don't have the academic credentials that we generally require to teach in a seminary, let alone lead one, so here's my thought. If you'd agree to join me here in the chancellery as my right-hand man, the vicar, you would be my eyes and ears on what's happening at the seminary. Of course, the seminary serves more than this diocese, so I need to be careful about not appearing to be presumptuous about seminary programming and politics, but I do want to have a say about seminary admissions policy and the curriculum being taught.

"My personal bias is that young men need to learn more about living as priests in their communities, about acting as examples of a Christlike life in more ways than the performance of ritual. What I am proposing to you, Pat, is that you join me in trying to make our diocese a place of goodness, a force for good in the Catholic community and beyond. I know that's a big task, but I think I've been sent here for a reason, and I really could use your help. As vicar, you'd also have a lot of say-so in the diocese related to assignments, discipline, the internal workings of the diocese; also, advances such as a more effective use of the laity and a closer look at what roles women can assume—of course, within the parameters set by Rome.

"It's a big job, Pat, but from what I've read and Stan has said, I think you could be up to it. Although you may not realize it, your experiences so far have well prepared you for this task, even your occasional run-ins with my predecessor. Also, you can teach courses at the seminary, if you wish, relating to the practical ministry. By that I mean teaching our aspirants about living a Christian life, a hands-on approach in how to be a priest in our changing communities. I'm sure I can get the other bishops to agree to putting you on the faculty."

The bishop paused as Pat sat very still, his mouth agape. The bishop continued. "I'd also like you to work with me as we develop new approaches to our ministry. As you know, fewer men are coming to seminary these days, whether that's due to the decreased participation by people in the rites of our faith, probably complicated by the broadening scandal of child sex abuse in the Church, or some combination of factors. Our need for priests of holiness and goodness is unabated; we need a way to attract the right people, and once we enroll them, to provide a pathway to ordination that suits them to the tasks ahead. This is a huge challenge, I know, Pat, a sea change, but one that is vital to our ability to carry out Christ's work, at least in our lifetime. And, finally, Pat, I know there will be pushback from some of the older priests who may think they'd be better at administering the diocese than you. That part will be on me."

Feeling dizzy, Pat stuttered, "But, Bishop, I have no academic qualifications, not the right education, and no relevant experience that would qualify me for such an assignment. And, Bishop, I really don't think I'm personally worthy of this task. I think I'm better suited right where I am, with the inmates, trying to help their struggles back to lives of grace."

Turner didn't scoff at Pat's protestation but, instead, remarked, "From my conversations with Stan and the little bit I see about you in your file, I'd say you're a perfect match to the challenge, Pat, in many ways you may not see. Please go home now. Pray and think about it, and let me know in a few days what you think. I know too, Pat, that taking on this new assignment would mean an end to your work at the penitentiary, but I promise that if you can do this, I'll work with you to find a great replacement for that important work."

With that, the two men shook hands and Pat left, confused and dazed. He decided he'd first talk with Father Stan, his mentor and confidant. When he got to the seminary, Stan invited him to lunch in the dining hall, at a table apart, apparently Father Stan's habitual roosting place at mealtime.

"Let me ask you first, Father, as I think you know what's inside me more than anyone else, do you think I'm really worthy of this position? You know my life, my secrets."

Stan was quick to reply. "Pat, there's nothing about your life that would disqualify you. In fact, your momentary fall from grace followed by your resolve to remain a priest demonstrates to me a commitment honed by experience and a humanity, which are both gifts you will bring to this challenge. Your ministry to the inmates at Suffolk prison, your outstanding parish work, particularly at St. Cecelia's, and most importantly the contributions you made to our youngsters by helping to cleanse the Church of those three priests who needed to be ousted from our midst. Do not concern yourself about your suitability, Pat."

Father Stan added with a twinkle, "So long as you remain committed to a chaste life, particularly now as you will be living closer to the center of gravity."

"But what about my lack of administrative experience, or any leadership role in the Church? I've never even been the rector of a parish. Won't those deficiencies make me suspect to many priests in parish work?"

"Perhaps," responded Stan, "but, if so, the naysayers simply become part of the challenge you have been chosen to undertake. You have the intellectual ability and the scope. And I know from our conversations over the years that your view of the priesthood is one of action, of service in the mode of Christ. And anyway, Pat, the diocese has civilians in leadership positions dealing with the budget, physical plant, and the like. Your role, as the bishop explained to me, will be to work closely with him on strategic initiatives, and I think that, in him, you'll find a kindred spirit. He's very concerned about the sort of men we're attracting to the priesthood and then once they come to the seminary, how well we're preparing them to actually serve as priests. While you don't have the academic credentials, I believe that your energy, your commitment to ministry, needs to be imbued in the men who come to us to be trained to be the deacons and priests. This is a call I urge you answer, not for your own good but for that of the Church you have vowed to serve."

Sobered by Stan's words, Pat thanked him for his frankness and, as usual, for his wisdom. He had the good sense not to talk with Stan about whether this choice would be his preference. He knew such thoughts were selfish. Nonetheless, they were there. Pat and Stan parted with Pat saying he was going to think about it during the weekend he was intending to spend in Duncan's Cove with his family.

Once back in Duncan's Cove, Pat opened the discussion with Maggie by describing the call from the bishop, his impressions of Turner, and how Turner's presence could represent the opportunity for renewal in the diocese. When he told her that the new bishop wanted him to be his vicar, Maggie's first question was, "What's that?"

"Think of it as a chief of staff, Maggie. The person who carries out the boss's program, in this case the bishop's."

"Sound like a lot of power, Pat. Is that what you want?"

"No, not at all," responded Pat with an emphasis that surprised him and Maggie. "To me, the further I get from actually serving the people, the less fulfilled I may feel. I've never had an administrative position in my times as a priest and I've never sought one. I think I've been very fortunate in my assignments and now, with this new initiative in Kingston which I'm so excited about, what would happen to that? No, this is not an assignment I want but what does that have to do with it? Aren't I supposed to go where I'm called?"

"Well, I suppose, Pat, so long as you stay a priest, but haven't you learned a lot about life since your ordination? Maybe being a therapist, working with children, could be your calling. In an odd way, maybe the bishop's call might get you thinking about your role as a priest and whether that's the best way you can serve God. Certainly, his administrators on earth haven't made it easy on you."

Pat was not expecting this response from Maggie.

"Can we just stay focused on what the bishop is asking me to do, Maggie? I know you have concerns about the way the old bishop treated me, but that's different. Right now I just want to talk about the job the bishop is offering me. I don't think being the bishop's right-hand man is the best way I can serve, but maybe I'm being selfish, looking at it only from my perspective."

"Well, Pat, if you don't mind me saying, there's nothing wrong with thinking about yourself once in a while even though that may be unfamiliar territory for you," she said with a smile. "Would you like to have a family confab to talk about this?"

"Yes," replied Pat. "That's a really good idea. Could we do it tomorrow? Is that too soon?"

"I don't think so. Let me make some calls and maybe we can have a cookout here," suggested Maggie.

And with that, Pat thanked Maggie and said he thought he'd take a walk. Once he got to Sean's bench, the harbor laid out in front of him, a calmness came to him, borne maybe from the familiarity of the place and perhaps too from the sureness of the seascape facing him. Although he did not come to any conclusion, he felt readier to discuss it with his cherished family, to consider the prospects with less passion, more centered. Sean's bench had done its job.

When Pat got back to the house, Maggie reported, "I've reached Susan and Bill, and Ruth and her spouse, Beth, and all of them are looking forward to having an impromptu cookout."

"Did you say Ruth and her *spouse*, Maggie?" Pat queried. "What's this about Beth being Ruth's spouse?"

"Don't get excited, Pat. We just consider Ruth and Beth to be spouses since they now live together and, I think, they have started an adoption process, hoping, maybe, to get a child from China. I don't know if they're actually married, though, since I don't think it's legal, but I heard them talking about trying to get a license for a civil union as I guess you can do that in some states. Anyway, Pat, they're obviously a very committed couple and we, I mean me and the rest of the family, really love Beth. She fits right in. Is that going to be a problem for you, Pat?"

After thinking a moment, Pat replied. "You know, of course, Maggie, that the Church is opposed to gay marriage, even to the notion of homosexuality."

"Yeah," said Maggie, with salt on her voice. "Isn't that an irony when I hear there are even gay priests?"

Pat wasn't ready for that comment but he recovered. "Look, Maggie, the Church has its doctrines, which I cannot publicly challenge, but you know me—I'm not a morality cop. All my life, particularly as a priest, I've been more interested in doing than judging. Others can be the rule enforcers. I don't judge Ruth and Beth, and, between us, I'm very happy for the love they share. Please just don't say I said so. The Church is working through these issues and I don't expect resolution anytime soon."

"Fair enough," said Maggie. "So long as you don't have a problem with Ruth and Beth, I won't put you on the spot with them as I know they're very edgy about what others think, particularly people they care about, and you're high on that list."

"Nice of you to say, Maggie, but what makes you think that?"

"Oh, in the past couple of years, I've seen a lot of both of them. Beth bought a boat, which she lobsters once in a while, just enough to have a few traps out and to tend them. Nothing big because her job is pretty busy, but she shows up at the coop now and then and when she does, we always wind up talking. She knows how much Ruth has always looked up to you and they're worried that deep down you might not approve. You can see how they might think that, being a priest and all."

"Of course," said Pat pensively. "When they're here I'll be especially welcoming. I think it's important they know that, for me, family's first."

"Okay, Pat, good idea. You do the grill and I'll make a large salad, and if time, an apple crisp for dessert as I know it's a family favorite. I remember how much Sean loved it, bless his soul." And so, dinner was on.

As the family drifted in and found Pat at the grill, they exchanged hugs and fell into easy banter, either about the state of fishing or about the latest sports trades. When Pat saw Ruth and Beth coming down the side walkway to the backyard, he handed the tongs to Chris and left to greet them with a warm smile and hugs to both. "Nice way to get rid of your grilling duties, Pat," Ruth chided good-naturedly.

"Yes, pretty deft of me." Pat was quick on the uptake. "Seeing you just made me forget all about that mundane duty."

"Better not tell, Maggie," Beth chimed in. "I'm sure she's counting on you 'cause good food is a hallmark of this house."

"Okay, okay," said Pat. "But then you have to hang around me for a little, as I haven't had the chance to talk with you for a while and I want to hear all about your new boat, Beth. You might have heard that I'm a fisherman of sorts."

"Yes, Maggie told me about that, Pat, and that sort of scares me a little. I don't know that I want to be snared in any of your traps," she wryly responded.

"No worry, Beth. I confine my fishing to the sea unless it's for compliments. I'm never too proud to fish for one of those."

Groan, Beth and Ruth audibly guffawed.

"Sorry, but I really do want to hear about your boat. I think it's great that you have one."

"It's ours together," deftly tested Ruth. "What do you think of that?" she probed.

"Well," said Pat, not taking the bait, "so long as you agree who's captain and you have a good understanding about finances and usage, it should work, I think, but if I really want a chance to go out, who should I ask?"

"Oh, that's easy, big brother, it's really Beth's; she's the fisherperson. I'm just sort of a financial backer, but when we go out together, she does all the work while I sit back taking in the sights."

Once Chris announced that the steaks and salmon were ready and all were seated, Maggie asked Pat to say grace. "Let's give Chris a workout," Pat responded. "We could all use a blessing from the next generation. Let's see what you have, Chris."

"Aw, Uncle Pat, you're just trying to see if I still say grace. Well, I do, for sure when I'm home. So here goes: Bless this food, Lord, and bless all of us who gather together today. Keep us close to each other and to you, Oh Lord."

"Amen," said all in unison. "Well, look at you," Susan said, "reverent and lyrical all in one. Good on you, Chris." And with that, the eating began.

Susan started the conversation. "Pat, Maggie said you were home, not just to take a break, but because you wanted to have a family meeting to talk about something. So, Father Pat, talk."

"Well, thank you for that nice introduction, Susan," Pat smiled. "And yes, there is something I want to talk with all of you about. To cut to the chase, the new bishop has asked me to become his chief of staff, or vicar, as the Church calls it, and I'm not sure I want to do it."

There was a silence in the room, a void as though the air had been sucked out of the house.

"Wow," both Chris and Susan then exclaimed in unison. Susan added: "What's there to think about? That's a huge promotion isn't it, Pat?"

"Well, I suppose you could think of it that way, but you know me. I've never been one looking for moving up, for the kind of recognition that comes with higher office or power."

"Then, if that's the case, Pat," Tom jumped in, "what's the question? If you don't aspire to move up in the Church, then thank the bishop and say 'no,' unless you don't like being the prison chaplain anymore."

"And what about that project you have going in Kingston? I thought that was important to you," added Maggie.

"Right on both scores," said Pat. "I'm still running a group at prison. I enjoy the opportunity to work with the inmates and bring them whatever peace or solace I can and to do little things for them to lessen their loads. And, for sure, I'm excited about the transition house that's coming along in Kingston, and the programs for released inmates and maybe even the community we may be able to run from the house. But that's all about me, my wants. Isn't that a little selfish of me? I am a priest, after all. And, this new bishop seems like a very different kind of leader. He's straightforward, not full of himself, and seems oriented to what we priests are supposed to be doing and not so much on rules and regulations of the Church. I like that in him."

"Well then, Uncle Pat, sounds like you have a tough choice," Chris said. Maggie added, "As you know, I've become increasingly skeptical of the Church after the revelations of the clergy sexual abuse and the now too frequent headlines of such misconduct throughout the world. And, of course, all this is happening while at the same time the Church seems to be stuck in its male dominance. Do you still want to be part of that?"

"Yeah," chimed in Beth. "There's no place for Susan and me in the Church. Sorry to say this to you, Pat, but we've quit going as it's obvious we're not welcome."

"And even if we weren't gay," added Ruth, "what's the point of any woman staying in the Church when the pope has made it clear that women will always be second-class citizens?"

"Okay, I get it," said Pat, exasperation in his tone. "I knew I could depend on your honesty when I asked for this little séance. This is a lot for me to absorb. I do know that we can't solve all the shortcomings of the Church now. You know that I agree with most of what you're saying about the abuse and the role of women in the Church, and those things truly bother me, but please assume for this conversation that I'm still committed to the priesthood. Your comments about the failings of the Church don't help me decide whether to stay with the prison and leave the path I've taken so far to join the bishop."

"Okay, you're right, Pat," Susan spoke up. "You didn't come here just to give us the opportunity to vent about the Church. Let's focus on you. What do you want for the rest of your priesthood, Pat? Are you ready to leave the prison, to go on to a new challenge? What do you think you could accomplish at the chancellery that could make any difference and that would make it worth your while to leave what you have so enjoyed doing?"

"Well," said Pat, "thanks for putting it that way. For one, the bishop wants me to play a role in how the seminary goes about recruiting and accepting candidates. It's obvious we've had some problem priests who have caused great harm, an irony since we're supposed to do just the opposite. So, if I could have a small part in developing a process to weed out trouble at the gate and help gather in some good candidates, that would be satisfying. Plus, the bishop said he'd like me to teach a course about living as a priest, unlike courses in ritual or even church history or dogma. He thinks we need to be orienting priests more to a life of service. That's always been my approach and I think I'd welcome having the opportunity to have some impact on future priests in that regard. And finally, I get a really good feeling about this new bishop. He talks like he wants me to be not just his aide de camp, but more than that, a sort of collaborator in whatever new initiatives he comes up with to make the Church more relevant to the community. I suppose that's sort of intoxicating for me."

"Careful there," Bill chimed in. "That sounds to me like power, something you have always said you don't care about, and, bless you, something you've resisted when your heart told you to."

"My conscience, I think you mean, Bill, if you're talking about my role in the trials, and I agree. But, Bishop Fuller knows about that. He said my difficulties with the diocese about the sexual abuse cases was one of the things that attracted him to me. I think that's a good omen and some indicator that this man may be willing to go out on a limb where moral right is concerned. I find that very desirable about a person in his position."

"Yes, and I just won the lottery," responded Beth, with a bitterness-revealing smirk. "I wouldn't hold your breath on that one, for the new guy to have any impact on the Church's view of women or its obsession with anything having to do with gender or sex."

"Oh, I'm not naïve about that, Beth," Pat responded, a little peeved at her sharpness, "but I think incremental changes...inches turn into feet and yards and sooner or later into miles, so I won't dismiss the good work this bishop seeks to do, even if it's not what you want and the Church itself needs. I'm not saying you should be patient. That's your judgment to make. I'm just saying that my sense is I can trust this man and that with him we might be able to make some changes, create some new initiatives that could benefit the community. You know, for better or worse, I think I am committed to this vocation. So, for me, the question is what's the best way for me to continue on my chosen path, and not whether I took the wrong fork way back when."

With that, Maggie spoke up. "You know, Pat, we all love you and frankly admire you for your steadfast commitment to your vocation even in the midst of the recent scandals, and we admire the stands you have taken for children. So we're with you whatever you decide, so long as you still have time to come back to Duncan's Cove once in a while to see how we common folk are getting along." Laughter then, interrupted by Beth. "And, to be sure, Pat, I want you to come fishing with me on *The Sea Pride* as I hear you're not a bad boat handler."

"Is that your boat's name?" asked Chris.

"Yep," responded Ruth. "Do you like it?"

"It's okay if you like double entendre, I guess. If I ever get a boat I think I'll name it *Seascape*." More groans followed.

Pat then stood, as if to make a point. "Please know that I am with you completely on these issues, and whatever I decide about where to go next and wherever that may take me, you can be sure I'll try to do my part, as little as it may be, to nudge this big ship into a better direction."

With that, Maggie announced that dessert was served and the conversation changed to family chitchat and the latest happenings in Duncan's Cove. A few hours later, after all had left, Pat said good night to Maggie and returned to his basement quarters to bed.

The next morning, Sunday, Pat attended Mass at Holy Family and, after stopping briefly in the vestry to say hello to Father Mark Stapleton, a newly assigned priest fresh from seminary, he decided to walk to Sean's bench to calm his soul as only the view of the harbor could do. And, as usual, resting on Sean's bench eased Pat's mind and lifted his spirits. He left feeling more centered. Later that day, he asked Beth if they could take *Pride* for a ride as he wanted to see how she handled. She happily accepted and around 1 p.m., on an incoming tide, Ruth, Beth, and Pat steamed out of the harbor, Gay Pride pennant flying from a short staff at the bow and the ensign aft.

Invited to take the helm, Pat was pleased with how ably the boat handled, her single diesel moving her along at a comfortable twenty knots, her well-turned bottom and rising bow handling the seas with ease. Once out of the harbor, Pat returned the helm to Beth and went aft to sit and take in the sights and smell of the sea he loved in the embrace of his newly extended family. "God is good," he thought, as a salt spray licked at him. The *Pride* did well too, beating back into the harbor against the tide and into a stiffening breeze, more spray now as the boat punched through the chop, holding steady as Beth capably navigated to the mooring field. As they motored back to shore in Ruth's skiff, the *Pride* now left to the sea and tide at her mooring, Pat felt his soul and mind clearing. He never felt as close to God, he thought, as he did when salt spiked his face in a freshening breeze.

XXI

CALL TO DUTY

The next morning, Pat presented himself at the chancellery and asked to meet with the bishop. When he got there, Turner was in his office, sitting in his recliner chair. He smiled as Pat entered, saying he had been expecting him. "Good to see you this morning, Patrick. Would you like to go to lunch? We can talk while we eat." Pat wasn't sure how to respond to this suggestion as he knew from diocesan folklore that Turner's predecessor would never deign to eat in a local restaurant with a lowly priest, preferring to have the kitchen prepare his favorite dishes and eat alone, as he most enjoyed his own company. Quickly regaining his balance, Pat said, "I'd love to do that, Bishop."

As they left the building, he was completely unprepared when they came astride a somewhat beat-up Chevrolet of uncertain vintage.

"Hop in," said the bishop, "and tell me where to go." Pat was flabbergasted.

"Whose car is this, Bishop, and what happened to the Cadillac in which Bishop Ryan was always chauffeured?"

"Oh, that," replied the bishop. "As soon as I saw that beast of a car I asked that it be donated to the senior center in town, where they can probably use it to get people to and from their appointments. It was too large and pretentious. In fact, I'm thinking of selling this grand chancellery building and renting office space for the staff while I find myself a more modest apartment, befitting a priest. Lord knows, the diocese needs the money because of this abuse epidemic. What do you think of that, Pat?"

"Above my paygrade, Bishop, but I'd guess you'd get both kudos and raised eyebrows. Some people may welcome the move for the sense of humility and oneness with the people it projects, but others will be aghast and maybe threatened if you downsize into more modest housing because they love the grandeur and majesty of the Church that this building symbolizes."

"Well said, Pat, and I guess I know that, but change sometimes is forced on us. I think we're at that time now. But how about lunch? Where do you want to go?"

"I know just the spot, Bishop." Pat replied. "A bit of a drive but worth it. Do you like lobster?" Pat and his new friend drove to the seashore, and there they enjoyed lunch together in a place on the edge of the sea, within walking distance of Pat's favorite perch.

"Well, Pat, what have you decided? Do you think you'd like to come aboard?"

Pat responded, "Yes I think so, Bishop, but first could I show you something I've been working on? It involves another drive, this time to Kingston, but I'd really like you to see this before you make a final decision about me.

"I already have, Pat," said the bishop, with curiosity. "So why do I need to see something in Kingston before I make up my mind all over again?"

"Please be patient with me," said Pat. "I know you have decided, but I'm not sure you really know who I am, what you might be getting, and I think I'd feel a lot better about a decision if I know you have seen this other part of me."

"Now you have me really curious, Pat. How about this coming Thursday? I think I can get free most of the day."

"It's a deal, Bishop. I'll pick you up at 9 a.m. sharp."

On the next Thursday, as Pat rode up the chancellery drive, the bishop was waiting for him, dressed as an ordinary priest, none of the trappings of his office evident in his garb. "Is this a VW beetle?" asked the bishop.

"To be sure," Pat, answered, "tried and true, 120,000 miles and still going. Got when my last car, a gift from my grandfather, died on the road. Heater's a little weak in the winter and windows work better than the air conditioning, but it gets me back and forth. Sorry if it seems small to you."

"Not at all," the bishop replied. "If it does the trick—what else could you need? But, if you're going to work here, you'll need something very dependable so you can get out to all the parishes. I think that's one thing we need to do, not like my predecessor: be out, be seen all over the diocese and not holed up here or someplace like it."

"Well, whatever you think, Bishop, but I can't be driving around in anything more splendid than your vintage Chevy," Pat laughed.

"Now that's a real puzzle, Pat. We'll have to pray on that one," the bishop laughed back.

They drove in companionable silence for the hour it took to get to Kingston and stopped in front of a building obviously under renovation.

"What's this?" asked the bishop.

"This is, or shortly will be, Grace Hall, Bishop—a transition home for recently released inmates from Suffolk. I'm so excited about its promise, Bishop. At Suffolk, I've seen men be released and then shortly later returned in emotional tatters, despondent for their failures. I've been concerned about the problem of recidivism, men violating the terms of parole or probation or committing new crimes soon after release and winding right back in prison. It's a revolving door for nearly a quarter of inmates, Bishop, and I want to try something different from the typical halfway house to see if it can make a dent.

"So, this will be not just a place for men to live but it will also be a center of learning and preparation for life in the community, and for substance abuse counseling and other mental health assistance, job training and placement, and, very importantly, for family reunification whenever that is possible. For me, Bishop, this is a dream come true. Let's go inside and I'll show you the layout."

Once in the building, as though on cue, the newly installed building-wide speaker system began intoning the lyrics of "Amazing Grace":

Amazing grace! How sweet the sound
That saved a wretch like me!
I once was lost, but now am found;
Was blind, but now I see.

'Twas grace that taught my heart to fear,
And grace my fears relieved;
How precious did that grace appear
The hour I first believed.

Turner just turned to Pat in appreciation for the nice touch. "Amazing Grace indeed, Pat." As they continued into the interior of the building they saw a hive of craftsmen, but none too busy for a tradesman here and there to give a shout out. "Hi, Father Pat. Like how we're coming along?" To which Pat responded, "Looks great," and, "Thank you so much for your generosity in giving your time and expertise," sometimes calling back to the person by name. On the first floor, framers were sheetrocking rooms and hallways. Pat asked the bishop to stop at one, a large room. "This one, Bishop, will be called Angel's Room, a place for residents to come to pray, meditate, or just think—a quiet room."

"Nice touch, Pat. I like the name."

"Well, I think it will be a much-used space and, most importantly, I really wanted to have one room named specially for the man who lost his life in a robbery. He had just been released from Suffolk. This room's in his memory and maybe the lessons we can learn from it. I think there will be a plaque about Angel on the wall."

The bishop just nodded as they continued, now ascending to the second floor where carpenters were hanging doors and finishing windows while painters were bringing spaces to life.

"You don't know this, Bishop, but most of these men—carpenters, electricians, plumbers, sheet rockers, and painters, all the trades we need—they're all volunteers who belong to one of the churches, or the synagogue or mosque who jointly support this project."

"Tell me more, please, Pat. This is really meaningful. Exciting too."

"Let's talk about it at lunch, Bishop. They're waiting for us at St. Cecelia's. I hope you don't mind but I called ahead to a friend of mine there, Father Jerome Robinson, the curate, and he has enthusiastically responded. They're looking forward to showing you the church and rectory. And, we also have a special treat for you, Bishop. I hope you don't mind surprises."

"Not if they're good ones, Patrick," the bishop said, looking askance. "I guess this will be a good test of whether I can trust you."

Yes, for sure, thought Pat to himself.

When they arrived at the church, they were greeted first by Monsignor Cunningham, now the rector emeritus in residence, awaiting the designation of his successor by the new bishop.

"Greetings, Your Excellency," Cunningham, said. "My name is James Cunningham, the former rector of St. Cecelia's now in retirement but helping as I can until you send us a new leader. We're so pleased you have come to see us. Can we first visit the church and then we'll go to the rectory where I know Father Robinson has laid on a nice lunch for you?"

"And, I hope you'll join us, Father?" the bishop asked with his head slightly turned. "Oh, no," Cunningham responded. "This is Father Jerome's show, Bishop, you'll see."

From the church, they walked next door to the rectory and then to the dining room, where a group of men and women were standing, obviously awaiting the bishop's appearance. Pat did the introductions, first pointing out Jerome as having been ordained two years ahead of him and now a fixture at St. Cecelia's and then, one by one, to the rest. They warmly welcomed the bishop. "Shalom" from one, "Salaam" from another, handshakes all around.

"Such an amiable group," whispered the bishop. Pat was beaming.

Jerome invited all to have seats, and once in place, asked the bishop to say grace. "Oh no, Father Robinson, I am a guest in your house. Please lead us in prayer." And so Jerome spoke: "God of all, as we welcome our new bishop to St. Cecilia's, please bring blessings on him in his new challenge. We thank you, God, for your bounty, and we seek your guidance in the work we share." Listening, Pat thought to himself how adroit of Jerome to offer a grace fitting for all in this group of multiple faiths.

With grace finished, Rabbi Shuman said with cheer, "We hope you're not here to take Father Jerome away from us, Bishop. He's such an important part of our interfaith work in Kingston." The bishop just smiled as food was passed around the table, a family-style meal. Midway through, Pat asked if anyone would care to tell the bishop about the interfaith group, what it has accomplished, and about the construction downtown.

"Happily," chimed Pastor Stevens. "Several years ago, at Father Jerome's invitation, we, or our predecessors, came together and agreed to form an organization to tackle urban problems common to all our congregations. Since uniting in this effort, we have been operating two daycare centers, one at St. David's Episcopal and the other here where children of any faith, or none, are welcome from 8 a.m. to 5 p.m. We feed them, make sure they exercise, and have other activities for them as the teachers devise. In each of our daycare centers we have several volunteers, enough to create overlap so we have adequate coverage all day. These centers now allow so many parents to work, as before the cost of daycare was too great for most because they don't have high-paying jobs."

"How wonderful," exclaimed the bishop. "Where did you get all the money to make this work?"

"In spite of its looks as a town that's seen better days, Bishop, Kingston is actually on the mend," Pastor Meyer responded. "New businesses are coming to town, and with that more people of means. And there are the old-timers as well. Each of us has pockets of generosity in our congregations, and many have responded to the call. We are blessed, Bishop."

"And that's not all," added Pastor Hall. "Early on, we knew adequate, affordable housing was an issue, so, as a group, we have worked with the Town to beef up regulations regarding tenancies, and we have also been successful working with some owners and builders in the creation of affordable housing. As part of this effort, we also have a volunteer social worker, actually a person who retired recently, who knows a lot about making the system work. She has helped many of our residents in their quest for assistance, whether disability, veterans, or from whatever agency might answer to their particular needs. That's been a big help."

The bishop was clearly impressed. "Well, all I can say is congratulations to all of you. What a fine example of interfaith cooperation, an area dear to me, as that's been part of my ministry during my priesthood and one which I hope to continue in my new role."

"Bravo," cheered Pastor Stevens and Father Stevenson together as though on cue.

"But what about the new building downtown?" asked the bishop. "Father Pat has told me something about it but it seems such an enormous, ambitious project. How are you managing to support it?"

"Yes, for sure," responded Imam Ihbram. "Maybe your driver could outline it for you; it's really his baby."

Laughter followed and then Pat spoke, first of the problem of recidivism and the failures of hope and opportunity that plagued recent releases from prison, and he went on to talk about the plans for Grace Hall. "As an aside," Pat said, "maybe one of the hardest agreements we had to make as a group was to come up with a name for the place. Some here wanted saints' names—put me in that group—others more secular names so as not to scare off potential funders. But after a while, I think it was Rabbi Shuman who came up with the name Grace as it has meanings for all of us across the board—Christian, Jewish, and Muslim, so that's it. A place of grace, of goodness, and a blessing. I think we're all very happy with our choice of name."

"Amens" all around the room.

Once lunch was concluded, and the other guests had said their warm farewells, the bishop and Pat bade goodbye to Jerome and left for the drive back to the chancellery. They were quiet for a while until the bishop broke the ice.

"I think I know why you brought me out here, Pat. You want me to make Jerome the rector."

Pat laughed. "No, I hadn't thought of that, Bishop, but what a great idea. I just wanted you to meet this group and particularly to see Grace Hall, as my heart is in that project, an idea borne of my work in prison ministry, an idea I don't want to abandon."

"Oh, I get it, Pat, you wanted me to come to see for myself why you can't come to work with me."

"I'm not sure," Pat responded somberly. "I'm torn. I've never been an organization man. Instead, I think of myself as someone on the front lines of our work, and I'm afraid that by leaving it, I could actually lose my drive, what makes me a priest. Maybe that's selfish of me. I'm a little confused about that."

"I think I understand, Pat," the bishop responded quietly. "And no, it's not selfish. Just human. As I told you when we met, I had to leave community work to accept this position, Pat, and believe it or not, that was not easy for me to do. I will miss that work, but I think part of being a priest, at least for me, is responding to a new challenge, so long as it's not against my moral gyroscope, my conscience. In that way, Pat, I think you and I may have some similarities, but here's one big difference. I can sense how important the interfaith project in Kingston is to you and I don't have to ask you to leave that to join me. Being the vicar of the diocese does not have to be all deskwork or all-consuming.

"We have good staff, Pat, financial people, administrators who look after the nuts and bolts. What I sense in you, Pat, is a good person who can help me lead this diocese, to guide our priests into more pastoral work in their communities. The kind of unity I sensed at St. Cecelia's is inspiring to me, Pat, as it would be to anybody. Imagine if such an interfaith effort could be replicated in some of our other cities and towns. What a great role for our Church in the community. So, let me assure you, Pat, if you join with me, I will not take you away from the work in Kingston. Indeed, I'll be looking for you to expand that sort of interfaith effort throughout the diocese, and I'll support you in that effort."

Pat was buoyed by the bishop's promise as it fed into the narrative he had begun to construct about this new leader. "That sounds wonderful, Bishop, and it's good to know you don't want to closet me away from the community, from the parishes of the diocese."

"To the contrary, Pat, I see you on the road a lot. In fact, I'm now sure this relic of yours, rattling us back to the chancellery, won't be up to the job. We'll definitely have to do something about that for you."

"Well," said Pat, "I have a nephew who would probably love it. I'm not sure this old friend is ready for the junk pile just yet."

Pat went quiet for a moment and then responded, "Bishop I think it would be a great honor to serve the diocese and the Church at your side, and I'm so happy about Kingston. I just have one other concern."

"Oh, my," smiled the bishop, "my new aide de camp is a negotiator. And what's that?"

"It's a most sensitive subject, Bishop, but one that has informed my priesthood for quite a while now, and it concerns the sexual abuse of children by priests."

"What a terrible scourge," the bishop somberly noted, "and one that appears to be growing as we see now not just in this country but abroad. It is an issue of great magnitude to the entire Church. I know people in Rome are working on policies to address the Church's response to it."

"Well, Bishop," Pat responded, now with less hesitancy to his voice, "and I say this with respect, I don't think we can wait for Rome to cure the ills in our backyard. I'd like us to act ahead of the curve."

"What do you have in mind, Pat?" The bishop cocked his head.

"For starters, Bishop, I suggest a zero-tolerance policy. That is, if any priest or anyone else under diocesan control is credibly accused of molesting a child, that person must immediately be placed on administrative leave and, where appropriate, dismissed if the charges are shown to be true. And, if the claimed behavior is criminal, the authorities must be notified without delay. And, finally, Bishop, I hope we can develop a pastoral program for victims, not a response driven by lawyers who defend the diocese against civil claims, but one motivated by the Gospels, by love. In short, an approach of concern, or caring unburdened by voices calling for self-protection."

"Keep talking, Pat. What would you do with the people who are accused?"

"Well, if there's a criminal referral and then prosecution, the criminal justice system will probably take care of that question. But if there is no prosecution and we still feel the claims are credible even if not proven, then a period of counseling and monitoring in place would be appropriate. No transfers to another parish where a claim may be buried. I know we'd have to carefully develop an appropriate policy, a response to this coming crisis, but I think it has to be motivated by a concern for victims, for the well-being of our parish communities, and not by a misguided sense that Mother Church needs to be protected from scandal, as we have seen that tactic is counterproductive. Sorry to seem so vehement, Bishop, but this issue is dear to me, and if I could play a role on the diocesan level to steer our ship on a more Christlike path in dealing with this issue, I would find that very fulfilling."

"I'm with you, Pat. And, here's what we can do. As soon as you are installed as my vicar, I will make public note that you have been charged with eradicating the scourge from our diocese. And you know, Pat, given what I think I'm learning about you, just maybe you'll come up with an approach that others may find worth following."

"That's wonderful, Bishop. Then please count me in if you still want me with all my conditions."

"Welcome aboard," replied the bishop.

"Amen to that," sighed Pat.

"Now as your first job, tell me about Father Jerome Robinson. Any negatives to making him the rector of St. Cecelia?"

"None that I could say," replied Pat. "He is obviously beloved in that community. A great leader of the church in Kingston. What else do you think you want to know about him? Do you feel you want to know about his personal life?" Pat asked with just a slight hesitation as he had a momentary flashback to his intimate dinner conversation with Jerome at the Thai restaurant in Kingston.

"Well, I guess not. I mean if you have any information he's been inappropriate with kids, that would be extremely important, but I'm sure you wouldn't think so highly of him if you knew anything like that."

"And, I don't think I'd want to find out that he has a wife and family stored someplace," the bishop continued.

"Oh, no, nothing like that," Pat now broadly grinned. "I think he'd be terrific."

The bishop smiled back, shrugged his shoulders, and said, "Well then, consider it done."

EPILOGUE

On the following weekend, Pat returned to Duncan's Cove where he offered Mass on Sunday morning at his home parish. Later, in the afternoon, he walked alone up Fish Trap Hill to Sean's bench. Early October, the colors along his way had changed-now golden rods, clusters of white and purple asters, shades of red, the shedding of maple trees. As he sat looking out at the harbor, pleasure boats gone, a few lobster boats at rest, he finally felt at peace. Soon Maggie joined him, and together, holding hands in an unspoken kinship, they looked out to the sea.

ACKNOWLEDGEMENTS

To Bill Byrnes, Miriam Gardner-Frum, and David Ruffner, for your wise counsel on aspects of the work's subject matter; to Jack Walker, Jim Bishop and Sarah Bishop, for your careful reading, insights and course corrections as the work progressed from draft to print; to my editor, David Aretha, the folks at Booklocker and 99Designs for your expertise in helping me navigate a world foreign to me; and to Kathrine, for your thoughtful counsel and unending support, thank you.

CPSIA information can be obtained
at www.ICGtesting.com
Printed in the USA
LVHW021256040121
675400LV00003B/257

9 781647 190422